ELSIE HAWTHORNE

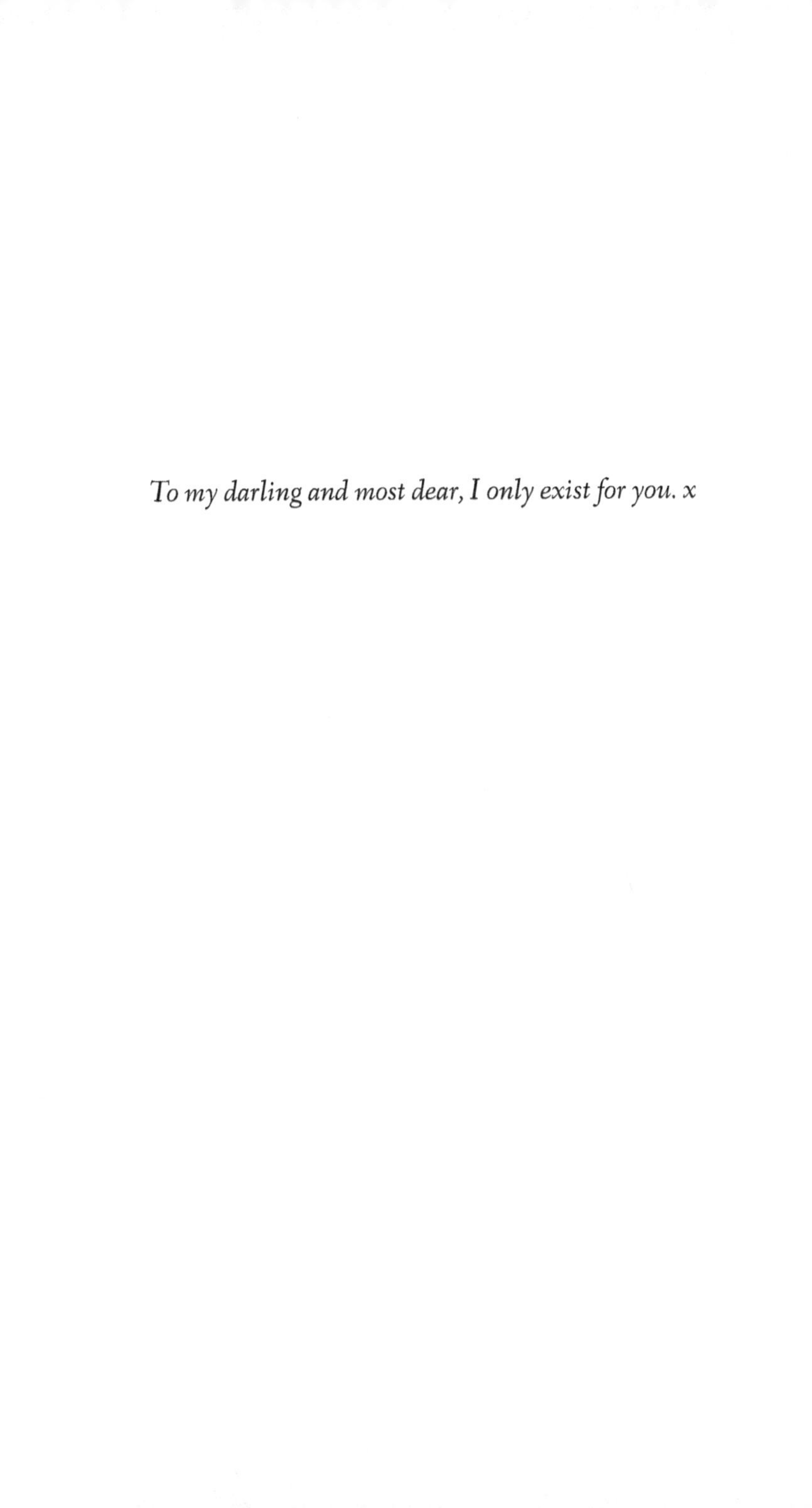

To my darling and most dear, I only exist for you. x

Author's Note

THE CITADEL
(SUNTIDE COURT)

THE CITADEL HOLLOWS OUT
THE MOUNTAIN, DESCENDING
DEEP INTO THE DARK STONE.

THE LIBRARY

SCRIPTORIUM
SCRIBE QUARTERS
INFIRMARY
LIBRARIAN QUARTERS
TO THE LIBRARY'S HEART

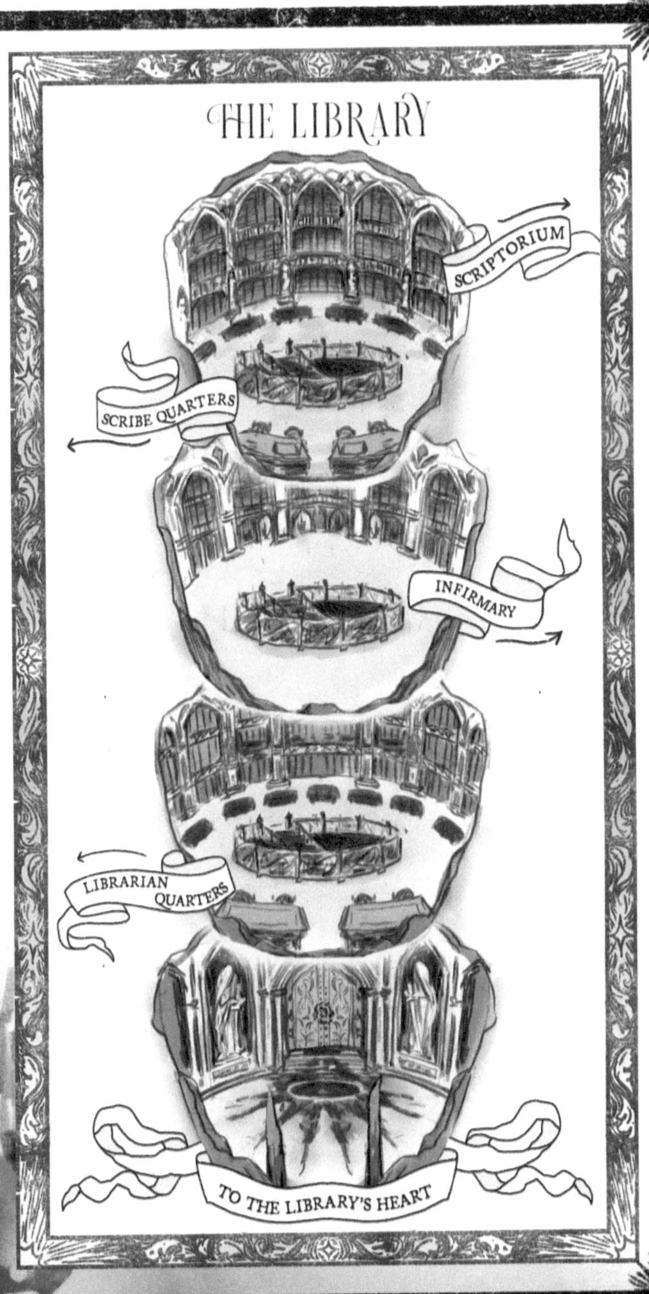

Chapter 1

Lorel

It's a warm day in the scriptorium, the wing of the Library devoted to the production of books. It's my first day back since the *incident* and naturally, my sister has sought me out to ruin it. On this particular morning, she perches on my desk, her silk skirts draped perilously over my paints and charcoal.

Her voice cuts through the quiet of the scriptorium, bouncing off the dull stone walls. Each section of the scriptorium sits surrounded by shelves on all sides except for where it opens with high arches onto an open courtyard that lets in dim, filtered light. Never full sunlight, of course. Never a glimpse of the stars through the clouds at night. Our desks sit in orderly rows. There are four in my section, giving us ample elbow room among the tall shelves that surround us.

This is a place of silence, I sign to her.

"You know I can't read your little hand signs," she says. "Use your tongue. Properly, like the rest of us."

I glare at her. So do the other scribes in my section,

Trefor and Sybri. There are the three of us, under Elris, our illuminator. Orielle seems impervious to us all. We are but lowly scribes in her eyes.

"Your Librarian turned me away when I came to see you. Am I not allowed to see my sister?"

You know you're not. Particularly when you're speaking in the scriptorium during the working hours.

I ensure I sign slowly for her, but she just stares at me blankly. There's no reason for her to not know the hand signs by now. I've been a part of the Library since I turned sixteen. I'm twenty-six now and in the last stages of my apprenticeship. She really should know the rules of the scriptorium at this point. Not in the least because she doesn't seem willing to let me go.

A noise of frustration catches in the back of my throat. It is entirely against the rules to voice it, but that hardly matters because it doesn't come. I've not been able to make a single sound since the incident six weeks ago. It's not just the loss of my voice, but a complete silencing. It doesn't matter what hour it is. Working hours, leisure hours, mealtime. I couldn't utter a word even if I wanted to. I am cursed.

Not that I want Orielle to know that. It is why I have refused to see her, after all. That and the strange presence of the curse in my chest, resting below the curse mark that had appeared across my skin. It doesn't like it when Orielle is near. I can't think why, not since she's such a *joy* to be around.

I pull out my chair, heedless of Orielle's skirts. She doesn't take the hint.

"*Lorel,*" she says, catching my chin. I twist away from her, recoiling at the sudden touch. The last thing I need is for her to pick up on anything different about me. "I merely wish to check that you are alright. It's hardly my fault if I can only catch you here during the day hours."

My hand signs in response are as swift as my tongue would have been.

This is when you always turn up. Don't pretend any differently.

The elegant roll of her eyes is all I get in response, but what did I really expect? Orielle is a talented mage and courtier devoted to the circus that is the Suntide Court, and my life must seem small and insignificant to her. I don't even know why she bothers to visit anymore. Perhaps I should be glad of it, but I can only feel ungrateful at the intrusion.

Orielle, golden child. Grey-eyed and clever enough to rise through the ranks of the Dawn King's ruthless courtiers. Tall and shapely. Always perfectly dressed, every hair exactly in place. Always with her chin tipped up.

I have just enough fae blood to make my pointed ears irritating to lie on. Orielle has enough to make her a prodigy. She belongs in those lantern lit halls. My dark-haired, pale self is happiest in the Library's shadows. Out of sight, and as far out of mind as I can get.

Which unfortunately, is never as far away as I would like. Unlike Orielle, extra attention is the last thing I want. The whole ordeal of the past few weeks has been a nightmare.

"You seem in fine form. I can't see what all the fuss was about," she says. She settles herself more firmly on my desk, as if I don't have a job to get on with.

The crude hand sign I use to tell her to move is clear, even to her.

Orielle wrinkles her nose, looking around at the other

scribes settling into their place. Elris will be along soon, and I don't want him to think I'm slacking.

Move. I need to get to work.

Orielle makes a noise to express her distaste. "Is this really where you want to be, Lorel? A mere existence among *scribes*?" she says. It echoes loudly in the chamber.

The King have mercy on me, I'm going to kill her. Why is she like this?

I want to be a scribe. I am content here. I have no ability for anything else and I can barely cast a permanent ward, let alone a proper sigil.

My hand signs are frantic. She understands them about as well as she understands me. There's no point in such an outburst. Even so, my hands shake with the fury that only a sibling can conjure.

I doubt I could have picked a profession more distasteful to her. My lack of magical skill bars me from most things she'd deem worthy. Of all the things I could be, this is something I am capable of. I'll never excel at it. I'll never rise to be an illuminator with my own team of scribes. I am lucky that sometimes Elris trusts me with the initial wash layers, but I know I will never be as skilled as he is. I don't need it hammered into me every time my blessed sister appears to express her disappointment at my mediocrity.

If I'm such a disappointment, why can't you just leave me alone?

Even if she does understand my hand signs, they're so rushed I'm not sure even a Librarian would manage it.

Orielle's face closes off and I worry I've gone too far.

And then a cool hand slides over my shoulder. Another grips my upper arm and there is the press of a much taller body behind me. I shiver as if I have passed into the dark alcove.

"Lady Orielle," comes a smooth voice, as cool as her hands. "I am afraid I must ask you to leave. It appears you are upsetting my scribe."

Dawn King have mercy on me. We've attracted the attention of a Librarian.

Orielle has turned to marble. Cold and impassive. Immovable. It's a look at what she must be like day-to-day. It is my least favourite version of her.

"I hardly think it your concern when I come to speak to my sister," Orielle says.

I lift my hands to reply. The Librarian's hand slides down my arm to still me.

"Scribe Lorel belongs to the Library and is in my care. As I told you when you came by earlier, you are not entitled to interrupt her work."

There is a spark of indignant fury in Orielle's eyes. "But she was not at work then, was she?"

"Lady Orielle," says the Librarian, and the way she says it has me shrinking like I'm sixteen again and have accidentally spilled ink across the desk. "I will only ask you once more. Remove yourself and do not step foot in my Library again without the appropriate applications."

"You cannot restrict me—" starts Orielle.

"If you continue to make such an infernal racket in the scriptorium during the working hours, I am afraid I will be forced to restrict you entirely from the Library. Do not try to force my hand. You do not have any power here," the Librarian says. Her hand is tense on my shoulder. It's almost possessive.

I suppose it is a claim of sorts. I am a scribe and I belong to the Library.

Orielle is complete and haughty outrage. Colour sits high on her cheeks and her eyes are bright.

"Fine," Orielle snaps, casting the word louder than required. Of course, she will not bear to allow the Librarian to have the last word. She doesn't hurry to remove herself from my desk, slipping off in a soft sigh of silk on silk.

I can't move my hands to sign a goodbye. There is no point anyway. My heart aches with regret to watch her go, just like it does every time we part poorly. Which is most of the time.

The Librarian doesn't move once Orielle is gone. Her fingers tap lightly against my arm, and I notice her perfume now. It envelops me in a cloud of moss and old stone. A deep earthy scent with a touch of night blossom. She leans in, her mouth against my ear. My heart stutters.

No one seeks the attention of a Librarian. We scribes avoid it at all costs. A late fee paid to a Librarian is one paid in blood. An excess of noise in the Library itself was an invitation to lose your tongue. To cause damage to a book didn't even bear thinking about. I dread what my punishment for this ruckus will be.

Her breath brushes cool against my ear, like she has spent too long in the depths of the Library. Perhaps even as deep as the Library's mysterious Heart, that dark ever-changing labyrinth where only the Librarians ever tread.

"Scribe," she says and it sends a chill like the grave down my spine. "When you are done with the day's tasks, I would like a word."

Dread sits cold in my stomach. If Orielle has brought a Librarian down on my head, I will kill her myself. If I survive.

"*Don't* keep me waiting."

· · ·

I cannot shake the cold feeling of relentless dread that has seeped into my bones. It turns my stomach on itself until I wish I could beg off the day's work and be anywhere else. Elris gives me a worried look as he passes me the day's pages. He pushes his pale hair back as he crouches next to my desk, hazel eyes unguarded.

Colour washes, he signs, attempting a smile that he surely means to be comforting. It comes across as wretched as I feel. He's taking pity on me. Taking notice of the tremor in my hands that will make the detailed work of copying outlines an impossible task.

Of course, there are still myriad ways I can make a mess of filling in the delicate washes for the backgrounds of the illustrated pages. Fortunately, Elris' style is a more romantic, fluid thing that is unlikely to suffer from the fits of panic that will no doubt plague me through the day's work.

The hours give me no quarter, the minutes rushing after each other relentlessly. All too soon, the bell chimes softly, calling the end of the day. With it come the voices of the scribes rising and echoing in the chamber. My voice doesn't join them.

I am a coward, so I busy myself in the stacks. Pretend that I'm laying out my work to dry while the other scribes clear out. Maybe I should have asked someone to wait for me, to be sure I *do* come out from my meeting with the Librarian. It's too late for that, though. It's far, far too late.

Chapter 2

Lorel

THERE'S NO GETTING OUT OF THIS. THERE IS ONLY ONE way in and out of the scriptorium— past the overseeing Librarian's office. The door is wide open in silent invitation. Deceptively warm light spills out into the stone lined corridor, as if the mythical sun might be shining through. It is a farce. The exit sits on the lowest level of the scriptorium and is dug deep into the mountain stone. Even if the sun still shone, it would not reach here. I take a deep, silent breath to settle my nerves before I step up into the doorway. I might as well be stepping up to the sacrificial altar. I half-expect the sacred cup bearer to be standing by with her poisoned chalice, the Dawn King standing by with his sacrificial blade.

I wonder if the Librarian is the chalice or the blade.

I recall her fingers pressing into my skin. It catches at the edges of my thoughts, my skin prickling against it.

"Scribe," commands the Librarian, from where she leans against the front of her desk. "You may enter."

I resist the urge to sign back that I'd rather not and instead I step into the room. The door clicks shut as it closes behind me and *fuck*, the last thing I want is a private audience. The Librarian gestures me forward and my feet obey. She towers over me easily and I would so dearly love to flee.

I've never seen her before, in all my years training in the Library. I would have remembered if I had, because she is eerily, terrifyingly beautiful. It's the kind of beauty that devours, scouring you out until nothing but bones remain. Long dark hair, long dark robes. Dark, fathomless eyes you could fall into. Red lips curved into a predatory smile. My heart hammers in my chest and I fight to stop the shaking in my limbs as I sign to her.

You wanted to speak to me.

The Librarian tips her head, the neatest frown touching at her brows. "It is the end of the workday, scribe. You may speak with your tongue," she says.

Dawn King strike me. Why did Orielle have to do this to me? I wish I could remember the lie I had come up with this morning for just this situation, but any sensible thought has entirely deserted me.

The Librarian closes the distance between us and I have to tip my head up to see her. I'm surrounded by her perfume again. It sends all my senses awry. Surely she can hear the way my heart is pounding from here. Like a mouse cornered by a gleeful cat.

I would prefer not to.

She hums, thoughtful. "Just as obstinate as your sister." Her hand comes up, pushing my glasses back into place. "These past few weeks have been quite unusual for you, haven't they?"

I open my mouth to reply, before remembering I can't and snapping it shut. It is far too obvious for someone as keen-eyed as her.

The Library has taken good care of me.

Another hum from her. Her long, elegant fingers brush my skin as she tucks my hair behind my ear. It's impossible to prevent the way I shiver at her touch. As if I had walked over my own grave.

"You are curious," she murmurs. I freeze in place as her fingers trail to rest against my pulse, where it hammers against the press of her fingers. Her smile widens. My breath is a shuddering, silent thing.

No more curious than dust. Her eyes flick down to watch my hands and catch on my mouth as they flick back to my face.

"You do yourself a discredit," she says, her tone low and dangerous. Her fingers run along the edge of my jaw, stopping to grip my chin and tip my head back further as she pulls me against her body. My breathing is uneven. Resoundingly silent in the quiet office space. The Librarian gives me a curious look, and then her thumb is against my lip, pressing into my mouth. Her free hand slides over the back of my neck, holding my head firm. I gasp silently as she pushes my mouth wider.

"Hmm, you still have your tongue," she mutters, as if I am some kind of unusual curiosity. "You cannot make a sound at all, can you? And I would wager not one of them cared to notice." Her thumb rests against my lips, her cool fingers gently caressing my jaw. Her eyes are dark and fathomless as night shadows, trying to pierce into the very heart of me. Trying to see the curse that rests inside of my chest. It is a dead weight of suffocating dread if I think of it for too long.

And now I am thinking of it, it starts to stir. I realise I have been standing here, willingly, for too long.

I pull away from her, and she lets me go easily, cool fingers slipping from my skin as it blooms with warmth. I fear I might be blushing. I press myself against the cool of the stone behind me and will my heart to calm down. I might as well ask the sun to shine.

It is merely an unfortunate side effect. My hands tremble a little as I sign, and I hate that.

"Of the incident, yes," she says, looking at me thoughtfully again. "I would rather like to know more about that." It is not a suggestion, the way she says it. That's too bad.

I can't remember anything. And it is the truth. The last thing I remember I had been sitting at my desk. There had been an elegant book in my hands. I can't recall how it had gotten there but it was so beautiful, even in my memory. I had picked it up and tipped the cover open.

The next thing I had known was waking in the infirmary surrounded by physicians and Librarians, my entire body aching. I had several broken ribs, cuts and marks down my sides from my own fingernails, and the last signs of a breaking fever. I also could not speak. I could not cry out. I could not gasp, or scream. Just complete, enduring silence. That had hurt the most.

They had assumed it was shock and that it would wear off in due time. It had not. And the Librarian was right. No one had really noticed. I had tried so hard to make sure they hadn't.

"You make yourself more and more interesting, scribe," says the Librarian.

I promise I'm not trying to.

She smiles. It is as horrific as a Librarian's smile promises to be. It's how she would smile as she extracted the cost of a missing book, in blood or flesh or bone.

"How delightful," she says. The look she gives me then makes me feel like I am mere moments from being devoured. I catch an edge of amusement in her gaze and I think she might be laughing at me.

"Well, I should not keep you any further from your evening meal. Go. You are dismissed." I'm not prepared for the sudden end to this confusing interaction. The Librarian turns away and the door behind me swings open again. I should go. If I am late, I run the risk of going hungry for the night. I'm still hesitating, waiting for the trap when the Librarian looks back at me.

"Scribe," she says, holding my gaze. My breath is caught somewhere in my chest and passing out seems like a sudden and real threat. "Have you lost the use of your limbs too, or do you have something else to say?"

I don't bother to sign a farewell this time either. I turn tail and run, putting as much space between us as I can. Trying to outrace the fact that I am not as upset by her as I should be.

I had thought waking from that fever, with no memories and the weight of something horrific and cursed upon me had been bad enough. It was nothing on waking from a fitful sleep clouded by dark shadows and nightmarish figures. The weight of that was a dread that settled over me like a shroud, as if I were preparing for a funeral— only the funeral was mine.

I lie for far too long in my little chamber, staring at the patterns of the natural stone in the ceiling. Like most everything in the Citadel, it has been carved into the stone and the walls show the natural striation of the rock. There are no windows, nor the illusion of them, in the scribes dorms, though I have memories of the grand illusory windows in the Keep.

The large rug that greets my toes when I finally drag myself out of bed is more dust than anything else. The room is furnished with my bed, a wardrobe, a washstand, and a desk that I rarely use these days. When I want to keep sitting at a desk I stay late in the scriptorium. At least there I can use my paints.

I don't know why I waste my time and supplies painting so much, as if I am some sort of artist. It's like playing pretend. Pretending to have the audacity to think I could ever be an illuminator. It is entirely foolish, and a waste of time. A ridiculous fancy for a scribe who is no better than she ought to be.

I hurl myself from the bed, pushing my thoughts aside. They are far too grim for first thing in the morning. I cross to the washstand in three steps, which is the farthest distance across the room. It isn't much, but it is at least a space of my own. A little sanctuary from the terrors of curses and Librarians. If only they wouldn't follow me into my dreams.

I wash up with the cold water from the washstand and throw my wardrobe open with more force than is necessary. It is filled with an unimaginative collection of black woollen shifts, grey wool surcoats, and grey woollen hose that I wear year round to protect against the cold underground air. I have two pairs of brown boots to swap between, though I only wear one pair, lest I wear through both and end up without shoes entirely.

This small space is everything I need. Everything that I am content with. I don't *want* anything more than this. I pull out a set of clothes for the day and strip off my sleeping shift.

The curse mark is a dark black ink blot across my chest. It's stark against my skin in the ancient mirror on the washstand. Bigger now than it was when I woke a week ago. It had only been a small blot, then. It's the size of my palm now. Not a single soul had remarked upon it, and when I'd asked the healer, Lune, to look, she'd only looked at me confused and assured me there was nothing there.

I look down at it now, press my fingers against it. Where the skin should be warm, it is cool to the touch. It is very much still there. After a lifetime of feeling cursed, it's strange to know I truly am this time. I turn my back on the mirror and pull my clothes on, covering up the reminder of the day everything had gone horribly wrong.

I smooth out any creases and check myself in the mirror before I go. With its dark, degraded edges, I do not look out of place at all. Short bobbed hair, dark and neat. Stern dark brows, always too serious. Large round glasses perched on an unremarkable nose. Perfectly acceptable figure with no real points of interest that had suited me just fine so far in life. Entirely uninteresting. Exactly as I wanted to be.

I take up my lapel pin from where I had discarded it the evening before. It indicates my place and affiliation and grants me the protection of the Library and its Librarians. Reminds anyone else of my station, if they bother to look. Very rarely did anyone bother to look.

I pin it in place and flick my pocket watch open to check the time. I've missed the morning meal. I hadn't wanted to talk to anyone after yesterday anyway, but the morning will be harder for it. I hate missing a meal.

For now, I'll need to be swift so I can enter with the other scribes. I doubt the Librarian will be watching the scriptorium again, but the last thing I need is to catch her attention again. I hope she's already forgotten me. That something else, something more interesting will catch her attention. I just need some luck. Unfortunately, I fear I may never have had any in the first place.

Chapter 3

Lorel

I FIND SYBRI AND TREFOR IN THE CROWDED HALL AND fall into step beside them.

"Morning, Lorel," says Trefor, grinning broadly. He's always far too cheerful. Brown eyes always alight. A slight creature with steady hands.

Good morning. If either of them thinks it strange for me to be signing, neither comment. I push my glasses back up my nose as I fall in beside them.

"That was rotten luck yesterday," says Trefor. I catch both of them giving me a look over, as if making sure I have all my limbs.

Sybri nods in agreement. She's tall and willowy with dirty blonde hair and calculating amber-gold eyes that give me a sympathetic look. "I'm glad to see you survived the encounter."

If I can just avoid a repeat, that would be wonderful.

"Let's hope she won't be down here again today. I've not seen her down here before," says Trefor, confirming my suspicion from the day before.

"Unless she's taken an interest?" says Sybri. "Though surely she has better things to do."

Surely.

Unfortunately, my luck is indeed rotten. Or I am more cursed than I thought.

The door isn't just open. The Librarian is standing there, leaning in the doorway with an air of boredom, watching us file past. The urge to run swells back to life, and I keep my head down and will myself to keep walking forward. The rush of sound in my ears drowns out the rest of Sybri and Trefor's conversation.

"Scribe," the Librarian calls and with the way she says it, I know she can only mean me. She could at least have learned my name. I ignore her and a moment later, stumble over the air at my feet. Sybri catches me before I can test out whether my teeth will win against stone.

"Are you alright?" she asks. Trefor looks over her shoulder, concerned.

I'm fine, just tripping on my own feet.

The Librarian's shadow falls over us, blocking the light from her office. The flow of scribes continues around her, each of them trying desperately to avoid.

"Scribe Sybri, Scribe Trefor, do you not have somewhere to be? Or do you intend to be tardy?" Both of them pale a little, though Sybri still seems unwilling to release me. We both know she doesn't have a choice. Neither of them are willing to learn what punishment a Librarian like her will give for being late. Sybri gives my arm a squeeze and then Trefor is pulling her on with an apologetic look. I don't blame them in the least. It's hardly their fault that I've come to a Librarian's attention.

Librarian.

I press myself back against the wall. Her lovely face is

set in a frown and fear that I have disappointed her wars with the desire for her to forget I exist. I must be losing my mind.

"Scribe. Are you well?" she asks. I want to hide my shaking hands behind my back, but I need to reply. Curse this fucking curse.

I'm fine. I need to get to my desk.

"You do not look fine," she says. Which is rude. I looked perfectly fine when I left this morning. If I am not fine now then it can only be her fault.

How am I supposed to look? Even the hand signs feel snappy and frustrated. Turns out I can control my hands about as well as I can control my tongue.

The Librarian laughs, a soft thing that is far sweeter than it ought to be. "As if you have taken your morning meal would be a start." *No.* She can't possibly *know* that. "Though there is little to be done about it now, nor about your sleep schedule." She reaches out, her fingers hovering a breath away from my cheek and the dark shadows under my eyes.

I should get to my desk.

"Hmm. If it is too much scribe, you need not push yourself," she says. For a moment I think she might be exhibiting genuine concern, and then I remember that she is a Librarian and their only code is that the scribes are theirs to torment.

I'll be late. I have as little desire to find out the penalty for being late as Sybri and Trefor do. Though of course, it would not be my doing.

The Librarian holds my gaze for a moment more, and then her hand is withdrawing. She steps back, the flow of scribes now a trickle of late comers.

"Very well, then," she says. And then her head whips

around, her hand striking out to catch a running scribe by the collar of their surcoat. The scribe tumbles to the ground at the Librarian's feet.

"We are not so uncouth as to *run* in the scriptorium, Scribe Maxim," she says.

I do not stay around to see what happens next. I do not know Maxim, but I offer up a silent thanks to him for giving me the chance to slip away. A desolate wail follows me, and I wince. If it is between me or him, well, sorry, Maxim.

I make it to my desk before I let myself crumple into my seat, hiding my head in my hands and willing the tremors to stop. Fear of a Librarian is normal, but this kind of response that causes my heart to race and the blood to rush to my ears? It must be the only sensible response my body can muster as it tries to tell me to run and keep running.

I jump at a hand on my shoulder, but it's only Elris, his face a beautiful picture of distress.

Are you alright?

He crouches next to me at the desk, rolled paper tucked under his arm.

I'm fine. Just tell me what you need done.

Colour washes again.

He unrolls the pages and slides them onto my desk. The shock of that neutralises the surging fear that had been running through my veins.

Again?

Elris grimaces as he signs back. *I fetched the Librarian yesterday. I hadn't realised Librarian Sila had started watching the scriptorium with such enthusiasm.*

I blink at him. I skip over the fact he's trying to make up for his blunder with a task he knows I enjoy, because I realise then that I hadn't known *her* name.

Her name is Sila?

Elris' face does something strange then. It's an expression I can't quite parse. *Don't get attached*, he signs.

It's a warning I don't need, because I hadn't even considered something so absurd.

I only hope that she forgets me. The sooner, the better.

Some of the tension eases from Elris' shoulders. He gives me another apologetic smile before moving off to take up his own seat.

I settle the pages across my desk, deciding how best to tackle them. My desk is wide enough for two pages to sit side by side, so that I can move between them while they dry. At the top of the desk, assorted pots of paint are nestled into cavities to keep them steady. A quick once-over tells me that there's nothing I need to replace before I start.

My brushes hang where I had clipped them yesterday to dry and I collect them up, depositing them in a glass holder. I'll need fresh water, and to tuck all but the first two pages into the rack hanging under my desk. The tasks are comfortingly familiar, among all the turmoil. I've been doing this for years now, and there is an ease to laying down the colour Elris requires.

Perhaps it is because of the ease of the task that it leaves my mind blank to pick up each and every thought that flits across it. No matter how pleased I am with the way the colour breaks across the paper, or how delighted I am at the way two colours curl together at a particular point, I cannot stop my swirling thoughts. And there are so many of them.

The Librarian, Sila, I can do nothing about, except continue to be my boring self. Even the incident with the book doesn't make me that interesting. It isn't like it's rare to find a cursed book in the Library, after all. It isn't even unusual for harm to come to the residents of the Library, or to anyone in the Citadel for that matter. It's just how it is.

Surely she will grow bored eventually. Dread settles like ice in my chest at the thought. I tell myself it's just the curse.

The curse *is* a problem. Recovering from touching a cursed object is one thing, being cursed by an inanimate object is another. So much for being boring, because the Librarian surely *knows* I am cursed. It's one thing to think I am unwilling to speak from shock or hardship or injury. It's another to know I cannot make a single wisp of sound. I can feel the phantom touch of her cool thumb pressed against my mouth. *Fuck*, I need to think of something else. I need to think about the curse instead. If I can solve that, then maybe I can solve my Librarian problem.

I go through the motions of the morning, clawing my way through my memories for any clue or hint as I go. Pages set out to dry, new pages started. Brushes cleaned, paints tidied, desk wiped down.

Then comes the midday break, where I notice a sweet bun that was not on the menu has been placed on my tray. I'm tempted to ignore it, but it's one of my favourites— a sweet bread with the little salty berries that grow in the deep caves under the Glade. I should leave it untouched.

Instead, I eat it with reluctant aggression as signed conversations happen around me. It's fresh and annoyingly good. I resent its existence in my life.

When we return to our desks, Elris assigns me some pages for copying. I'll need to do the first pass in graphite, before going over it again in ink. I take up the knife to sharpen my pencil. I'm still thinking on the book and the curse. Maybe if I can find the book, it will have some answers.

I realise I haven't seen the book since the night I opened it. Someone must have returned it to the shelves. I fumble my pencil and it clatters to the floor.

Elris looks up as the blade passes neatly through the flesh of my left hand. I barely feel it. The knife is so sharp and the shock is immediate. Blood wells in the cut. I can't make a sound in response, and that makes me want to laugh. I might be tumbling very quickly into hysteria.

I push my chair back with a screech against the stone, trying to prevent the blood from spilling over my desk and the fresh paper.

There are very few reasons a scribe might be allowed to break the work day silence. Fortunately, this is one of them. Elris breaks it with a dignified and emphatic, "*Shit*, Lorel." It's a close enough summary of what I wish I could say. "Trefor, fetch the Librarian— *Fuck*." Elris groans as our eyes meet.

It's too late to stop Trefor, and we're both kidding ourselves if we thought I could sneak out of here unnoticed while my hand is bleeding everywhere. Dawn King have mercy, so much for not drawing attention to myself.

Sybri has grabbed a clean paint rag, one of the clean, crisp white ones. She takes my hand, wrapping it as tightly as she can over the wound. My blood is thin and bright red as it soaks through.

"We'll need to take you to the infirmary," she says.

Elris carefully takes the knife from my other hand, as if I can't be trusted with it any longer.

"At least it's a clean cut," he says. "Sybri, are you able—?"

Librarian Sila appears in the walkway, Trefor looking pale and apologetic behind her. "Illuminator Elris, you may return to your work. I will take this from here." She says this like she might be talking about any number of unpleasant tasks— like being civil or politely asking someone to keep their voice down. Elris clamps his mouth shut, nodding.

Of course, Librarian, he signs, stepping back.

Sybri lets go of my hand like she's been burned, and with the look the Librarian has just levelled at her, I don't blame her in the slightest. The Librarian's eyes drop to the stone at my feet, taking note of the blood on the floor and my poor abandoned pencil. I eye her warily.

"Come," she commands. I have no choice but to follow.

Chapter 4

Lorel

THE LIBRARIAN STALKS DOWN THE CORRIDORS LIKE A night terror. I have to take at least two steps to her one to keep up. I clutch my injured hand to my chest. The infirmary is not far, situated where the edges of the Library meet the Glade— another of the Citadel's factions. The Citadel has five factions, all of them burrowed into the side of a mountain and stacked in together, except for the Dawn King's palace— the Suntide Court that pierces through the mountainside into the open air.

Lune, the closest person I have to a friend, is stationed in the infirmary today. She's sitting at the desk that marks the entrance to the room full of rows of beds and illness that I had spent the last few weeks in. I am rather loath at the idea of returning. Not in the least because I cannot speak and have a curse living inside of me and I think this must actually be some kind of divine punishment.

"Lorel— Librarian Sila," Lune says, brown eyes widening where they peer out from under nut-brown hair bound back by a scarf. The Librarian stands behind me and places her hands on my shoulders. The press of them is cool even through the wool of my clothes and I suppress a shiver.

"Cupbearer. I did not expect you would be working in the infirmary," says the Librarian.

"I am not the Cupbearer every day of the year," says Lune, frowning. "What have you done to Lorel?"

The Librarian scoffs. "I have done nothing except allow her to work when I ought to have sent her back to her bed. She is clearly not recovered from her ordeal."

No, I'm not, because my ordeal is ongoing and ever present and exactly the size and shape of one overbearing nightmare of a Librarian. I hold out my hand to Lune, who comes forward to take it.

"She has cut herself on a pencil sharpening knife."

Lune's expression makes me want to hide away in the shadows, never to be seen again. "*Lorel*, how were you even holding it?" she says, exasperated.

"As I said. She is not well today," says the Librarian. I fear she is right. I am not clumsy by nature, but I *had* almost thrown myself to the floor today, and now I had cut my hand open. Perhaps I should have followed my first instinct to run and hide in my bed.

"I will see to it," Lune says.

"And then send her to rest," instructs the Librarian. "I need to return to the scriptorium. I do not want to see you back there, scribe." Her fingers dig into my shoulders for a moment, and then she is gone. The absence of her presence is like the lifting of a blanket. It was smothering me, but I'm disappointed nonetheless at its loss.

"Well, let's get you stitched up," says Lune with a wry twist of her mouth.

.   .   .

The barely painted walls of the reception area turn into wildly colourful murals depicting plants of healing and the Dawn King's benevolence. They cradle the infirmary within them, rows of beds partitioned by folding screens, though Lune doesn't lead me there today. Instead, she takes me off to a small room to the side. It is decorated in a style similar to the infirmary, and the lamp Lune lights with a quick sigil is much brighter than the low light in the space we had come from.

Lune is adept at her sigils, as most with fae blood are, but her true talent is as a healer of magical ailments. She cannot heal a cut, but she can see the magical pathways of the body. Alas, for me, my injury is merely a physical one.

The cut, anyway.

A bench lines the wall in a neat impression of disarray, topped by shelves of little jars and bottles, tools and bandages. There's a bed in here too, an armchair and a tall stool.

Lune drags the stool over to the chair. "This will be much more private," says Lune. "Sit."

She indicates the armchair, and for once I do as I am told. I know it's going to need to be sewn up and I am already dreading it. Anyone who could easily heal a wound of the flesh such as this is kept for the use of the courtiers. I really should have been more careful.

In a way, Librarian Sila is right. I'm not well. I just didn't think a curse was really an ailment. Thus far, Lune had not been able to sense it, but I can feel that cold sense of dread resting in my chest. The curse slumbering. I can almost imagine it like a cat, curled up and waiting for something.

Lune stops in her muttering and gives me a puzzled

look. "Are you quite well? You're being awfully obliging," she says.

This is what I was afraid of. Lune is far too observant. I cannot sign properly with one hand and Lune won't understand the shorthand I could passably use otherwise. What signs she does know are mostly to do with her profession. Not with, you know, horrific curses. I just shake my head at her.

Lune sits beside me and takes my cut hand. It is as bad as I feared and as clean as expected.

"Well," says Lune, cheerfully. "It could be worse. You know you can speak in here. I won't tell your Librarian."

I give her an alarmed look. She is not *my* Librarian. I just shake my head and keep my mouth clamped shut.

"Very well," says Lune. "You'll just have to listen to me prattle on then."

Lune makes good on her promise, while she sews me back together. I grit my teeth, unable to make a noise. Not even a hiss at the pain, which somehow makes it all the more agonising. Lune's careful gaze misses nothing, even as she talks. I'm grateful she does— at least one of us should make noise over this and her chatter is distracting enough. Just. Nothing seems irreparably damaged, and I can only thank the Dawn King for that.

Lune wraps my hand to finish, and it is painfully obvious that even if I wanted to I could not return to the scriptorium. My hand is useless in this state. I go to stand when Lune is done, but a gentle pressure on my shoulder sets me back in my seat.

"No," says Lune, stern. "I've patched up the most grizzled of the Dawnguard, for much smaller injuries, with far more protestation and drama. Even if you didn't want to talk, I expect you to make *some* sound. Your face was certainly *trying*."

It was foolish of me to think such a thing would go unnoticed. Scribes may not speak during work hours— it was simply how it was done— but very rarely are they truly silent. Even if my throat had been scoured out— which had happened to another scribe once— I could not have stopped myself from trying to cry out through it.

I look around for something to write with, miming for a pen. I should tell her. Maybe she will know something, have at least one helpful thought tucked away in that head of hers. I haven't been told much about what had happened to me. I'd hardly been able to ask many questions, after all. I didn't even know who had found me.

Lune passes me a pen and a board with paper clipped to it. But when I have it, I don't quite know what to write. How do I put it into words? It's not a type of self-inflicted madness, I don't think. One can't prevent themselves from making a sound when they make an involuntary gasp of air through sheer will. Can one?

The look I give Lune when I look up must be desperate, because her face softens into something like pity. I *hate* it.

"So you can't make a noise. Since when?" Lune is using her healer voice.

Since I woke up here, I scrawl across the paper.

Lune frowns, which is preferable to pity. "When they brought you here you had broken ribs, broken fingers, dark angry bruises and little cuts dug deep into your sides," she says.

This, at least, I knew. The cuts had been from my own fingernails. I just couldn't understand why I would have done that to myself.

"Plus an awful fever."

Do you know where they found me?

I hadn't asked much when I had woken here. The fever had still been clinging, and I was lucky I could remember my own name. It was like something had taken a torch to my memories. They'd come back for the most part. Only one part was still missing. The gap between opening the book and waking in the infirmary.

"In your room," Lune says. "You were found pressed against the wall, jammed into the corner. Or so I was told. I wasn't on the roster that day. If it hadn't been for the fever burning you up, I think they would have thought you dead."

I stare at her. How in the King's name had I gone from the scriptorium to my room? I push my glasses up my nose and set to writing again.

And they didn't find me with a book?

The writing is painfully slow with my off-hand, my bound hand trying to balance the writing board.

Lune shakes her head. "If she did, then it wasn't passed on." Cold dread rises up from the stones, chilling me from my toes and raising the hair along my arms.

She?

I already know the answer, even as Lune gives me a resigned look

"Librarian Sila is the one who found you. If you want answers, you should ask her."

Chapter 5

Lorel

Lune sends me back to the dorms to rest and so I cannot go and find the Librarian. She wouldn't be pleased to see me back in the scriptorium, and I don't *want* to go and find the Librarian. If I start asking questions, she'll only grow more curious. There must be another way to find the answer.

I search my room, in case the book is hidden away somewhere. If I had been found here, crushing myself against the stone, then perhaps there is a chance it had fallen behind some furniture. I know even as I search that it isn't. I sit on my bed and rub my hands down my face, thoughtlessly. The regret is swift and painful. Whatever salve Lune had used to numb the pain is starting to wear off.

The memory of the Librarian's fingers pressing into my shoulders makes my heart race. Fear, probably. Definitely fear.

No, I could not ask her. I would exhaust all other possibilities first.

I wrack my thoughts.

That night, I had stayed late in the scriptorium to practice, preferring the silence there to the silence of my room. I had just set everything aside and tidied up, and there it had been. The book. A trap set to entice me. And I had fallen for it.

The book had been properly ancient. Slim with a red leather cover, the foil peeling, the spine cracking and threatening to crumble. By rights, I should never have touched such a book with my bare hands. I knew better than to open it. I had just wanted to have a peek, to see what kind of illustrations it held. It had been placed on my desk, after all.

It had no title, or if it did, it had long been lost to time. There was barely the impression of one, so old even the leather had forgotten the tools that had marked it. I had cracked the cover ever so slightly— and then there was nothing. No impression of what the book contained. No memory of leaving the scriptorium. Nothing at all about what had happened in my room.

But I could remember the book, and that was a start. It was *something*. I hadn't seen any sign of it in the scriptorium. It was not in my room, and I refused to believe the Librarian had it. Perhaps even if she had it would have been returned to the Library. Tomorrow then, during the working hours when *the* Librarian would be watching the scriptorium, I would go find *a* Librarian and see if they could help me find the book.

"You don't know the contents of the book or its title?"

This Librarian looks over his glasses at me with clear disapproval. Dark-haired and dark-eyed, Librarian Mercias is tall, broad-shouldered and easily irritated. Under other circumstances, the latter fact would amuse me. Today though, it does not.

He towers over the raised desk, looking down at me. They're all so cursedly tall, and I have to wonder if this is a boon given from the Library's Heart. Perhaps it helps them reach the top shelves, or maybe it's just for looming over scribes.

I rub my glasses clean before setting them back on my nose. Librarian Mercias' dark eyebrows twitch in irritation, as if he can hear my thoughts. Impossible, but for the fact my face has always given me away and my own lack of patience is clear even in my hand signs. I grit my teeth. This whole conversation has been painful, and not just because of my injured hand.

No. That's all the information I have.

"Then I'm afraid I cannot help you, Scribe Lorel," he says. He settles back into his chair as he says it, lounging. I know this Librarian well. He often watches the scriptorium, and he's always an absolute prick. "Knowing that it may have been returned to the Library in the last six weeks isn't enough to go on."

You must have a record of returns.

"Perhaps," says Librarian Mercias, examining his nails. "I hardly see the value in the request if you can't tell me the contents."

If you would just look—

Librarian Mercias holds up his hand. "No. You lack information, have no request permit and are *not* a researcher. Move along, scribe." He returns to shuffling at the papers on his desk. A clear dismissal.

I refuse to move. I will bore a hole through his wretched head if I have to. He sighs as he looks up and there is a fracture of something like pure fatigue in his expression— but his eyes aren't on me. They're on someone behind me.

No. Surely not.

"Mercias," croons Sila, draping an arm over my shoulder. I freeze as her fingers caress the side of my face. She's haughty, in a way someone can only be when they so entirely outrank another. "You cannot possibly be denying my scribe her request?"

Her body is cold where it rests against mine and I feel my heart kick up again. This woman is going to kill me. Librarian Mercias crosses his arms over his chest.

"Sila," he says coolly. "You cannot expect me to grant this so-called request without the appropriate paperwork."

Sila laughs, and it's as cold as she is. "Oh, of course I wouldn't. No, I will take Scribe Lorel's request from here, unless you have any objections?"

I cannot see Sila's face, but hearing her say my name makes me feel like I've walked over my own grave. So she *does* know my name. I direct my spark of irritation at Mercias, who could have just allowed my request and spared us all.

Librarian Mercias's face is nearly unreadable, but there is something of Elris' warning in his eyes when they flick to my face. I don't need the warning. What I need is to get out of here before Sila drags me off into the depths of the Library and feasts on my heart or something.

"None, but you are wasting your time, Librarian Sila," he says.

I feel the way Sila's fingers press against my skin a little at that. Flexing. How curious. "We shall see," she says. Her grip on my shoulders tightens as she turns me towards the door to the Greater Library.

I should be thrilled to walk through them. Instead, I'm only concerned I won't be walking out of them again.

I've only ever seen the edges of the Greater Library from the reception that sits at the entrance. It is not for the likes of scribes to wander about the Greater Library or anywhere beyond it.

The central chamber soars up high. The tall stained glass dome must break the surface far above, and dim light filters down. The walls are lined with shelves full to bursting with books and layers upon layers of these balconies spiral high up the chamber, and all the way down into the dark as well. I itch to look over the edge to see how deep it goes. The Librarian's fingers are firm as she directs me up the nearest set of stairs.

We walk until she is satisfied, though I could not say if she *is* satisfied. She simply decides to stop at some point, finally letting go. It feels like I might have bruises where her fingers have pressed into my skin. I back myself against the nearest bookshelf, and instantly regret it as she angles her body to block me in.

"Now, little mouse, why are you scurrying through my Library? I was under the impression I had instructed you to rest." She runs her finger along my jaw, tipping my chin up.

I had been trying not to look at her directly because it makes me feel breathless. I scowl back at her and raise my hand to sign.

Aren't you meant to be watching the scriptorium?

Sila laughs softly. It's joyless, doing nothing to soften her expression. "Why would I bother today?" She lets my chin drop and steps back slightly. "Tell me, what book are you seeking?"

I don't want her help. I didn't want to involve her. She makes my skin prickle and my heart race, as if all of my senses are telling me to get as far away as possible.

It might seem she is being kind. Helpful even. But it will come at a cost. It always came at a cost with Librarians.

Why do you want to help me?

Sila tips her head. "Why should I not help?"

You're a Librarian. Being helpful isn't usually in your nature.

She smiles at that, and it splits across her face like heartbreak. It turns her into something heartrendingly beautiful. It is a terrifying reminder of how dangerous she is. There are ghastly faetales of beautiful ghosts that exist only to steal souls, and that is what she reminds me of.

"Why don't you just tell me what you're looking for, little mouse," she says.

I fold my arms, shoving my hands under my armpits. I'm restless because maybe she has the answer, and all I need to do is ask. I'm reluctant, because the whole point of this exercise was to avoid her. My mouth moves to shape the sound of frustration that I can't utter, and then my hands are out, moving with the same irritated energy.

Fine. It's an old book, slim, not much bigger than my hand. Red leather cover. It might have been returned some weeks ago.

Sila tips her head back the other way, like a curious bird. "After the incident?"

Yes.

"A red leather cover. With foil?"

Yes.

"Ancient and cracking along the spine?"

Yes—

"It is not here," she says.

How can you know? You haven't even looked. Curse this wretched bandage for making my signs clumsy in my frustration. A hot thread of anger lances through me. She's playing with me with no intention of helping me at all. *If you're not going to be helpful—*

"I didn't say I would not be helpful," she says, pressing a

finger to my lips. I blink at the touch, cold against the warmth of my skin. She frowns, holding her finger there even though it's my hands that do the talking. "What is the connection between the incident and the book?. . .Ah, the book *is* the incident."

I purse my lips against her finger.

"You were not found with a book," Sila says. "But you were reading a book in the scriptorium earlier that evening, weren't you?"

I stare at her, startled. *How do you know that?*

Sila smiles knowingly. "I was there, of course. How curious. You know, I had forgotten the book until now. I have not seen it since." Her finger taps my mouth as she thinks.

Sila must have been watching the scriptorium that day. But I had been there after hours, and I'm sure I'd never seen her until after the incident. I would certainly have remembered her.

Books can't just disappear.

"That's not entirely true," Sila says distractedly. "Books do all sorts of things when the fancy takes them."

You must be joking.

"I am a Librarian, scribe, I do not joke." She slides her finger across my lips, taking my chin between her fingertips. I swallow, mouth dry as she searches my face intently. "Something is missing here."

I don't know if she means in me, or in the story. Maybe both. It's probably both.

I can't remember that night.

That seems to catch her off guard. As if I have given her the wrong answer to a question she did not ask aloud.

"What do you remember?"

I opened the book, and then I woke up in the infirmary.

"Did they tell you how I found you?"

Yes.

There is the smallest fracture of *something* in Sila's expression. There and gone again, too quick for me to know what it was. Her fingers flex again, grip tightening slightly before she drops her hand to take my injured one. She lifts it, holding it gently in one hand while her fingers run softly over the bandage. It makes my breath catch in my throat, silent as it always is now. She looks up at me sharply.

"You should go rest," she says after a moment. "I expect to see you back in the scriptorium tomorrow."

And with that, I am dismissed.

Chapter 6

Lorel

THE FOLLOWING MORNING, I FEEL UNSETTLED. My dreams had persisted with dark, shadowy, barely remembered things. The curse in my chest doesn't stir. At least *it* appears to have slept well.

I arrive early to the scriptorium, uneasy and longing for its quiet sanctuary. Perhaps my dreams were trying to warn me, because there is a figure sitting on my desk.

"Lorel," Orielle says, standing. I feel like I should check her temperature, make sure she's not running a fever herself. She never stands for me.

Librarian Sila was very explicit that you shouldn't be here.

I'm not sure why I bother, but some part of me wonders if Orielle knows more than she lets on. She's vain and rude, but she's not stupid. She did not reach the heights she has accidentally.

"I just wanted to see my sister, and make sure she was alright," says Orielle. "I shouldn't have let myself get so worked up, but not being allowed to see you for so many weeks was intolerable. I still don't know what happened to you."

I don't think it would have helped you to see me.

"You're *my* sister, Lorel," she says. "But since you joined the Library, it's like you're going further and further away from me. And I cannot follow you."

I cannot just walk into the Keep, the way you just wander in here.

The Keep would never allow my presence in the way that the Library tolerated Orielle's. Having the Dawn King's blessing, they saw themselves as above the other factions. They lived a different life there. Spending time in the King's Court, entertaining him, entertaining themselves, keeping an eye on the rest of us.

It was where I had been raised, first by our parents, and after they had been taken by the night cough, by Orielle. It had been my home. But my sigils and wards are weak, muted things. Without magic, there had been no place for me there.

Orielle purses her lips. Her eyes are a little too bright and damp around the edges. "I can see you still refuse to speak, though your work day hasn't yet begun."

I'm sorry but I can't.

Orielle wraps her arms about herself, stepping closer with a deep sigh. "I miss you, Lorel. I miss my little sister. I thought you might have died." She puts her hand to her mouth, taking a deep breath.

I'm sorry.

It doesn't matter though. If she understands or not, she makes no sign. Just gives me a watery smile and looks like she wants to hug me. I'm a failure of a sibling, because I don't reach for her. I'm not a little girl anymore, far from it. It would be better for us both if she just forgot about me, but I know Orielle well enough to know that isn't in her nature.

Orielle takes a breath, and it rattles through her, the noise sparking something like jealousy in me. She brushes past me as the other scribes start to file in. I don't think she wants to deal with Sila again. I don't blame her, honestly. I don't know what to make of Sila either.

With Orielle gone, I settle at my desk and notice that one of my paint pots is slightly ajar. Curse me for being so careless. Thankfully, it seems unharmed by my lapse in judgement. The paint master, Striger, would have been furious if I had wasted a whole pot so carelessly.

I'm mindful of my bandaged hand as I go about my day. Lune wants me to make sure I keep moving it, gently. With the fractures I had sustained prior, it was just more of the same. Though of course, I am going to be more mindful if I handle a knife again. Though I'm not sure that Elris will let me near anything sharp for some time.

Today's work is a map in the final stages. It's a huge piece of work that Trefor has been copying over the past weeks in preparation. It's divided up into intricate pieces, the original work copied in careful detail. Each of us has a piece or two of the edges, with a beautiful grand border to fill in. We'll block in the base layers and Elris will complete the finer details. It's a shame we won't ever see the final piece assembled. Others will put it together in its final place in one of the Library's reading rooms, where scribes are not allowed to go. Something this grand will be for the Librarians, rather than the average scribe or researcher.

I point my brush, wetting it with my tongue and shaping it with my lips, and set to work filling in the border with the most vibrant red. Once Elris finishes it with the gilding, it's going to be a beautiful piece of work. I paint and as the initial excitement of the piece wears off, the day starts to drag.

I stare at my brush, hovering over the page. I try to put brush to paper but my arms feel like lead. Barely half the workday has passed, and I feel *exhausted*. If Sila finds me like this, she's going to kill me.

I stare at my hands and at the brush. It feels like I need to use every little piece of my available consciousness to put the paintbrush down. Getting it as far away from the piece as I can before I inevitably drop it. A shiver creeps up my spine and that familiar feeling of dread begins to stir in my chest, as if in warning. It feels as slow as I do.

My fingers start to tingle as I stare at them. It's as if I have never seen hands before. I try to flex them, but all they do is twitch back at me.

Something is horribly wrong.

I can barely parse the thought. I will myself to turn and look around, to call out for help. I can't scream, but I don't remember why. With slow determination, I manage to turn my head. A cold sinks into me as I do, like the grave rising to meet me. Welcome me.

Trefor lies over his desk, eyes wide and glassy. His brown hair flopping over his forehead handsomely. He stares past me into a place I cannot see.

Not yet. My chest begins to ache. There is blood dripping from his mouth and nose. How long have I been dying for that Trefor is long gone? His flesh pale and sickly grey. There is a map piece pressed under his cheek. The last piece he'll never finish.

Bile rises in my throat and my skin feels too hot. Something warm trickles over my lips as blood trickles from my nose. I won't die over Trefor's last work. It's the least I can do. I hope.

My vision starts to blur and I will myself to push away from my desk. There's a vague, murky screech of wood on stone and I can only hope it's me. *King's mercy.* What of Elris? Sybri?

Me?

I tip sideways, but the impact of the cold flagstones never comes. There is only the cool, solid press of a body catching me. The murmur of someone speaking, slow and indistinct.

Only the dark, heady scent of moss and earth and a sweetness that reminds me of death.

And then there is nothing.

Chapter 7

Sila

A SCREECH OF WOOD AGAINST STONE CARVES ITS WAY through my thoughts. The sound is a warning, sending a wave of alarm washing over me. Like diving into winter-chilled water. Like sipping poison. It goes as quickly as it comes, replaced by a familiar and comfortable irritation.

The scribes. The Dark Lady curse them if someone is merely dragging their chair across the flagstones. I am on my feet without a second thought, in no mood for carelessness. I might have to take an ear for it.

My boots click swiftly across the stones, the occasional scribe peeking out from their sections and quickly ducking away when they see me. That, at least, is as it should be. I make my way in the direction of the noise, unease growing in me as my footsteps take me closer to the section my scribe works in.

And then someone screams. I hasten my pace.

My heart cannot race like hers can, but it can still scream in protest. Still constrict and contort itself in word-less agony. In fear, an old friend that has been absent for a long while. When I step between the shelves, I find a sedate kind of chaos. The screaming scribe cuts off at my appearance. My scribe, Lorel, sways in her seat. A thin red trickle of blood leaks from her nose, dripping over her lips. Her eyes, usually so sharp, are unfocused behind her glasses. She blinks slowly and then her body is crumpling, her skull destined for impact with the floor.

I should let it happen. Let her head hit the ground and crack over the stones. The insignificant trickle of blood should mean nothing to me. But it's so bright and vibrant. So full of life.

I am moving again, carelessly and without thought. If I *had* thought for a moment, then surely I would have let it happen. It would solve a problem, fulfil my Dark Lady's command. I catch her body with my own and she is a pale scrap of a thing in my arms. Her head rolls back against my shoulder, her mouth open, her body a dead weight. I can feel it through my fingertips, see it in the eyes of the dead scribe, folded over his desk. Poison. Pain strikes through the heart of me.

Someone has tried to poison my scribe. *My* mark.

"You, Scribe Mella," I say to the living scribe. "Find assistance for these two. Get them to the infirmary immediately. If you ask questions, or fail, I will have your eyes for disobedience."

"Y-yes Librarian, I— uh— Scribe Trefor—" she starts.

"Is dead, leave him. He does not need us. Now *move*," I command. By the grace of my Dark Lady, she moves, calling out to break the silence. I lift Lorel into my arms, and give the other scribes no further thought. I would have gone already, but I will never hear the end of it from Mercias if I let the blond one die.

Lorel's head rests against my shoulder, her breathing laboured where it flutters against my skin. All I need to do is stop and let her go. Let her follow her fellow scribe into the dark. But while I curse myself as I walk, I do not slow.

There is something unbearable in the thought of her heart stilled.

For months now, I have watched her. She was just one of many scribes. Delightful to torment as they are, she is no different from them. There was nothing to suggest that she might be the one my Dark Lady had marked for death. There was no reason for it to be her.

I watched her, night after night, practising late, missing her meal times. She was so determined. And only I knew it. It was our little secret, her quiet unspoken ambition. Such a sweet thing. An ill-fated thing, too.

This is not even the first time I had found her dying, though she claimed to remember nothing of it. I could only envy her that. I fought to not think of it, for to do so was to invite feelings I should not be having.

Naturally, I thought of it often.

I found her clawing her way through her own skin and crushing herself against the wall. I should have killed her then, but she had reached for me when I approached. Pressed herself against my body desperately and I had convinced myself that her illness was not the sign I was looking for. I had so badly wanted that to be true.

It is impossible to deny it now. Lorel is the one my Dark Lady wishes dead. Shadows take me, I need to just let her die already.

Instead, I shoulder through the doors of the infirmary. Every part of me recoils at the thought of her cold and still and beyond my reach.

"Healer—" I call out. Gella, one of the junior healers, appears at my shoulder. "Poison," I tell her.

"Dawn King have mercy— Clairabel, fetch Lune. She's

in the apothecary," says the Gella, calling out to another healer nearby.

"Right away," Clairabel replies. She drops what she is doing to scurry out the back of the infirmary.

"Bring her in here, Librarian," Gella instructs, leading me to the private rooms off to the side.

"There are others," I tell her as we walk down the hallway. "Two more if you are lucky."

"Let's hope we are," Gella says, throwing open a door. "Here. I'll send Lune along."

I lay Lorel down on the bed, with a care I rarely afford anything. As if she is some fragile thing, as likely to shatter on a cushioned mattress as she is on stone. And she is so fragile, with her fleeting little life and her bat-wing flutter of a pulse.

I kneel at her bedside and push her hair back behind her ear, her skin soft and burning under my fingertips. Somehow, she is still breathing. I take her glasses off, impatient that the Cupbearer is taking so long.

I set her glasses aside on the bedside table and hover there. I could smother her in shadows, and she would never know. She wouldn't suffer. There would be no awkward questions, given I suspect she should not even be alive. I doubt anyone will expect her to survive.

My fingers twitch, and the shadows thicken for just a moment, and then the Cupbearer is at my side with all her usual noise. At least her care for Lorel, for my scribe, is genuine. I let the shadows go. It is out of my hands now.

"I leave her to your care, Cupbearer," I say, turning on my heel. I can be of no use here, just standing there staring at her like a light-struck rat. If there is anyone who can help her, it will be the wretched Cupbearer. There is no one that could administer the correct antidote better than the King's poisoner herself.

I step aside for the other healers and scribes as they rush past me. I gather from their hurry that, for now, they all still breathe. I do not care about them, though. I shouldn't care about any of them.

When I am finally alone in a corridor, I pass into the shadows, embracing that dark space in between. No one will be able to hear me scream here.

How many months had it been since I started watching her? I had been presented with so many opportunities. My scribe is so prone to misfortune that she should have been easy to do away with. I tear at my hair and it comes away as shadow. I scream from deep within my chest, letting loose every bit of frustration. Somewhere under my heart, one of my two tethers is stretched taut. There is one for the Heart of the Library, to which I am pledged as a Librarian. The other ties me to my Dark Lady, Queen of the Eventide Court. The only thing keeping me anchored to the world and the only thing preventing me from fading away like so many of my kind before me.

It is pulling at me, tugging at my soul, and stretching to breaking point. Time is running out.

I will have to kill her tonight. Because if Lorel does not die, then I will.

Chapter 8

Lorel

It is dark.

I am cold.

I'm grounded in a void that I think must be the place we go when we're sleeping. Still tethered to the world. Not dead then.

Not yet.

The dark moves, shifting like smoke against my skin. Soft. Gentle. I repress a shiver and open my eyes to a place absent of light. It presses in, overwhelming me.

The curse that rests in the cavity of my chest stirs. A candle gone out. A cat stretching lazily. I thought I was cold before, but the temperature drops again. Colder. Darker. Something brushes my jaw. Holds it tenderly.

A cold blooms in the back of my skull, running down my spine like ice.

You need to wake up now.

The thought is not mine. It isn't even really a thought—more of a feeling. A stranger's presence in my mind, like nothing I've ever encountered.

I don't want to wake up. I want to stay here in this darkness forever. It's cool, and my skin is burning. It feels safe. It cradles me. I close my eyes and relax into it.

The new unknown presence reaches in, cutting through the void. It pushes aside the darkness, grasping at my face, my hair, my eyes. The curse inside me pushes against my chest and throat, trying to tear itself free. Like it has done once before.

The illusion of peace is torn apart as the strange forces tear at my flesh and rend through my bones. I try to scream. I remember that I can't.

The cold voice speaks in my mind again.

I am not done with you yet.

I do not wake easily. I drag myself from the depths of sleep, clawing my way back to the world of living. The room I wake in is not my own. The bed beneath me is less comfortable than my own and smells faintly of pine. The walls are carved from a different stone, painted with delicate forest motifs and healing herbs. The light is blessedly dim, so I am not blinded when I open my eyes. I still struggle to make sense of what I'm seeing.

I can see her clearly, leaning over me. The Librarian. Sila. She isn't looking at my face, she's staring at my exposed chest where my shift has been pulled down. Her fingers rest against my skin, cool against the fever still burning within me. They rest softly against the dark bruise-like mark. It's almost the span of a hand now. It has grown.

Her eyes flick to my face, and light catches the edges of a long, cruel blade. The top hovers above my chest. My breath catches, my heart kicking up again.

I blink, and there is no blade. Only Sila, with her fingers pressing gently into my skin. Her dark hair is a curtain flowing over one shoulder, her eyes are a little bright in the low light. My addled mind must have imagined it.

"Oh little mouse, what have you done?" she whispers. My skin still feels too hot, too sticky. I don't understand her question. I don't understand how she can see the curse mark when no one else has been able to.

Sila spreads her hand across my chest. She takes a deep breath, and then she's tugging my shift back into place. How have I come to be lying in the infirmary again?

Blissful ignorance doesn't last long. Trefor's face, wide-eyed and staring in death, comes back to me. Blood. Paint. Poison. Someone had poisoned us. Oh mercy, Elris and Sybri. I try to push myself up and find myself being pushed back down.

"Your friends are safe," Sila says. She looks quickly regretful as she corrects herself. "Illuminator Elris and Scribe Sybri are recovering. Scribe Trefor was not so lucky. There is nothing you can do for them now. You need to rest. I can feel the heat from your skin. Your fever still rages."

I feel too hot.

"I know, little mouse. You are not well. Rest, I will watch over you," Sila says softly.

Why?

I fumble the sign, but she seems to understand.

"Because I must," Sila says, helping me to sit. Her arms come around me, pulling my body up to sitting. Her skin is so cool. It eases the way my flesh burns.

She helps me to drink some water and when the glass is empty, I roll towards her body without thinking. My cheek rests against her shoulder and I sigh without a sound. It feels so good. I must be truly out of my mind, but I can't bring myself to pull away. I'm falling back under again, the lovely shadows beckoning me to rest. Sila's fingers comb through my hair.

"Lorel?" she murmurs. My eyelids are so heavy that I could not possibly open them. Sila lowers me gently down against the pillows. I sigh again, loud in the darkness, as the cold press of her body leaves me.

I drift on the edge of that darkness, waiting for it to take me under as it wraps around me. Presses cool against my skin. Pulls me closer as I go under, and do not need to think any longer.

At some point, the fever dreams break, crashing against the shore of my consciousness one last time before fading away. I fall into a proper sleep then, dreamless and restful. When I wake next, it is a gentler thing. I am not in my own room, the stone above different from the stone my room is carved from, the sheets smelling faintly of pine. I have a vague sense that I have woken here already, but it is hazy and edged in shadow. I think someone had held me.

I push myself up from the bed, any noise from the exercise stolen away by my silencing curse. Fuck, I hate that.

There is a familiar weariness in my limbs. I'd been a sickly child and the feeling in my body is no different from the many times I had woken from a fever in the past. The door to my room opens and my breath catches silently in my throat. My heart skips.

It is only Lune. She smiles at me, tired and raw around the edges, with dark shadows under her eyes that would rival a Librarian's. I don't know who I expected it to be.

"You're awake," she says. "Thank the King. This whole week has been a mess." Lune drags a nearby stool to my bedside. I shuffle back against the headboard, unable to hold myself up for much longer. Lune leans in and pushes my hair back. Her fingers are warm against my skin. "Your temperature is better. Elris and Sybri have been awake for a few days now, but you were the only one to take with a fever." She cups my face with her hand, and I feel a slight tingle across my skin as Lune uses her magic.

Her eyes refocus on my face, and she smiles. "All clear." The tension in her shoulders doesn't entirely leave her, but she relaxes a little. "At least I won't lose any more of you. I don't think the Librarians would be very pleased with me if I did."

Trefor. My throat burns at the memory. I close my eyes and rest my head against the headboard. Lune squeezes my shoulder. I'm too tired to cry. I wasn't friends with Trefor, really, but we were all together day after day and he'd been a talented mark maker. What a foolish accident.

"I've only seen one Librarian this past week, and he was incensed. I fear for your paint master," Lune says. She pours me a glass of water. I frown at her as she passes it to me. It's cool against my skin, like the hands of the Librarian had been against my chest. As they held me.

Sila. The Librarian had been here when I had woken earlier.

"There's pen and paper if you have questions," Lune says. She *knows* I have questions.

Has Librarian Sila been here?

"Not since she brought you in," says Lune. "She seems to always be there when trouble strikes you, doesn't she?"

I chew on my lip. She does. She had found me after I had read the book. She had known, even, that I had read the book. Until the other day, I had never seen her before, but she seemed to know an awful lot about me. I groan silently. I thought if I could just be my dull self she would grow bored with me, but I've had her attention for far longer than I realised. *Fuck.*

I'm doomed.

How is Paint Master Striger involved?

"The poison. It was in your paints. I guess the question is whether it was an accident or intentional," says Lune. My stomach turns at the thought. The Paint Master was an agreeable man, as far as people were allowed to be agreeable in the Library. I couldn't imagine him intentionally poisoning us, but nor could I imagine him being so careless. This was beyond the games and torments of the Librarians, if what Lune said was true. Librarians did not need excuses or traps if they wished to cause harm to a scribe.

There is a knock at the door, and another healer's head pokes through the gap.

"Lune?" she whispers. "There's another one."

Lune's face falls. "Can you find someone to bring Lorel something to eat? I'll be out in a moment."

Once the door closes, Lune puts her head in her hands. Her fingers press into her skin. I lift my pencil, but I don't need to ask the question.

"Night cough," she says through her fingers. "It started with the researchers, and now it has spread to the scribes and the papiers within the Library. It's come up overnight in each of the other quarters too, and the afflicted are starting to fill up the infirmaries. It's moving so fast."

It has been years since an outbreak of night cough, but the memories of my parents as the cough tore through their bodies never left me. It was believed that dark spirits, wretched enemies of the Dawn King, stole in to infect the afflicted while they slept. True or not, it is no wonder I am in a separate room.

Lune takes a deep breath and lets it all out. That must

be nice. "Get some rest. I'll be back when I can," she says, standing. She puffs up the pillows to make it easier for me to sit up. She ignores any of my protests. It's easy enough to do when she can't hear them. And then when she is gone, the chamber is silent. There isn't much to it. Just the bed, the wooden stool and the little table with the carafe and glass.

I wish I could be in my own room, in my own bed, but even that wouldn't stop all the swirling thoughts. It's like someone has opened one of the cliff side windows and sent papers flying about the room. Only each piece of paper is a thought, and it's impossible to connect them as they wheel about.

The poisoning should have felt accidental. Entirely plausible that it could be a mistake. Only with how many times I had been in the infirmary these past weeks, it was getting harder to believe it *was* an accident.

Chapter 9

Lorel

IF I WAS GOING TO BE HERE ALONE FOR SO LONG, someone might have thought to leave me a book to read. Not that I could really keep my eyes open. I think it might be late afternoon when I'm startled by another presence in the room, sitting on the edge of the bed.

Sila. I blink away the sleep from my eyes, looking for my glasses. I realise after a moment of searching that she is holding them in her hands.

"Good afternoon, little mouse," she says. Her smile is soft, and yet somehow still menacing. There's a gentle click as she moves, setting my glasses carefully on my nose. "There, you look slightly less vague."

I can see her more clearly now. The permanent shadows under her eyes seem deeper, her skin paler. She almost looks *tired*, which can't be possible. With her so close, I struggle to breathe. I can't help but feel that something has gone terribly wrong.

Is everything alright?

Sila doesn't respond immediately, staring at me for a long, drawn out moment. Her eyes drop to my chest and I have to start the whole process of remembering how to use my lungs all over again as she reaches out. Her fingers tug the tie of my shift undone, and push the fabric aside. I am drowning and surely delirious. Without a doubt, this must be a dream. No, a nightmare.

Her fingers press against my skin. I have the vague sensation that this has happened before.

"You have a curse mark," she says, as if she already knew this. "How?" She keeps her fingers pressed there as she looks back up. Her dark gaze is piercing. It allows no room for falsehood. Some very sensible part of me is telling me that I need to run.

You can see it?

No one else has been able to see it. Not any of the Librarians who saw to me after the incident with the book. Not even Lune with her magical touch.

"Yes," she says, through gritted teeth. Her nails dig in a little before she pulls her hand away. "Someone has a claim on you. How? Do not make me repeat myself again, scribe."

So, I am a scribe again.

The book. It appeared after I read the book.

"I didn't see it when I brought you here," she says, her lovely face grim as she frowns.

It wasn't so very big to start with. And...it was hardly the only mark on my skin.

Somehow that turns her frown into a fully fledged scowl. It makes her face look like murder.

"No, it wasn't." The room feels darker for Sila's presence. The shadows are deeper. The air is colder. "And now you have been poisoned."

Surely it was an accident.

"If it was, we will never know," Sila says.

My blood turns cold.

What happened to Paint Master Striger?

"Mercias tore his throat out. He'd had three days to explain himself and still refused, and Mercias was...upset." Sila finally turns her gaze away from me. I swallow hard. My breath would be rattling through me if it could.

That was what Librarians did. Took what they were owed, gave with strings attached. Did not bother with things such as mercy.

Did he say it was an accident?

She catches the movement of my hands, and when she turns back to me, her face is perfectly composed again. "Mercias? No."

I had hoped when I came to the Library that I would be so unremarkable, so incredibly ordinary that I would never have a Librarian's eyes fall upon me. I had chosen to study here, because it suited my temperament. I have to remind myself now that the Keep would have been no different. Arguably, it might have been worse.

Not Librarian Mercias. Paint Master Striger.

Her face is perfectly still this time, and I realise she has such a lovely voice that makes her delivery all the more horrific.

"No, he said nothing at all. And now, he never will," Sila says. She lets out a long breath. "I did not intend to wake you. I will leave you to rest." Her hand rests on my thigh, with only the wool blanket and my shift between us. Sila goes to move and I grab her. I cannot have been think-ing, otherwise I would not have dared to do it. I release her as if I have been burned.

"Scribe?"

I have far overstepped, but she has not answered all my questions. My heart races like it always does this close to her.

Do you think it was an accident?

Her face is inscrutable, her gaze opaque. "I do not know," she says. "Rest now. I will watch over you."

I settle back against the pillows, feeling anything but tired. My eyes drift closed anyway, and I do not hear the door as she leaves.

I can't stop thinking of her fingers pressed against my chest. They had been so cool against the heat of my fever ravaged skin—

I no longer have a fever, though.

Lune had said she had not seen Sila, but I had. She had been there, leaning over me. She had seen the curse mark. I had thought I had seen a blade.

But no, there hadn't been one.

Had there?

"Lorel? Are you awake?" Lune whispers. It's pitch dark in the room. I hadn't bothered to refresh the sigil on the lanterns, not that it would have done much good if I had tried. It must be late, since there isn't much light filtering in behind Lune either. Without light, who could really tell how much time had passed since Sila was here. My shift is still in disarray. I sit up, and the bed frame creaks as I retie my shift. The noise of the movement must be enough for Lune, because she steps into the room and swiftly relights the lanterns.

"You'll need the light," she says, holding out a letter. The paper is lovely under my fingertips, the kind that someone who wears pretty dresses and attends parties in the grand hall of mirrors might use. I take up the pen and paper by the bed.

My sister?

Lune nods. "She caught me on a break, as the Librarians have been refusing her entry."

She has no respect.

"No, but she never has. I wonder if the Lightkeepers know that?" muses Lune.

If they don't know yet, then there is no helping them. Thank you. I hope she has something sensible to say.

Last I had seen her, she had been rather contrite. It had been uncomfortable. The letter doesn't make me any more comfortable.

Dearest Lorel,

They've told me you are in the infirmary again, but they will not tell me why. I hope Lune can deliver this letter to you. I hope you can still read it. Is it a fever, again? What are they doing to you in there? I'm terrified that they will not tell me if you were to die. That I would not find out until long after the fact. I don't care that they think you belong to the Library— you are my sister, first and always, and they cannot expect me to abandon you.

I will never abandon you. I hope you know that. Please write back to me, and tell me you are alright? I know I ask much of Lune, but I doubt they would be willing to part with her services in the Library infirmary. I am sure she would carry a note for you. You are lucky to have her as a friend in that place.

I love you. Please be alright.

Orielle.

Dawn King and the stars above. *Fuck.* I rub my temples.

"Is it bad news?" Lune asks. I pass her the letter to read.

There's little private enough to try to hide it from her. Lune's frown deepens as she reads. "Have they been preventing her from seeing you?"

Only when I am unwell. Though that is standard for the Library. Otherwise, she keeps turning up in the scriptorium.

Lune looks up from the letter, alarmed. "*How?* You can't just wander into the scriptorium."

She has no respect.

Lune purses her lips. "I bet she speaks in there too, doesn't she? King's grace, she doesn't help herself." She passes me the letter back. "I'll carry a note to her. That's no hardship."

It's a hardship for me though, because I do not know what to write back. I love my sister, but I had made my choice, and accepted all that it had entailed. I can at least write back that I am alive. The curse mark feels cold, chilling the skin over my heart. The curse under my skin stirs. I can't say how long I will be alive for, but for the moment I am.

I use the paper to scrawl a quick note back. I do not have my sister's talent for sentiment. I can only hope she remembers that and doesn't feel too hurt by its brevity.

Lune takes the folded note. "I'll pass this along to her, so she has more than just my word," she says.

Thank you.

Lune reassures me that I can return to my own room tomorrow, and then leaves me to rest again. I feel too rattled to sleep. The thought of returning to the scriptorium, returning to work as if nothing had happened, is uncomfortable. Trefor's empty desk sitting beside me as a reminder that will only be made worse when someone new comes to occupy it. An accident like this one is tragic.

But I don't think it was an accident.

I think of Orielle, sitting at my desk and lying in wait for me. The loose paint lid. I had thought I'd been careless with my paints. The last weeks had rattled me and recovering had been hard. My hands had seen better days. But I wasn't clumsy. I wasn't careless.

I stare at my hands, the bruises and the swelling long since faded, just the cut and the stitches standing out against my palm. I need to get to the scriptorium. I don't know what I might find after a week away, but everything led back there in the end and I am determined that this time I will find answers.

Chapter 10

Lorel

SOMETIMES I WONDER WHAT IT WOULD BE LIKE TO wake to daylight, instead of the cold dark of a room under a mountain. It does no good to think such thoughts, but they come anyway. I like the shape of my life that I have moulded for myself, but the sun does not shine outside the Citadel anymore than it does here. It had, once, but now the land was covered in a cursed fog that never lifted. A warning, the Dawn King would tell you, that there is no life to be had outside the Citadel.

I sit on the edge of the bed, testing my legs in the dark little infirmary room. I'd done a little moving about the room in the time since I had woken, and I hoped they wouldn't fail me now.

Lune has left to bring me a change of clothes, since I couldn't very well walk out in my undergarments. Otherwise I would have left already. I was tempted to do so anyway. I was so *tired* of this room.

The door creaks open and I look up, but it isn't Lune returning with a change of clothes. Instead, Sila stands like a long mark of darkness in the doorway. Stands there holding *my* clothes. I stare at her.

"I thought you might like your own clothes," she says, closing the door behind her. It is unnervingly thoughtful.

Thank you. My hands fumble it a little.

Sila crosses the room to set my clothes down on the bed.

"Have you eaten yet?" she asks.

What?

It takes a moment for me to catch up with her words.

Yes, breakfast.

"Good. Come, let's get you changed." Heat sears my cheeks and it must show because her mouth curves into one of her horrifically lovely smiles. "Oh, surely you're not shy, little mouse."

I'm not. Sort of. Maybe. Taking my clothes off around other people just isn't something I tend to do. I'd never even tried to be intimate with someone. No one was *interesting* enough to warrant bringing myself to be naked in their presence. No one had shown any promise that they could do better than I could do myself. My cheeks must be the red of a Barracks forge. Why was I thinking of this *now*, of all times?

"I can leave if you like, Lorel," she says.

Dawn King strike me, it isn't like she hasn't seen most of me at this point anyway. There is no need to cause more of a fuss than I already am. I push myself up from the bed and my legs wobble. She catches me as I stumble. Strong arms hold me firmly.

"Steady there, little mouse," Sila says, her mouth far too close to my ear.

I purse my lips, but I'm not foolish enough to think I can stand on my own so easily. I grip Sila's forearms and feel her wiry muscles shift under my palm. It's an unexpected pleasure. Librarians always wore long black cloaks, with the full intention to look like stalking nightmares, I'm sure. Sila's cloak always sat over unfashionably wide, billowing sleeves that would have been in style five centuries ago. I tip my head back to look up at her and she's watching me curiously. I can't quite decide what the look in her eyes is.

There isn't any time to puzzle it out, because her hands grasp the fabric around my hips and lift it over my head. The cool air hits my skin, and I shiver against it. I clutch my arms around my chest.

"Arms up," Sila commands. I do as I'm told, and she drops a clean linen shift over my head. I tug it down over my thighs, unsure why I am so nervous. Sila swats my hands away from the ties, tying them for me.

I can dress myself.

"I'm sure you can," she says, motioning for me to slide my arms into the sleeves of the woollen dress she has picked out for me. I give her a look of dismay. The thing buttons all the way up the front, and I cannot manage it with my hand...which she surely knew. Her mouth twitches in a satisfied sort of way as she tugs the dress around my body and starts to slip the buttons closed. If nothing else, she is far quicker with it than I have ever been, so I suffer it in silence. As if I have a choice about the silence part.

When she's done, she's kneeling at my feet and, for once, I look down at her. I regret it almost instantly when she smirks back at me. She drops a pair of wool slippers in front of me, and I brace myself on her shoulder as I step into them. I don't know why I'm holding my breath as I do.

"Hmm, perfect," she says, looking up at me. I might as well have a fever again at this point. Maybe I still do.

When can I go back to work?

"Never, if I had my way," she says cheerfully as she

stands. My thoughts snare on that and I think I must have misheard her. She settles my glasses on my nose. "Come, let's get you back to your room."

I know the way.

All I get is a thoughtful hum in response. And then a playful tut when I try to walk across the room and stumble again. I should have tried harder yesterday to be less useless.

Sila catches me again, but this time one arm comes around my back and the other scoops up my legs. I throw my arms around her neck, terrified that she'll drop me. She just laughs softly.

"I have you," she whispers. I can't even sign back the insult I want to throw at her right now. I try to push away, but Sila is strong. She holds me as if I am nothing more than a piece of damp paper. "Scribe Lorel, if you cannot make it across the chamber, you will not make it back to your room. Do you want to stay here?"

I pull back, the better to look at her. Her face is... not unkind. I think she would put me down, only she would put me back in the infirmary bed and leave me there.

I want *my* bed. I want *my* room. I'm tired of being here. I shake my head to answer her and she smiles, satisfied. The door opens itself and I cling to her again as she walks. I hide my face in her hair and it has the subtle fragrance of star flowers, the little bloom grown for making funerary incense. I should feel more upset about this. Particularly as this is about as embarrassing as it could get.

Not in the least because if I am trying to lose Sila's attention, I think I am failing catastrophically.

Chapter 11

Lorel

I'M STILL TRYING TO MAKE SENSE OF IT ALL HOURS later. Sila had set me down, and helped me back into bed and I had turned my back to her. Hidden my face in my pillows until she had left. Childish, maybe, but there were too many thoughts in my head and not enough ways to say them.

I've let the room fall dark, not bothering to relight my lantern. My sigils always faded quickly when I lit them. I was used to it. Used to so many things.

Always trying so desperately to be overlooked. To disappear into the shadows. I had no desire for greater attention.

But something about Sila's attention is different, because no matter how mortifying I thought it was to be carried to my own room, I cannot deny that I had felt safe. That at this moment, I need that more than I can say.

The coming-and-going of footsteps and voices dies down in the hall. I hope that means that everyone is settled for the night, because now would be the perfect time to visit the scriptorium.

No one should be there at this hour. Even I have never

stayed there this late. It would be empty and quiet, and I could search in peace. I couldn't stay lying here wide awake in the dark forever. I would surely go mad. I needed to be doing something. I still wasn't quite sure what I was looking for, but it all led back to the scriptorium. The book, the knife, the poison.

I sit up on the side of the bed and set my glasses on my nose before I slide my feet into my boots and tie them up. My last attempts to walk hadn't really worked out, but I was determined. I was going to get to the bottom of this, one way or another. I just hoped I wouldn't have to drag myself there.

I manage to shuffle to the door and crack it open. It's a start, but it's going to be slow going. That's fine, I have all night after all.

The hall is clear, just the hallway lanterns and the shadows they cast to keep me company. I keep close to the wall as I slip out into the hall and set off for the scriptorium. It *is* slow going, and I have to stop and rest more often than I would like.

That's the problem when you spend six weeks abed, then follow that up by being poisoned and spending another week abed. All your strength deserts you. I'd always been weak, but it didn't need to be so cursedly obvious.

I take the stairs carefully, the shadows thick around the edges. I have walked this path at least twice daily for almost ten years now, thank the King. It's no hardship to find my way down the stairs in the dark and I reach the bottom without incident, only to have something run over my foot. I stifle my scream unnecessarily. I can't make a noise. And it's just a rat.

I'll tell myself that, anyway. I don't dare investigate it any further.

The larger corridor towards the scriptorium is unlit, as if to remind me that I shouldn't be here. In the Keep, it wasn't all that uncommon for someone to find a body, or blood, as they went about their morning. The occupants of the Library were usually more circumspect, but I really didn't want to come across one now. Or become one.

I shuffle along, and the mountain creaks and groans. Usually relegated to background noise, the sounds are amplified in the quiet. The snap of a door shutting has me pressing myself against the wall for a moment, but no foot-steps follow it. Perhaps I should not have done this in the dark alone. If only I had asked— No. Don't be stupid.

The arched entryway to the scriptorium looms out of the darkness. There are very few places that are locked in the Library, because the true deterrent was invoking the wrath of a Librarian. Which, as Striger had found out, is exactly as horrible as it sounds.

I rest for a moment under the arch. It's different to see it in the dark, with little more than my weak lantern light. All the arches and lines of the carving cast long, deep shadows. There's a shift in them, for a moment, that sets my heart racing in the dark. I'm certain if anyone were near, they'd be able to hear it, it's beating so loudly. I press myself into the shadows, but nothing comes.

I continue on past the Librarian's office, and the spot where Maxim had been warned not to run. I hope he had heeded the warning. You only really got one, after all.

My desk sits on the first level of the scriptorium, on the nearest side. Our section has been roped off, the paints and brushes removed. The map had been taken away some-where. I hoped we could finish it, one day, though it would always be missing the piece that Trefor had died over. What an awful way to go.

I set my weak lantern down inside the rope and crawl under it, because I lack the dexterity to duck under it in my current state. I drag myself up, holding onto the sturdy bookcase, and look around. Now that I'm here, I'm not sure where to start. The red paint responsible for the poisoning is gone and, they had likely found Striger's supply contaminated.

Except that I hadn't topped mine up recently, and I had used it only a couple of days earlier for the washes on the Book of Faetales. So it must have been added after that.

And if I'm correct, not just to mine. I doubt that Striger or whoever it was that had done this would have risked contaminating the paint masters' supply before the poisoning. It would have been done after. It was meant to *look* like an accident. That was why it had been added to Elris, Trefor and Sybri's paint. That was why it was in the paint at all.

There are far easier ways to take out a room full of scribes. *Fuck.* Someone had tried to poison me, and they'd killed Trefor. They would have killed the others, too. Just collateral to cover up their target. And maybe I'm delusional and Elris truly has a secret worth killing for, but with my recent track record, that is not likely. The truth sits in my chest, cold and hard. I remember my sister sitting, contrite, on my desk.

Something falls at the far end of the scriptorium, hitting the ground with a sharp metallic ring. It could be just another rat, but the hiss of cursing follows and I'm certain that rats have not yet mastered the art of swearing. Not yet, anyway.

There are people here, and I need to get out. Now. There are more noises. The sounds of a scuffle trying to be kept quiet. Meaning there was more than one of them, and they were not on speaking terms. The noises echo off the walls, and I can't be certain where they come from, only that I need to move *now*. Before they block the only exit out of here.

I kill the sigil in the lantern and sit to peer around the bookshelves before I crawl back out from under the rope. There are shadows on the wall at the end of the hall, moving closer. One shadow breaks free of the others and they give up on being quiet entirely. I duck back behind the shelves, holding my breath even though there isn't a chance it'll give me away. Footsteps ring out down the hall.

"Enough fucking around! Just stop him and we'll clean it up after," says a man's voice.

"*Fine.*" There's a noise, something sinking into flesh, a strangled cry, and then a body hits the ground next to me. Thank the King I can't cry out. His face grinds along the stones. I don't know his name, but I recognise him as a fellow scribe. I stare too long as blood pools under him. He stares back, unblinking.

I need to move— no, hide. *Fuck.* Other footsteps echo down the hall. His attackers see me as soon as they stop to check the body. I shuffle back and the scribe on the floor moves. Throwing an arm out toward me. He starts to drag himself across the floor. *Fuck.*

Lantern light blooms across my face as his assailants appear in the gap between the shelves. The taller of the two, with dark hair, sets his boot on the scribe's neck. He puts his weight into it with a sickening crunch. The scribe stills, but he's already given me away. The second man, with brown hair, is holding his lantern up and smiling at me. I am not surprised to see they both wear the Lightkeeper insignia.

"Davos," he says, sounding pleased. "It's her." The man that I can only assume is Davos looks up from the dead scribe and his grin matches the brown-haired man's. *They know who I am.*

"Aren't we in luck then?" he says.

Move Lorel. I try to push myself up from the floor, push myself away towards the open arches of the courtyard that sits in the centre of the scriptorium. My limbs fail me, and all I manage is to scramble pathetically across the floor. One of them grabs my hair, dragging me up and back towards the light.

Fuck this. I don't need to be able to scream to cause a racket. I kick out at whatever I can. My wooden desk screams for me as it is shoved aside, grating against the stone. A glass jar topples from a desk and shatters. I reach up to dig my nails into his hands.

"You little b—" His sentence ends with a wet gurgle. His hand loosens and I stumble to the floor. His body lands at my feet as I push myself out of his way. Blood wells from his mouth, his neck cut open. Fingernail marks gouge down the side of his face. A dark shadowy figure stands over his corpse.

"Hello, little mouse," Sila says, low and dangerous. I try to remember to breathe as I look up at her, standing between the two dead Lightkeepers. I hadn't even heard her dispatch the first. I hadn't even heard her arrive.

She's not wearing her robes. Instead, she stands there in skin-tight trousers and her old-fashioned billowing-sleeved blouse. Her fingers are extended with long, bloody, talon-like nails. Her eyes are black from edge to edge, and a dark ichor runs down her cheeks.

Her mouth moves in a smile that doesn't reach her fathomless eyes. Bright red blood is splattered across her face. In her hand is the long, cruel blade from my memory, dripping with thin red blood. Something sensible, like fear, seizes my lungs. Traps the air in my chest. I freeze in place. She's far more dangerous than any Lightkeeper. I could never hope to outrun her.

Sila pushes the Lightkeeper away with her boot and all I can think is that I've seen people move dead rats with more care. She kneels, and the blade disappears in a wisp of dark shadow. Her talons retract as she reaches out to take my face.

"Did they hurt you?"

I flinch at the unexpected gentleness in her voice. My scalp feels tender. If anything, her face turns darker. She tips my head forward, running her fingers through my hair with alarming tenderness.

"Perhaps I was too merciful," she murmurs. Blood sticks to my face as she takes her hand away.

She's too soft. Too gentle. So dark. So lovely.

My hands shake as I try to form the signs I need.

I've seen your blade before.

"Ah, you did see me that night," she says. She purses her lips, looking regretful. "Just know that I could not do it, little mouse."

You were going to kill me.

"Yes."

Just like they were.

"Yes."

Then why did you stop them?

Sila looks me in the eye, steady. The shadows deepen around her, her eyes darkening again. Her features stretch unnaturally, and she is even taller. A looming shadow.

My heart races. My lungs release. The curse in my chest stirs, as if trying to make itself comfortable. I should try to run. She had tried to kill me.

I don't know what it is I've done that so many people want me dead.

Sila holds out her hand to me, in a gesture that reminds me of valiant knights in old faetales.

"Because I could not do it," she says. "But you clearly cannot be trusted with your own safety. Come with me."

It's not a question.

Or what?

"Or I will take you anyway," she whispers.

I don't know where she wants me to go, but I want answers, and Lune is right. Every time I stumble, Sila is there. Rescuing me. She needn't have made her threat, because I want to go and I can't face this all on my own.

I take her hand, resting my pale fingers against her long, bloody ones. She smiles. It is a thing of nightmares and rips the air from my lungs.

"Hold your breath," she says.

The shadows whisper as she pulls me against her. I take a deep breath, and jam my eyes shut, and let the darkness take me.

Chapter 12

Lorel

SILA HOLDS ME TIGHTLY AND, EVEN WITH MY EYES closed, I can feel the darkness pressing in, trying to smother me. My lungs burn, threatening to burst from my chest if I have to hold my breath for a moment longer. I *can't* hold it much longer. It's stifling and oppressive—

And then the darkness is receding. Sila's arms loosen, resting softly around me in a protective circle as I gasp for air, the action entirely void of any sound. I rest my forehead against Sila's shoulder as my chest shudders. The room spins and her solid form is grounding. It had only been that morning that Sila had carried me to my rooms. Left me to rest. How had it only been mere hours ago?

There's a plush carpet under my knees, and dull light from a sigil-lit hearth. I haven't seen one of those in *years*. Wherever I am, this isn't a place for scribes. I tip my head to the side, taking in the room. It's almost like some kind of storage closet, though it's far too large for that. The furniture too fine. There are books and papers piled on almost every available surface, including the armchairs and the lone footstool. The only truly bare spaces are the gap on the rug that we are currently occupying, and the chair behind the desk that dominates the space. Through the double doors to my left I catch sight of a bedpost, a robe slung over the end. Sila's robe.

Dawn King help me. Sila's *rooms*.

Sila laughs softly as I look up at her. It softens her expression, her eyes crinkling at the corners. My hands are still wound tight into her blouse and I let go as if burned. My glasses sit askew on my face, and I set them to rights. There are specks of blood across them that I'll have to clean off later.

"Are you alright?" she asks. Her eyes are back to normal now, though her face is still tracked with those blood-like tears. They're pooled at the corner of her mouth, stuck in her teeth as she speaks. She should be terrifying, splattered with the Lightkeepers blood too. She isn't.

Are these your rooms?

Sila nods. "It's the safest place for you, since I cannot seem to keep an eye on you else wise."

You've been watching me.

"Of course I have. In case you haven't noticed little mouse, people keep trying to kill you."

You amongst them.

Her face grows sombre. "I suppose you will want an explanation."

I think I deserve one.

"Do you not trust me?"

Not at all.

"Then why did you come with me?"

My hands hesitate in their reply. She had freely admitted to holding a blade over my heart with every intent to still it.

Because you didn't.

Because if anything, it seemed she kept preventing my death.

Why didn't you?

There is a fracture in her face, a glimpse of something sharp and aching, there and gone. She pulls her arms away from me now and takes my hands as she stands. She's gentle as she tries to tug me up and so she doesn't expect the way I settle all my weight into the ground, refusing to be pulled up. I try to tug my hands back, but her grip is firm.

Sila sets her mouth in a wry smile, running her thumb over the back of my hand and this time I could be as leaden as the stone around us and I would still go to my feet. As soon as her grip loosens, I tug my hands back.

You're going to have to answer my questions.

"I will."

But not this one.

"No."

Then you cannot expect me to stay here—

"Scribe—"

Don't scribe me—

Sila's sigh is loud in the chamber. "Lorel. There are some things I cannot answer for you."

I don't understand.

"You wouldn't understand— No, it is not because I doubt your intelligence. You would think me a liar."

Now I certainly do.

That wry twist of her mouth again. "Are you always this mouthy? Usually you're so circumspect."

Those men recognised me. They were going to kill me. They killed that other scribe. You were going to kill me— what am I supposed to make of that? Who will protect me from you if you change your mind?

"Oh, little mouse, it is far too late to change my mind,"

Sila says. "But let us make a bargain, if that will put you at ease."

A bargain? That is a faetale.

"Hmm, is it? Let's see, shall we?" Sila holds out her hand, clenching it into a fist and then opening it again, her palm fills with shadowy smoke. It drips from her palm. Curls in the eddies of the air.

This is absurd. You are not —

"While you bear the curse mark, I will not harm you. You will have my protection, and you will stay where I can do so," she says.

The shadow curls, as if listening to her words. It is impossible. A bargain is a fae thing, and there is only one true fae left— the Dawn King. There is no one else in the Citadel that could make such a bond.

Sila has fae blood, that much is obvious, but how much of her power comes from being a Librarian? A Librarian cannot walk through walls, or move through shadows. They do not summon blades, and while they can be horrific night-mares, I had never seen anything like Sila when she had wrapped me in her darkness.

"What is there to lose if it's not real? Take my hand again." I wanted to trust her. I wanted to feel safe here, because where else could I even go? There was nowhere else I *wanted* to go.

I reach out and grasp her hand and the shadow twists, suddenly sharp, cutting a clean line into each of our palms. I feel the warmth of my own blood, thin and red as it pools in our hands. Sila's is a deep, dark red that is almost black. It's cold and thicker than I would have expected. The shadow wraps around our hands like a handfasting ribbon, soft as silk. Sila clasps my hand, and her features lengthen, the light dancing across her face, her hair bleeding into the room's many shadows.

"While you are marked," Sila says, with a strange echo in her voice. Inky darkness drips down her cheeks. "I promise you my protection. Your turn, little mouse."

I can't speak aloud, and I have only one hand. It isn't like this is really happening, anyway. Though the blood pooling in our hands suggests otherwise.

I will stay where you can protect me, I mouth. The shadowy ribbons constrict tightly around our clasped hands until it almost hurts. I gasp, a sharp intake of breath as the shadow melts into my skin, sealing the promise as it heals the wounds it left.

Sila stares at me. It is a full minute until she lets go of my hand. Her fingers brush against mine as she goes. I inspect my palm and there is a shiny stripe of freshly healed skin. The only evidence on me of the bargain struck. It hadn't left another open wound across my writing hand, but—

It shouldn't have worked.

I look up at Sila, and she's smiling softly.

How?

"I am fae," she says, shrugging.

That isn't possible.

"I warned you that you would not believe me," Sila says. And she's right. She did. I'm still not sure I do, but there is a surety from the bargain that settles over me. Some part of the magic of it that leaves no room in my mind for doubt. Sila will protect me. I will stay where she can do so. Sila is a true fae.

I rub the scar tissue. Now there will be scars on both my hands. I look up at her, and she's watching me intently, face impassive.

How can you be fae?

I don't expect an answer, but this time she gives one. "I am old," she says.

You would have to be ancient.

Another shrug. "As pleased as I am that you are taking an interest in me, these are not the most interesting questions you could be asking." She's smiling again, just a soft curve of her lips and a gentle sparkle in her eyes, as if I amuse her. She's right. There are more pressing matters.

The poisoning wasn't an accident, was it?

My hands shake at the thought of it. I had almost died. Others *had*. Those men, the dead Lightkeepers, had recognised me.

I think of my sister sitting on my desk. An unpleasant suspicion grows in me. *He* couldn't be bothering with me now after so long, could he? Surely not. I redirect my thoughts— I can't think of Orielle or the court right now. My relationship with her is fraught, but I can't fathom that she might try to kill me. It doesn't seem right, but how well do I really know who she has become? How well does she know me?

"I do not think so. I think the men I killed this evening were tidying up loose ends. The scribe they killed must have been tangled up in it." Sila pauses, frowning. "I'll need to go and clean that up before the day starts, or Mercias will have a fit. Not, of course, that he has any grounds for it after his most recent behaviour."

I don't understand how you fit into it.

I still don't quite understand how *I* fit into it. There is nothing special about me. The Dawn King had confirmed as much when he let me leave the Keep. Only an incident with a book. And a space of memory, wiped clean. Fuck. I should have been more curious about what else was missing.

I'd been so focused on the book, I hadn't even considered what might have happened in the vacant space in between. Had I done something to cause this mess? The dreadful mass of the curse shifts in my chest. Or is this the past finally coming back to haunt me?

I flinch as Sila's cool fingers brush my skin. The light catches on the scar across her palm. She cradles my face in her hands as if it is a precious thing.

"Little mouse," she says, softly. I had gotten caught up in my thoughts. "There you are."

Sorry.

"You have nothing to apologise for," she says. "If anything, perhaps I do. I was tasked with watching the scriptorium. I was told I would know my mark when they appeared. I know no more than that. I do not know why you are considered a threat, and when it came to it, for the first time in my long life, I did not want to do it. I could not do it."

My stomach churns and my skin goes cold. The curse mark feels ice cold, and the chill of it prickles across my skin.

Someone gave you an order? The Library?

"No, not the Library," says Sila, hesitating. My silent breath catches. Surely she is not an agent of the Keep, too. "My queen."

I stare at her.

What? A queen? There is no queen.

Sila shakes her head. "For as long as there have been sacrifices, there has always been a queen, too."

That doesn't make any sense.

I have bound myself to a woman who thought a queen had ordered her to kill me. Sila has surely taken leave of her senses. And yet, she had made a bargain with me with horrific shadowy powers the likes of which belonged in myth and faetales. My horror must show in my expression, because her face closes off to me and her hands slide away.

"There is more to the world than your understanding, scribe," she says, her tone cold. It's all too much, all at once. There is only the King. None of this makes any sense.

"I need to go clean up the mess and find you something to eat. There is a washroom off the bedroom if you wish to use it," she says, turning away from me. "You can sleep in the bed. I never use it these days."

I don't want her to go. I don't want to be left alone here. I reach out to stop her and the fabric of her shirt slips through my fingers as shadows wrap around her. When they dissipate, she is gone and I am alone with only my whirling thoughts for company.

Chapter 13

Sila

I EMERGE FROM THE SHADOWS IN MERCIAS' LIVING quarters. His space is neat and orderly, as if he hardly spends his time in here. It is different to mine, a lot of dark wood and ornamental cut-outs, and everything made to feel sturdy and sombre. There is very little delicate about it. I imagine the most delicate thing in here is likely blond, scribe-shaped, and in his bed.

"Mercias," I call, crossing my arms over my chest.

There's an emphatic *fuck* from the bedroom. All the Librarians have fae blood— diluted by millennia, but still there. That is true of most in the Citadel, and it is what gifts them their magical inclinations. Before he became a Librarian, Mercias had other abilities. When he had pledged himself to the Library and become a Librarian, he had exchanged them for a greater boon. Still nothing like the power I wielded, of course, but useful enough.

Unfortunately, he still requires impractical things like sleep. Well, that is too bad. I need him.

"You're keeping me waiting, Mercias. You know I am not a patient woman," I call out again.

"You're not a woman, you're a fiend," Mercias hisses as he shoulders through the door, pulling his cloak on. "Sent from the dark as my personal torment."

I smile at him. "I need you to help with a cleanup."

Mercias looks at me properly then. Neither of us need light to see by, and the blood is obvious.

"*Fuck*, Sil— Librarian. What the King's name is going on? If this is an overdue fee collection, and you've killed them— "

"It is nothing of the sort. There were intruders in the scriptorium."

"Oh, of course. The scriptorium that you're suddenly so interested in," he says drily.

"Insolence does not suit you," I say lightly. He snorts in response. "They are related to the poisoning, and given your behaviour with Striger, I hardly think your argument has much integrity."

That sobers him up quickly. Good. I hate disposing of bodies, and I loathe cleaning up blood. I would not usually have been so quick to draw a blade. It was not even my second or third preference— if I was going to get blood everywhere, I would use my talons and tear them open. It was more satisfying. Still, I could not let the scribes return to work this morning looking the way it did.

"Where are they?"

"Down, Mercias. They are dead."

"How many of them?"

"Three. Two Lightkeepers and a scribe."

"Lightkeepers," Mercias hisses. "And a traitor."

"Mmm." I turn and lead him from his rooms, catching the way he glances back towards the bedroom before he goes.

In the hallway, I keep walking when he stops to lock the

door. He will catch up if he knows what is good for him. It does not take long for him to fall into step beside me.

"You should be more careful," I tell him.

"I can handle my own affairs. And the Head Librarian can deal with me as she sees fit," Mercias says. "You should worry about yourself."

I arch an eyebrow and look at him sidelong. "I cannot think what you mean."

"Oh, come on Si— *Librarian*. Your sudden interest in the scriptorium. Carrying the scribe to her room. The Head Librarian knows what I'm doing, and it won't be long before she realises you're doing the same. You're only getting a pass for now because no one can be certain."

"I hardly think I need a warning from the likes of you." He rolls his eyes at me, and I pretend not to see. Alas, he is no longer my student, and I cannot so easily punish him for his insolence. "And I am not bedding a scribe."

Mercias is silent for a long moment. "Honestly, somehow, that's worse. It's one thing to bed her, it's another to see you being— " He cuts himself off.

"Being what, Mercias?" I ask. I know he hears the dangerous tone in my voice. I know he always ignores it. It has always been irritating.

"Being soft," he says. "If you were bedding her, it would at least make sense."

"I do not see what that has to do with anything. You are hardly soft with yours," I reply.

"He would hate it if I was," says Mercias. Then, "Fuck."

We don't need to walk far into the scriptorium to find the bodies. They lie where I had left them.

Something seizes my heart in a vice grip, an echo of the agony and fear I had felt when I saw them try to grab her. If I hadn't been following her— it hardly bore thinking about.

I can still see the moment those animals had grabbed for her, had dared to lay hands on her. I clench my fists, the nails biting into the soft flesh of my palms.

Everything feels more intense than it has in an age. My fury is brighter than it has ever been.

I had acted without thinking and now Lorel is in my rooms, my bargain mark on her hand and that other wretched mark on her chest. She had looked at me with such confusion, the poor tired thing. I half expect her to be gone when I return. In which case the bargain mark will demand I hunt her down. I would hardly need the bargain to do that, though. It is clear she cannot protect herself.

Mercias looks towards the desks as he walks around the space, kneeling to examine a fallen sigil lantern.

"Sil— "

I narrow my eyes at him, and he sighs dramatically.

"*Librarian*, why were you in the scriptorium?"

"It hardly matters," I say.

"The Dawn King strike me where I stand," he mutters. "I'll try again— why was Scribe Lorel in the scriptorium in the middle of the night?"

"I suppose she could not sleep," I say with a shrug.

"And you followed her." It is not a question.

"She would be dead if I had not," I snap, flexing my fingers. I dislike the look on Mercias' face. Something like pity. He shakes his head.

"Fine, your scribe is a touchy subject," he says, moving to the nearest body. "They've not gone stiff yet, so it should be easy enough to take them to the guardians of the catacombs. They can deal with them."

"Do you recognise the scribe?" I pick up the nearest of the assailants' bodies, throwing him over my shoulder with ease.

Mercias grabs the dead scribe's hair and pulls his head back. He bares his teeth in a snarl.

"Yes, I know this one. I'll have to notify his kin." He looks between the two bodies. "You didn't kill him, did you?"

"No," I say, moving to pick up the second man. Carrying them is nothing, but touching them makes my skin crawl. They hardly deserve the respect that the guardians will no doubt give them. "They got to him far before I could."

Mercias hums under his breath. "That makes it easier, I suppose. And then there is no need to mention scribe Lorel."

"It hardly needs reporting," I say, as he picks up the scribe.

"The Head Librarian may be unwilling to interrogate you, but she'll certainly interrogate me," he says, gesturing me on. "What a mess. And in the scriptorium, no less."

I lead the way out and down to the catacombs. We'll come back to clean up the blood after. The thought turns my stomach. How easily I could be cleaning up my scribe's blood instead.

And I cannot figure out why, which is the worst part. I had suspected some plot with Striger, because it had all been far too neat. I had not suspected that Lightkeepers were involved.

Something about her had made her a target. The cursed book she spoke of had almost killed her. The poison had almost killed her. The scribe and the Lightkeepers had almost killed her.

I had almost killed her.

I had held my blade over her heart, like I had so many others before her, at the command of my queen. My tether to the queen had been stretched, taut and thin. It was what kept me anchored in the world— that prevented me from fading away— from losing myself. My constant companion for thousands of years. And then I had seen the mark on her skin, and everything had changed

Lorel had called it a curse mark. And maybe it is, in a way, but it is also a claim. A claim from someone else, something else. Something that was not *me*.

Something wanted her, but I wanted her more.

The tether had snapped, then, and I knew I had chosen, and I had chosen her.

She had woken a moment after, blinking softly at me, and I had known I would do anything to keep her safe. And so I will.

"Sila!" Mercias' voice comes from behind me, loud, as if he'd been trying to get my attention for some time.

"Ah," I say, realising I have walked too far. Missed the stairwell down. He just shakes his head at me, and says nothing more as he takes the stairs and I follow.

Chapter 14

Lorel

I am dozing when Sila returns. I had bathed and sat with my thoughts and I could only conclude that I am tired beyond measure. I cannot draw a logical conclusion to anything Sila said and yet nothing that is happening makes any sense. She was not the only one with an interest in my death. And now it seems she is the only one with an interest in me living.

If I had had more sense, I would have curled up in an armchair. As it is, I barely remember to pull my shift back on before I tuck myself into Sila's bed. The sheets are surprisingly soft, if a little dusty. They have the memory of her perfume, sweet against my senses and tangled with the smell of salt and earth. It shouldn't relax me, but it's comforting as I drift off.

There is a shifting weight on the edge of the bed, and the thing in my chest stirs like a cat disturbed from its nap. After a moment's pause, it settles itself again as if content that there is no threat.

"Lorel," Sila whispers, her fingers combing through my hair. Without my glasses, she's a little indistinct. The blood is gone from her cheeks, so she must have washed up while I slept. "Are you hungry? Or shall I let you rest some more?"

I don't need to reply because my stomach grumbles as if it has been waiting for someone to notice it and provide it with sustenance. I'm reluctant to move. I like the way her fingers feel in my hair, her nails gentle against my scalp.

Her face softens in a smile. "Come along then. Let us get you fed." She moves away from the bed and if I could make a noise, it would be the most melancholy of sighs. I rub the sleep from my eyes as I sit up, and I remember to fetch my glasses before I go.

She had been so prickly before, hurt and wary as she'd turned away from me, and now she's being so soft. I don't understand it. Librarians are not soft with scribes. They're not soft with anyone.

Sila has removed the books from a small table and chairs in the room's corner, unearthing it from the scholarly debris.

Are these all Library books?

I yawn wide and drop into a chair, stretching my arms high above my head and forgetting that I'm only wearing a shift. Sila's amusement is back, dancing in her eyes, tipping up the edges of her mouth. It seems her good humour has returned— though whether it is from dealing with dead bodies or antagonising Mercias, I cannot say.

"Some are, I think," she says. She leaves the room and returns with a tray. It is far fancier than the ones from the scribes' quarters, both the tray itself and the offering upon it. I blink at it slowly. There is a mushroom and vegetable stew, an assortment of pickles, a round of bread, and in the corner is a soft cheese. Only it's drenched in a sweet golden syrup that isn't something usually wasted on the scribes. I look back up at Sila, uneasy. This is surely not for me. She places it firmly on the table in front of me.

I suppose you don't have to pay late fees then.

Sila smiles, her teeth flashing dangerously through it. "They are welcome to try. Now eat."

Are you sure this is mine?

Sila makes a little huff of a laugh. "I am certain."

I hesitate for a moment more before deciding that if I don't, there is a real threat that Sila will feed me herself. I dig into the stew, and maybe it's just how hungry I am— because I doubt there is really any difference between this and my usual fare— but it's possibly one of the most delicious things I've ever eaten in my life.

Sila lounges in the spindle-legged chair across from me. She's not watching me, her eyes focused off somewhere across the room in thought. I reach out and brush my fingers against her arm to get her attention.

"Are you still hungry?" she asks. Her face is unguarded with a gentle smile, and it takes me a moment to remember why I wanted her attention.

I haven't finished yet.

"Hmm, I can see that now. If it is not to your tastes, I can find something different." Sila rests her head in her hand as she leans on the table.

It's not about the food. It's just, what do we do now?

"Oh, I thought you did not believe me?"

I don't know what to believe anymore. I can barely light a sigil properly, and I've probably only ever squished a spider accidentally. I've no idea why you all want me dead. Except maybe if it has something to do with this. I pull my collar down to display the inky black mark, only a few days older than when she last saw it and already closer to Sila's handspan than to mine. *I don't know if I believe you. I don't know if I don't either. It's a lot to take in. But... it wouldn't be the strangest thing happening right now, would it?*

There's a wry smile caught at the edges of her mouth again. "No, it certainly would not." Her eyes are fixed on the mark across my chest, and they close off, cold and unfathomable. "It is growing."

I think it will consume me.

"I will not countenance that," Sila says, sharp. She takes a deep, steadying breath. "You said you could remember nothing."

I can't. I picked up a book from my desk. I woke up in the infirmary.

"And you have not found the book yet?" Sila taps her fingers on the table surface, her mouth pinched as if she is coming around to a thought that does not please her.

No. I have no idea where it went.

She's silent, wrestling with something. She makes a frustrated noise in the back of her throat. "I think I know where to find it," she says eventually. She looks back at the mark and this time there is resignation there instead. I'm not so sure what to make of that.

How?

Sila reaches over the table, tugging my shift back up and tying it gently. "There is only one place to find such a book, and that is in the Heart of the Library."

"You are to stay within my rooms," Sila says sternly. "This is the safest place for you, and thus far, no one knows you are here. There is food in the kitchenette, and you can read what you wish." Her cloak is thrown around her shoulders, and I don't think I could disobey the tone of her voice if I tried.

Anything?

Sila smiles, a wicked growing thing. "Look to your heart's content, little mouse. I have no secrets from you."

I don't think that's true.

"I suppose I would not know. It depends on how well you can search," Sila says.

There is a reason I'm not a researcher.

Sila's mouth twists in wry amusement, and there is something lighter about her. "No, I suppose you are not."

You seem pleased.

"I look forward to finding out what you discover about me," she says. "Give me two days to make sure everything is in order, and then we shall find your missing book."

Two more days with a growing curse mark is better than the indefinite amount that I was facing before. It still worries me. Going into the Heart of the Library worries me too. Only Librarians can enter the Heart, nestled in the depths of the Library. Rarely did they take anyone else with them, because rarely did anyone else walk out again.

I will need to trust our bargain, if not her. Maybe I can find evidence of that trust hidden in her things, though. Find some reassurance that I have not made a terrible deal with some kind of horrific demonic presence from deep within the Library.

"Lorel?" Sila's fingers caress my jaw, tipping my head up to see her. She pushes my glasses back into place. "I mean what I say— do not leave this room."

I wet my lips, remember I can't speak, and nod. Sila's eyes track every movement.

"Good," she says, and as she steps back, the shadows reach out and swallow her whole.

Surely others notice her walk through the shadows, or arrive without using a door. Though perhaps they simply do not care to notice. It may not be worth noticing.

It leaves me standing in her rooms, alone and surrounded by books and scrolls and boxes and papers. I stare at the door. I *could* leave, but I doubt I would get far. And really, where would I go? To deliver myself to the Lightkeepers? To try and hide in the Glade? There is nowhere that Sila won't find me.

Somehow, it is a comforting thought.

I turn my attention to the room. Some books are coated so thick with dust that I can't begin to comprehend how long they might have sat here. My hands come away covered in it. Had they been here since the previous occupant? I circle Sila's desk that sits in pride of place amongst it all, as if I am trying to sneak up on it. It feels almost too personal to approach it. Too intimate to rifle through it.

I have no doubt that Sila has already been through mine. There wouldn't have been much of interest there, though. Just some embarrassing sketches and attempts at painting I'd likely forgotten to throw away. My heart aches a little, and it's silly, but I miss my paints. Miss my desk. Miss the scriptorium, even.

But this isn't the time for melancholy. I have permission to dig through a Librarian's things, and I won't let the opportunity pass me by. Some of the piles are as tall as I am, though I suppose that isn't a problem for Sila. I wiggle my way through and collapse into the chair. It's unexpectedly comfortable. I pass an eye over the stacks within arm's reach — well, my arm's reach— and then turn my attention to the desk.

It has a dark red leather top, worn thin in places, but cared for, suggesting that she must *sometimes* clear the desk. There are two drawers on either side under it, neither of them locked. A stand with a book open, and small stacks and piles balancing precariously on the edges. And in the middle of it all, a research journal in what must be Sila's hand. Never mind what it is she writes of, the script she writes with is *archaic.*

The Library contains almost two thousand years of our history, since the first sacrifice and the Dawn King's ascension. Tastes in handwriting and illuminating came and went, and a keen eye could date a piece based on those features alone. Elris' work builds on the style of his master, Illuminator Valen, but it is still distinct. And in the centuries that come after, it will anchor it in this time and place, because what came before and what comes after will forever be changing.

There is a current trending style, adopted some years back by newer scribes after an old manuscript had surfaced for copying and everyone had thought it beautiful. It had been truly, properly ancient. Dry and cracked and brittle. The preservation had taken three teams of scribes weeks of cleaning and copying. That manuscript is the closest thing I've ever seen to Sila's hand, and even then, the connection feels weak.

Those of fae blood, as most in the Citadel were, could live for a few centuries if they were lucky. Sila would have to be older by far for a script like this to come naturally to her. Older than that manuscript that had seemed so ancient.

I rub my fingers together, feel the dust caked to them. Not dust from a previous Librarian, but from Sila's neglect over decades, maybe even centuries. She had told me she was a true fae, and I had not believed her.

I am a fool.

I had been raised to believe there was no true fae left, except for his majesty, the Dawn King. Benevolent ruler of us all. But I am also a scribe, and I know how histories can be written anew at any time. How stories can twist a lie into truth.

I brush my fingers lightly over the journal pages, the paper fine under my fingertips. The words looping and swirling across the page, almost illegible. I look at the closest stack to me, at the spines and begin to notice a pattern, and a familiar hand.

These are not library books. These are centuries of Sila's journals.

Chapter 15

Lorel

IF I HAD THOUGHT THAT SEARCHING SILA'S DESK WAS too intimate, then I don't know what level of intimacy it is to sit and read her research journals. I circle around, first leaning over the desk to flick through the book currently propped open on the stand. I stare at it, mouth slack and eyes wide. It is a book on curses. Its pages record known cases and their details, and as I flick through it, my stomach churns. Very few of them end well.

I set it aside. Sila's desk is a place of orderly disarray and beautiful things. Everything seems cared for, but the only thing that appears to have its place is an exquisitely turned dip pen. It's worn soft where Sila's fingers must hold it, and sits nestled against the ink well on a stand. Sila favours a deep red ink, apparently. Somehow, I thought she'd use a black.

I finally come back to the journal. I remind myself I have permission to read it, even if it will take some time to decipher her handwriting with its elaborate curls and occasional shorthand. Her shorthand is archaic too, but as the hours wear on, I start to pick it up. Near the beginning, I notice my name and flick back to the start of the entry.

Known:

Lacerations to torso. Bruising, shoulders, neck, waist, knees, fingers. Broken fingers. Broken ribs. Fever.

The mark was found in her room, jammed against the wall in the corner. Assumed that she was trying to cool her skin with the stone.

The mark had dug her nails into her skin. Assumed that the broken fingers are because of her grip.

The mark would not let go. The mark did not make a single noise despite obvious injuries.

Additional information:

Burns to the throat.

The mark has woken, seems unaware of her surroundings. Unable to speak, the physician confirmed burns to the throat. Affliction is clearly magical in nature.

The mark is listless. Concerns about her mental state.

The mark continues to recover well physically.

· · ·

...

Additional information:
  Silenced.

The scribe has returned to work in full health. After further interrogation, the scribe confirmed they are not only unable to speak, they cannot make any verbal sound. Scribe confirmed silencing related to prior events. I don't believe this to be related to the burns in the throat. Requires further research.

The scribe was sent back to the infirmary after cutting hand with a sharpening knife. While the scribe appears in full health, she seems unsettled. Neglecting needs. Clearly did not partake of the morning meal, appears to be sleeping restlessly.

Additional information:
  Memory loss.

Lorel relates loss of voice and cause of prior violence to finding and reading a book. Confirmed loss of memory between reading a book and waking in the infirmary. Must try to locate said book to confirm suspicions.

Additional information:

Curse mark growing. Fever, repeated.

Lorel and her peers were poisoned. One scribe has died, and two are in recovery. Lorel has unusual symptoms not present in the surviving two. She is feverish again, and I have learned there is a curse mark upon her skin. She has confirmed it is growing at a rapid pace, and began six and a half weeks ago, when I found her. Unsure if the curse mark is damning or protecting her. Need to confirm where the curse mark comes from.

Book is still missing, in spite of a thorough search of the scriptorium, Library, and Lorel's rooms. Suspect I know the location of the book.

There is space for further notes below, and then it continues on with her research and theories. Almost two months of questions and answers that lead to more questions. Notes from books she's read on curses, magical ailments, anything, it seems, that she thought might be relevant. The curse stirs in my chest, as if it can hear me thinking of it. It settles again quickly and I feel as if I have been admonished for waking it.

There are further notes about me scattered throughout. They start with 'the mark' and end with 'Lorel' and I don't want to think too hard about what that means, because it was hard enough to believe that she was an ancient true fae. I had no need to entertain any other thoughts about her that I could not believe to be true. That way madness truly lies.

Her most recent notes in the journal grow increasingly

frustrated as each researched recounting of a curse victim ends in violent death. Only, as I read, I wonder if Sila's frustration has clouded her thoughts because in every historical account of a curse mark, the violence is always at the end. Mine began with violence, even if it came from my own hand. There is not a single mention of a curse victim almost dying at the inception of their curse— only ever at the end. In fact, by these accounts, they are almost always in good health and spirits at the start.

It doesn't change that Sila is right that the only place left to look for the book is in the Heart of the Library.

The Heart terrifies me as much as it excites me. You don't live in the Library and not wonder at its secrets. Wonder at going down all those flights of stairs and down again into the dark, where the gateway to the Heart of the Library sits. Only those attuned to the Library's Heart could open it, and the only ones attuned to the Library were the Librarians themselves.

The Library is, by all accounts, an endless, living labyrinth with a mind of its own. I have been told in the Keep that the Dawn King had made it to keep all our history safe. The Library-dwellers believe otherwise, saying that it had grown from a magic older than the Citadel's founding. Either way, the Dawn King's only interest is ensuring each year during the Ascension, the annual celebration of his coronation, that the Library continues to bow to him. And thus far, it has.

I look back at the journal, tracing the shapes of Sila's letters across the page with my fingers. There is no use worrying over it; the Library, the curse, Sila. If I have learned only one thing these past few weeks, it is that my fate is no longer in my own hands.

I pick up the next nearest book and start reading.

. . .

"Learn anything interesting?" murmurs a voice at my shoulder. I'd scream if I could. I'd been so engrossed in Sila's research notes on old faetales I hadn't heard her come in. Or, more likely, I'd missed her materialising behind me.

"Oh, that's an old one. Hmm." She's distracted by the book, mumbling about how something isn't correct anymore, and it gives me a chance to regain some sense of composure. "I should make a note and update that."

Sila reaches for her pen and ink, leaning over me so that I am swallowed by her hair and perfume, her arm and cloak slung over the chair back. The curse stirs again, as if opening one eye to check that all is well, and then settles. I grab at Sila's shirt, fingers wrapping into the soft silken fabric. My fingertips brush against her skin. It's as ice cold as the rest of her. I'd never thought on it before, but was that also a Librarian thing?

Sila goes very still, hand poised to take up her pen, and then turns to look at me. She narrows her eyes at me and I hold my breath, unsure if I've overstepped.

"Have you been in the same spot all day? Did you remember to eat *at all*?"

I release her shirt.

You only instructed me not to leave.

Sila makes a noise through her teeth to express her disappointment. "Your ability to care for yourself is woeful. Are all scribes like this?"

Are all Librarians like you?

"So it's only you that is so obstinate as to be reckless," she says. She turns back to her desk and quickly makes a note, blots it, and tucks it into the book I was reading.

It's hardly reckless to miss the midday meal.

Sila makes a sound that indicates she strongly disagrees.

"Up, I won't have you starving on me, little mouse." I give her a look to indicate that I think she's being tiresome, but I get up. It *has* been some time since I sat down. I should have at least gotten up to stretch. Sila brings through a tray again, and it suddenly becomes very clear to me that Sila must not eat.

The tray is a mix of things that one would never usually serve together. There is a round of bread, but the only thing to put on it is more of the soft cheese drenched in a puddle of golden syrup. A selection of very specific pickles. I don't know what has possessed her to pair it all with my favourite sweet bun. It's the strangest meal I have ever been served. My hesitation must be obvious, because Sila frowns.

"Hmm, have I chosen wrong? I'm sure these are your favourites," she says. "You seemed so pleased with the cheese yesterday." She is entirely uncowed, studying me with all the seriousness of a Librarian wondering why a book has been mis-shelved.

It's fine.

I try not to think about the fact that right down to the pickles, each of these is a thing I love. I had never thought to put them all on the same tray at once, though.

You have a lot of notes on me.

"Is that your discovery for the day?" she settles across from me again. She seems pleased when I start to eat, and for the barest moment I wonder what I have been so afraid of. And then I remember her standing over the Lightkeeper corpses.

I don't know why you're so interested in me.

"Hmm, it is curious, is it not?"

Yes.

She doesn't give me any further answer, and I don't

quite know what question I need to ask to get one. For the first time in my life, the silence makes me uncomfortable.

Are all these books your research journals?

"Most of them. There probably is a Library book or two in there somewhere," Sila says, looking around. "I'm sure I don't know."

If Sila doesn't know, then surely no one else ever will. It could be the beginning of its own library, if only it had any kind of system to it.

Do they mostly cover faetales?

The few I had looked in had, the last had been the most interesting to me because it cross-referenced faetales with historical records as Sila tried to make connections and highlight missing details. It was certainly not the kind of study that the Dawn King would sanction, so naturally it was entirely engrossing.

"Mostly. It's all you folk really have left of the oldest history. I've spent years at a time searching the Heart for more, but if it has what I'm looking for, it hasn't shown it to me yet." She's silent for another moment, and I wait for her to tell me what exactly she is looking for. Instead, she deftly changes the subject. "But no matter, we will find what we need for you because if we don't, I will raze the Heart myself."

Chapter 16

Lorel

THE NEXT MORNING IS MUCH THE SAME AS THE LAST, only this time Sila commands me to remember to eat alongside her instructions not to leave her rooms. Again, I consider what would happen if I left, and decide I'm not interested in finding out. I finish my morning meal, wondering if Sila has an endless supply of 'things Lorel likes to eat', and then turn my attention to Sila's things.

I could read Sila's research journals for days and not get bored, but I don't think I will learn much about *her* from them. And I want to know more. I want to know why she would threaten to burn the Library down for me, why she is keeping such thorough notes on my condition, and why she is researching how to cure it. I want to crawl into her mind and understand what it is that makes her face go dark when she looks at the curse mark.

Most of all, I want to know why each time she could have let me die, she didn't. Yesterday it had felt too intimate to sit at her desk. Today, though, that intimacy is what I crave. It's the same desperate compulsion that had sent me to the scriptorium. I should be wary of it, but I am tired of being wary. Growing tired of being afraid.

I start in the bedroom. I know she doesn't use it— not for rest, in any case. I don't think she needs to sleep, and I have yet to see her do so. The room is lined with overflowing shelves and only the wardrobe is in use, half open and dripping with her clothes. I expected her to be neater, if I am honest.

I start my search from one end and work methodically around the room, top to bottom. There are plenty of books, and more research journals, and assorted meaningless trinkets long forgotten and covered in dust. I search drawers and check for false bottoms— I find two with nothing more than an assortment of papers that must have been important once. I check panels for hidden hollows, go through any pouch or case I find and discover a wild assortment of pen nibs, dried bottles of ink, and more than one bottle that I think might contain blood.

I am halfway through the search when I hear the faint toll of the midday bell. I pause, knowing the admonishment that will come if I don't stop.

I do not stop. I am a woman possessed. A scribe in the middle of a task.

I am considering that the side tables to the bed might be the most likely to contain something interesting when a panel pops under my fingertips. I had tapped it only a moment ago, and had been sure it was solid and it is, in a manner of speaking. I lever a wooden box out of the space and the open end of it reveals a hefty book, lodged solidly into a space that, honestly, no one should ever have thought would accommodate it. It must have dampened the sound.

It almost crumbles under my hands as I shift it, parts of

the cover sloughing off, and I wince. It's a cruel fate for a book. Only, it isn't a book. Not quite. The cover comes away with a faint tingle of magic, an alarm or ward long faded. Inside, the pages have been cut through, carved out to fit a small wooden box. And while the book is old, the box is ancient. I've never seen its like. It looks as if it was painted once, but it's all worn away.

I sit back on the floor with the box in my lap. Every other little trinket has felt like the throwaway detritus of a long life. This feels different, not in the least because of how it was hidden within the shelf. Or that Sila had taken a knife to a book to hide it. I know this is exactly the thing I have been searching for.

There's no charm or sigil or ward on it that I can make out. Just tiny intricate carvings into the brass that have long since oxidised. I find a penknife that I had unearthed earlier and run it carefully around the edge of the lid, conscious not to damage it. I can imagine the alarm on Sila's face if she were to find me sitting here with another knife in my hands, but the thought only amuses me. I should probably be more worried that I have overstepped in my search.

The box's lid gives with a little click and falls open. Nestled in dust that might have once been velvet and wool is a gold locket. It's carved with the same style of marks found on the oldest murals and mosaics. I pick it up gingerly and wipe my thumb over the metal. The gold is cool against my skin. I recognise some motifs. While many of our rituals might have changed, the way we mark the loss of a loved one has not. It is a death locket, not so different from the one Orielle has for our parents. Only for it to be made in gold can only mean one thing. This death was a sacrifice.

I open it. A portrait on one side, and a lock of dark hair

on the other. The woman looks as if she could be Sila's sister, but even confined within the frame, the shadows at the edges reach for the lock of hair. Bleed together. Just like Sila's shadows. My blood turns cold at yet another impossible thing.

I should not be holding Sila's death locket in my hands.

Chapter 17

Lorel

THE REMAINDER OF THE DAY IS A DRAG. I PLACE THE death locket on the table and set about tidying up the mess I've made. It hardly makes a difference. Sila's room still looks like the burrow of a nesting dormouse. In the end, I tidy up more than my share of the mess, likely destroying a complex system of organisation in the process. The realisation that I'm not afraid of retribution is a sudden and shocking one. I try to remind myself that she is dangerous, but it's hard to do so standing here tucking all her things away. I begin to understand why it is such a mess. There's simply not enough space for everything that exists in here.

I make up a plate for midday, even though it is long past time, and find myself wishing that Sila would just appear from the shadows so that I could get some answers out of her. Two days ago I thought she had been locked up in the Library too long. Two days later, I think I am the one who has taken leave of her senses. I had thought what she'd told me was impossible, but it is me who is sitting here with a curse, unable to speak, after having faced multiple attempts to kill me. If it wasn't happening to me, I would have thought that was impossible, too. I think I have been desperate to hold on to some semblance of normalcy, but it doesn't exist anymore. Not for me.

The air stirs behind me and this time when her fingers thread through my hair and tug my head back gently, it doesn't take me entirely unaware.

"Miss me, little mouse?" she says, looking down at me. She's rather lovely from this angle. I shove *that* thought aside.

I've been waiting for you.

Her fingers comb through my hair with a slight tug, letting my hair drop away as she comes around to sit at the table with me. "What have you found today?"

Questions.

I nudge the box across the table, and Sila's eyes widen in something like delight. "Oh, I haven't seen this in an age."

I can well believe it, given the state I had found it in. Her expression is soft as she takes the death locket and clicks it open.

"I have once again underestimated your tenacity." She clicks it shut again and tucks it away. The gentle heartache in her eyes, the tightness in the corner of her mouth, goes with it.

I chew on my lip, a little nervous. I want this to go better than the last time she had revealed one of her secrets to me.

This is a death locket. For someone who was sacrificed. It's you, isn't it?

Sila holds my gaze, deathly still. I notice her shoulders do not rise and fall. She does not eat. She does not sleep. Her skin is as cold as ice. We were both more complicated than we looked, it seemed.

"It is," she says slowly. Cautiously.

Then... how? How is it possible?

The silence stretches out between us.

Please. I want to know.

Sila blinks slowly. "How lovely it would be to hear you say that aloud," she murmurs. Her fingers run idly along the edge of the box. "Your people have stories of dark spirits. Ghastly things that haunt the halls of the Citadel and bring sickness and famine in their wake. You also have tales of a ghoulish woman cast down by the Dawn King. I think these days you tell it that she wished to cover the world in darkness, but she was slain by the Dawn King and cast into her own shadows. When I was a girl, there was more to it. The woman was the Dawn King's queen then, and he cast her out into her own Court, a pale imitation of the Suntide Court— reflecting the sun's brilliance as the moon does. It was necessary to keep the balance. Words I am sure you have heard before."

I had. Almost once a year, as the warmer months drew on and sickness took hold, or when the earth withheld her bounty. Blood will always correct the balance. That is what they say.

Sila is silent for a long moment.

"I went to the altar willingly. I had lost much that was dear to me, and I did not wish to lose anymore. At the time, I thought it was an honour. Now it was so long ago that I'm not sure what to make of it. I drank the poison, and the Dawn King bled me over the altar." Sila tips her head back and in the low light, I can see the faintest line, usually hidden, running from ear to ear across her throat. She tips her head back down, and her lovely face is unreadable. "It was not so bad. Until I awoke in the Evenfall Court."

The Queen's court?

Sila smiles, a teacher pleased at her students' progress. "Exactly so," she says, her brows creasing together as she continues. "I cannot recall the queen's words exactly, only that I believe when the stories spoke of casting her out, they meant she was the first to be sacrificed on the altar. Through whatever bargain she and I struck, I was reborn as I am. As one of her wraith-like shadows. What remains of my first body still rests in the catacombs, in truth. She remade me anew."

Then... how did you come to be in the Suntide Court?

"Did you not guess yet?"

You were sent to kill me... but I am not the first?

"Yes," breathes Sila. "I am her eyes and ears in the Suntide Court, because my queen still has a grudge to settle with the man who murdered her. I have been here for centuries now. I have watched other wraiths fade, heard the stories change, seen Librarians born and been there when they died, but I persist and so she uses me to fulfil her wishes, to play her game."

The light in Sila's eyes is bright, fervent. It would be easy to believe her delusional, but I would be ignoring the evidence of my eyes. A bargain that shouldn't have taken, struck. A true fae that lives on by the grace of a dead queen. A locket to mark the death of a woman who was once beloved.

But you let me live.

Because this is still the part that does not make sense to me.

Her expression softens again. "Of course I did. How could I not? It's been a long, long time since I have cared whether someone lived or died. I do not wish to see you dead, Lorel." She pauses, head tipping to one side, features suddenly impossibly sharp. "*Shit.*"

Sila's hand snaps out and grabs my wrist, pulling me up harshly from the chair. My knee catches and I curse silently as she drags me to her bedroom and shoves me through the door. "Don't move. Stay quiet— well, don't knock nothing over." Her brows knit together for a moment. "Did you tidy — ? Oh, never mind." She pulls the doors shut fast, leaving me sprawled on the floor, still trying to catch up.

Then I hear what Sila must have heard. The metallic ringing of metal on metal that I would associate with the Barracks, not the Library. There is a sharp, heavy knock at the door. Two solid thumps that seem intended to let anyone on the other side know that the caller is being polite. Heavy enough to prove that if they wanted to, the door wouldn't stand between them for very long. I pull myself up to lean against the bedroom door, where an ancient keyhole gives me a clear view of the centre of the room.

Sila must be sitting at her desk. She makes no sound to acknowledge her visitor.

Two more thuds threaten the integrity of Sila's door and Sila clicks her tongue, impatient.

"I'm sure you know how to use a door, Vika, so use it," she says, sounding tired already. There's a rough laugh from the other side of the door before it opens. The woman who steps through gives all the appearance of someone in a very cheerful mood. It only makes her more terrifying.

I thought Sila was tall. I thought Sila was strong. This woman— Vika— makes Sila look like one of the Dawn King's most delicate courtiers. Her dark curly hair is cropped short, her eyebrows as dark and thick as Sila's. The planes of her face are as sharp and hard as she looks. The smile on her face is genuine, but incapable, I think, of being anything but cruel. Everything about her screams violence and every sensible bone in my body is screaming for me to get as far away from her as possible. She turns her back to my hiding spot, and the emblem of the Dawnbound is splashed across it. She's not wearing a weapon, and I suspect it's because *she* is the weapon.

"Is this all the welcome I get?" says Vika, kicking the door shut. "I return from a gruelling year at the Dawn King's watch tower and you can't even look up from your books for me?" Vika stands in the only vacant space in the middle of the rug. "Fuck's sake, Sila, this is a mess."

"No one asked you," says Sila. I can't see her from the keyhole. Vika sighs dramatically and does a turn about the room. I duck down, out of sight of the keyhole and try not to move. I do not want to be seen by her. *Sila* does not want me to be seen by her. "Have you returned all this way just to interrupt me?"

"Of course I did," says Vika, cheerfully. "Given the complete lack of a challenge in this insipid cesspit. By the queen, Sila, do you know how many of these idiots I've watched kill themselves out there?"

Queen. Did that mean Vika was another wraith? She certainly appeared to be. It was a wonder that no one had noticed.

"So what is it, then? You have come to ask me to spar because you are bored? Because if so, you have wasted your time," says Sila, sterner than the oldest Librarian. Well, second oldest Librarian, maybe. How Vika is just standing there with Sila speaking to her like that, I'll never know. If she spoke to me like that, I would shrivel up and beg for death on the spot. Her words are punctuated by the telltale sound of a blotter being used rather aggressively.

"Don't be dull, Sila. You've got to give me something, otherwise I'll be the one to start killing them," Vika says. There's a sound of restless movement, chain mail moving against itself.

"I'll not be goaded or flattered into it, Vika. Not by the likes of you," replies Sila.

"Fine. Then I will have to settle for a conversation with my oldest friend," says Vika. An armchair creaks as Vika settles in.

Sila laughs, cold and indifferent. "When have you ever ended a conversation with something other than your fists?"

"Oh, well, I think I had one last week... hmm, maybe not."

"Why are you really here, Vika?"

My heart thumps in my chest, and there is a burning in my thighs and calves as they begin to cramp. There's not a chance on this dark earth that I'm going to move.

"Can I really not pay a friend a visit?" Vika almost sounds hurt. Almost.

"No," says Sila. "You put us both at risk."

Vika's laugh is an unexpected and wholehearted bark of a thing. "Oh, that's very good," she says. "The only thing dangerous in this place is the incredible stupidity of its population. Each of them more idiotic than the last. The *captain* they've placed me with, Sila. When I tell you how much I have to restrain myself from crushing her pretty little face." Vika makes a noise of disgust.

"We all have trials to bear," says Sila, drier than a neglected inkwell.

"Oh, and what of you, Sila? I hear your mark has disappeared."

"Have you now?" Sila says icily.

"I'm surprised. How hard is it really to murder a sad little scribe? Don't you Librarians do that daily, anyway?"

"You are testing my patience, Vika," returns Sila.

"Look, I don't care if you want to play with your food,

Sila. Just make sure you finish the task. I don't want to have to do it for you." More movement.

"I'm sure I don't know what you mean," says Sila. I hold my breath, every muscle tense.

"I'm sure you do," replies Vika.

"Don't make threats you can't keep, Vika."

"I would never threaten a friend, Sila." Restless footsteps come closer to the bedroom door and it is a good thing I can't scream because when Vika next speaks, she sounds like she's right next to me. The curse in my chest stirs, and this time, it is alert. Watchful. All raised hair and twitching tail. "I'm hurt you'd even think that."

"Get out, Vika."

"Fine," says Vika, her footsteps moving away from the door again. "I was getting bored, anyway."

Just imagining the look Sila must be sending her has me quailing and hoping that the ground will swallow me whole. My heart continues to pound long after the door shuts behind her. I jam my eyes shut, willing myself to calm down. Not one, but two of them. *So far.* If I had any doubts left before, I have none now.

Chapter 18

Lorel

With a pack settled on her shoulders, Sila strides down the hall of the Librarians' dormitories and I trail behind her. The hall is all narrow dark stone with a vaulted arched ceiling and a dark plush red carpet running the length of it. Wall sconces, set low, light the way.

Sila has hardly spoken since Vika left. She had clearly been unsettled by the conversation. It worries me to think that there is something in the world that Sila is afraid of. It worries me, too, that Vika could so easily and carelessly walk these halls. Because her presence *had* been a threat, outside of all the bluster.

As we walk, I hear a scream echoing down the hall. Whispers. Occasionally, a wailing noise like the dead have risen, and maybe one has. I can't say what Librarians get up to in their rooms. I'm not sure I want to know.

I take two steps for every one of Sila's and even with two days rest, the walk to the Library tires me. I don't know how I'm going to make it through an endless labyrinth. I only hope Sila doesn't intend to take it at the same hurried pace.

The hall lets out into a common area, and I keep my eyes fixed on the hem of Sila's cloak, determined not to make eye contact with anyone else in the room. The last thing I want is to find myself surrounded by Librarians or whatever else lives in these halls.

The balcony edge of the common area looks out over the Greater Library. There are books here that I have helped make, somewhere among the towering shelves, but there is no opportunity to appreciate the view as I hurry to follow Sila.

She waits for me at the bottom of the stairs, imperious and even a little bored.

"Come along, scribe," she says, sharp. She turns on her heel and keeps up her pace.

If the intent is to have me look like an unfortunate scribe conscripted to assist her, then it is surely working. Though she hardly needed to make such a show of it.

The stairs spiral down behind the curved walls of the Greater Library, crowded with researchers, their assistants, and Librarians and their students. Sila pushes through, and they make way for her, stepping swiftly out of her path. A researcher flinches when she comes up behind them. I watch three different people turn pale and pointedly walk in the opposite direction. As we descend, the crowds thin, until finally we are alone in the stairwell, and Sila slows her pace. The darkness grows oppressive and thick. I can feel the tingle of magic on my tongue and against my skin, and I know it is my first contact with the Heart of the Library.

It's a shock, no different from missing a step in the dark, to come to the end of the stairs. The ground smooths out into worn down stone, opening onto a large chamber. The magic here is thicker, though not by much. It is as if the large circular door at the other end of the room keeps it contained, barely. Worse than all that is that it feels... familiar.

The curse in my chest shifts, as if settling into a patch of warmth. And it is warm. I press my hand against the curse mark and feel the heat against my skin.

"Sila, you have surely not wasted your time dragging a scribe here with you," drawls a voice across the chamber. I startle at the other Librarians' sudden presence.

"Poor Mercias. Are you on guard duty today? How very dull for you," Sila replies, striding out into the room to meet him.

Mercias stands idly, inspecting his nails and barring her way. "I'm afraid I can't allow you to take a scribe into the Heart, Si— Librarian."

Sila goes very still, giving him a dangerous look. "Do you think you have any authority over me, Mercias?"

"I cannot in good conscience allow you to take *that* scribe into the Heart. Not when she was so recently *poisoned*, and has been reported as absent." Mercias stares Sila down and I wonder if that's a skill he's had to learn.

He ignores me as I wander past them both, staring at the ritual marks carved into the floor. I'm hardly a danger, since I can't open the Heart's door.

What are these marks?

They feel familiar too. There is something strangely comforting about them.

"It's the key," says Sila, absently. "Step out of my way, Mercias."

"How are you—" Mercias starts.

I miss the rest of it because when I crouch to press my hand to the activation sigil, the ritual marks light up, pale blue like a binding spell. I squint against it, a loud rumbling noise filling the chamber as the door to the Heart slides open. There is nothing on the other side but thick, dark magic. It calls to me, tugging at my being. The curse is alert in my chest, all keen and eager senses.

Sila and Mercias stare at me when I look back at them.

I didn't mean to.

"You shouldn't be *able* to," says Mercias with all the tone of a man who had only allowed me to walk past because he hadn't yet learned to identify me as a problem, and now regrets it. And I honestly hadn't thought I would be *this* kind of problem.

Sila looks more pleased than anything else. "So it is the Library," she says.

"What do you mean, Librarian?" says Mercias darkly.

"It's calling to Lorel," Sila says. I turn back to the dark, watching the way it curls and eddies as if reaching out for me.

"She is a *scribe*," he says, sounding curious in spite of himself. "The Library *cannot* speak to her."

"Do as you will Mercias. I will be taking her into the Heart. You're welcome to wait till we return. I'll try to make it this side of the century for you."

He doesn't put up much resistance as she breezes past him. She catches me up with her body and pushes me over the threshold into the Heart of the Library.

For a moment, it is disconcerting to walk. As if perhaps my hands have been replaced with feet, and my feet with elbows. And for some reason, my eyes are on the side of my head, instead of where they sensibly should be. The walls of the hallway seem to be walls, and the floor is a floor, but something about them feels wrong. Perhaps because they seem to be on an angle. Sila's body presses against mine, and the feel of it, cold and solid, grounds me. Tips the world back to rights. Brings my thoughts back to where they should be.

"Easy now, little mouse," Sila murmurs. I give myself a moment to blink myself into existence in the new world forming around me. I have to check that all my fingers and toes are in the right places. The curse sits like a weight, warm, in my chest. Content. "Now stay close. The Library may have let you in, but that doesn't mean it will let you out again."

I stare at her in alarm as she steps around me to lead the way. The ground beneath our feet forms into an endless staircase that goes on forever into the darkness. That magical essence is stronger here. Ever present against my skin, and constantly shifting like a living thing. As I follow Sila, watching the sway of her cloak, the labyrinth seems to build out ahead of us. It stretches out, infinite and impossible. Perhaps I needed to rethink my definition of impossible.

There is a pattern to it, or so I think. It shifts before my eyes and it doesn't just rearrange itself, it rearranges my thoughts, too. I know it has changed, but my mind tries to convince me otherwise. It would be easy to go mad here. To lose yourself.

"That went better than I thought it would," Sila says, keeping her voice low. "Here, I can see you easily enough, but you'll need the light. It will only get darker the further in we go, and I suspect the Library will not give up its secrets easily."

Sila pauses and holds out the lantern she had hooked to the pack. It's unlit. She does not light it. I feel sick at the thought of even trying. I concentrate, marking the sigil on the glass. It summons a soft low light, like it always does. It's a feeble attempt.

When I look up, Sila is frowning at the lantern, her face cast in long shadows from the meagre light. Irritation itches at my skin.

If you wanted better, you should have done it yourself.

I snatch the lantern from her and stalk on down the stairs. It takes a moment for her footsteps to follow. She easily falls into step beside me. I can't even walk furiously away from her and her cursed long legs. I forge onward.

"Lorel. *Lorel,*" comes Sila's voice, a hiss in the darkness.

I stop dead in my tracks. Take a deep, silent breath, and turn back to her. Of course, I have no idea where we are going. My face flushes with warmth. Sila stands in an open archway, a few steps back, and it is only now I see rows of them along the walls of the steps. I hadn't even noticed the walls appearing. Sila turns towards the darkness, greeting it as an old friend, and I scurry to catch her up. I have no desire to lose her in this place. I blink as that emotion surges, too. A fear that I might be parted from her, rising unbidden and overwhelming before it recedes again. Returning to a level of concern that feels more appropriate for the situation. I plunge after her into the dark.

Chapter 19

Lorel

THE DARKNESS IN THE HALLWAY IS CLAUSTROPHOBIC, pressing in breathlessly on all sides. I follow along behind Sila, trailing like the barest shred of a ghost. The entrance has long since been consumed by the endless void behind us. The path ahead is undetermined and entirely opaque. Sila is confident and sure as she strides into the dark, boots clipping on the stone sharply.

I study the outline of her as I walk. She had called herself wraith-like, and down here with the halfhearted light glancing off the edges of her hair and cloak, she is. The light only serves to emphasise the dark shadow of her form.

And it is an entirely lovely form. Without warning, that sudden desire threatens to overwhelm me. It makes my heart race, and for a moment I think it will give out. My breath catches silently in my throat and I choke on it. A heady, overwhelming wanting sending me loose-limbed and desperate.

And just as quickly as it came, it dissipates. Bleeding out of me and back into the darkness. I falter, my toe catching on the stone. I fall to the ground in a pile, the lantern hitting the ground hard enough to likely cause a dent. Another emotion hits me, and this one I am all too familiar with.

Useless. Unworthy. You will hold her back.

The thoughts crowd me, and this time it is despair that threatens to overwhelm me. The knowledge that I am nothing more than a useless, sad little scribe. Something to be pitied. It is relentless. I can hardly see the lantern light. It must have gone out. I couldn't even keep my lantern lit. My chest aches and I can hear Orielle's voice admonishing me again. And again. And again. *Why can't you just be more? Don't you want to be more? You're betraying their memory.*

I want to scream back at her. I could. I could scream at the top of my lungs. Scream—

Long fingers wrap around the sides of my face, nails digging into the flesh of my cheeks and scalp. Cold. Shockingly cold. The pain, sharp as anything, cutting through the dark reverie. Everything is dark.

Where did the light go?

I should call for it. Summon it back to me.

I take a deep breath, dragging air down into my lungs, and one hand moves, smothering my mouth. I try to bite it, try to reach for the owner of those hands. How *dare* they? I try to find purchase with my nails and fists. I squirm against them. I wrench free, breathing deeply and the other hand moves, slamming my jaw shut and holding it fast. I struggle against ink dark eyes, welling over with blood. Light glancing off them. Sharp teeth, bloody and clenched. Blood sprays across my face. I am pressed against a body, firm and unyielding. I don't know this creature that holds me, know nothing but the dark.

"Lorel. Little mouse, please. Come back to me. Don't let it hold you in fear," it whispers into my ear. *It?*

Cold self-loathing sinks through me. Despair. Dark and overwhelming. As if I have already lost.

I should give up.

Yet I still struggle against my captor. Why are they even *bothering*? Nails dig into my skin, holding my jaw and face tight against the urge to scream. I don't know why they're trying so hard. I can't make a noise, anyway.

Oh.

The darkness clears. My little lantern light returns, offering a glimpse of Sila's horrific form, the one that I had seen in the scriptorium that night. Her breath caresses my cheek, a constant whisper begging me to return to her. Shadows wrap around me, holding me to her while she keeps my jaw shut. I go limp as all the fear and hatred and anger slides away. Disappears back into the dark. Her grip goes slack.

"Lorel?" there is panic in her voice. I rest my head against her collarbones, trying to catch my breath. The soft curve of her breast presses against my cheek. She lets out a breath. Relief, maybe. Her fingers comb through my hair, as gentle as anything. Reassuring. She doesn't move, just holds me there a moment as if she's trying to get her breath back, too.

"Are you alright?" she whispers. I nod. "I'm sorry. I should have warned you. I did not realise your thoughts ran so dark, little mouse."

When I lean back to see her face, her eyes are normal again, the darkness confined to the irises. Worry written stark across her features. The shadows— Sila's shadows— release me.

What was that?

"The Heart, playing its games," she says. "It is a dark and lovely thing, but it is dangerous, too."

Like you.

Sila stares at me, a soft smile playing at the corners of her mouth as I realise what I've signed. Warmth flares across my face for the second time.

"You are a wondrous thing," she says. She grimaces, her fingers gently touching where they had dug into my skin. "I'm sorry, I couldn't let you make a noise. Otherwise, you would be lost to me."

I shiver at what I have narrowly avoided.

Don't apologise for saving my life. Again.

The corner of her mouth tips in a grim smile. "Come, there is a branch up ahead."

How she knows that, I'll never know. Outside the circle of light, there is no ahead, no behind, only deep impenetrable darkness.

Sila pulls me up from the ground as she stands. "Try not to think too long on anything," she says, smiling.

Will it try it again?

"Only at the edges. It will ease as we go further in," she says. "Of course, then it will be replaced by other things." She does not elaborate on what those other things are. I shiver, wrap my arms around myself and follow as she walks on.

The points where her fingers had dug in sting, but they keep me grounded in the dark. They aren't nearly as bad as the cuts my own nails had made. Those I still had scars from.

Sila's definition of up ahead and mine must differ, or perhaps it is only that time seems meaningless in the endless dark. The stone walls, an imitation of the Library's halls, turn to rows and rows of shelves, packed to bursting with books and papers and scrolls. It isn't so different from how Sila organises her own shelves. I keep my mind carefully blank, focused on putting one foot in front of the other. There are brief surges of feelings again, but they no longer take me by surprise and I turn them aside easily. They lessen as we walk, just as Sila had said, until they no longer come.

We continue to walk in silence. I'm grateful for the small bit of light I have, otherwise I think it would be easy to become lost. Both in body and in mind.

Occasionally we pass a door, or an arch between the shelves. There are ghosts of things at the edge of my sight. A room of dancers, a pale imitation of the Dawn King's courtiers in the hall of mirrors. Children sitting on a rug in front of a hearth, the sigil light making them shadows as they play.

Hacking coughs rattling out of an open door. Children crying.

Even in the Heart they haunt me.

Sila comes to a stop beside me, holding out an arm to stop me from walking headlong into a wall. Here the corridor finally branches in an intersection that leads left or right. The corridor has grown larger as we've walked, no longer narrow, crowding tunnels. Instead, the ceiling is vaulted, arching high, meeting the tops of the shelves that stand more than twice my height. As if in answer to my thought, when I turn to look the other way, there is a ladder that I am certain wasn't there before.

Sila looks amused when I look up at her. "It likes you," she says. "Don't let it distract you." Her fingers find mine, threading through them tightly.

First Sila's attention, now the Library's. I had hoped to disappear into obscurity in the Library. What had I done to deserve this kind of torment?

Sila turns left, pulling me along as I cling to her. Everything is quite ordinary for a moment, and then at the edge of my vision, the shelves begin to shift as the other corridor *follows* us. I can feel a headache coming on as my mind tries to make sense of it. It tries to convince me that the corridor had always been there. No, not there— there. I keep my lantern cast on the ground, so that I can focus on putting one step in front of the other.

The curse shifts and settles again, a soothing kind of presence brushing against my senses. For once it puts me at ease, and it isn't much longer until the second corridor gives up its pursuit.

The monotony of the hallway winds on as Sila follows this turn and that. I keep a tight grip on her hand to keep me anchored. I'm terrified that if I let go, I'll be left adrift. If I were to get lost here, I doubt I would ever find my way out again. Which I am sure is the Heart's intention.

There's nothing to mark the passing of time. Objectively I am tired, and growing hungry, but I'm also not. As if time is suspended and me with it.

The air shifts ever so slightly, and my heart skips with it. As if it doesn't care what change is coming because it will take anything at this point. It changes as swiftly as everything else has, the shadows opening up into high, towering ceilings like the Library proper. Wide sweeping staircases lead up to shelf lined rooms. Balconies similar to the common area open up onto the open space and high above our heads hangs a dimly lit chandelier. Beyond the rooms and archways, the dark fog sits thick. I have no doubt that it would open on to more halls, more rooms, more corridors.

Sila brings us to a stop at the foot of the main staircase. She untangles her fingers from mine and I try to ignore how tightly I'd been clinging to her. It's hard to do so, what with how they're cramping.

I collapse onto the stairs, my feet aching now that we've stopped moving. Tired right through to my bones. I press my palms against my eyes and try to suppress the yawn that follows. I feel so very small, and we've walked so far already and I've no doubt we have so much further to go.

"Little mouse, here," Sila says, keeping her voice down. Her hand rests on my thigh, cool even through the wool of my dress. She's kneeling on the step below with a wry smile. "I don't imagine they're very satisfying, but you should eat something." I take the little parcel she's offering me.

Wrapped in the cloth is a dry, dense flat bread. It's the kind of thing made to be edible for a long time, at the expense of being actually edible. It's sweet and a little salty. It'll have to do. Sila passes me water and I try to wash it down.

Where are we?

"Where we are supposed to be," Sila says, as opaque as the surrounding darkness. "The labyrinthine Heart of the Library is constantly shifting and changing. The only way through is to know where you want to be going, and to go there, regardless of what the Heart throws at you."

How helpful.

A smile plays at the corner of her mouth. "So long as I know what we are looking for, we will find it. Trust me, little mouse, I won't lead you astray."

Won't you?

The cramping in my fingers is easing, the aching in my feet fading, but my limbs feel heavy still. The thought of moving on is an unpleasant one.

"Not in here," she says, smiling. "Now come, before you fall asleep and turn to stone."

. . .

The hallways and rooms and staircases are certainly more interesting than the endless corridors, but when I follow Sila through the hallway that I swore we entered through for the third time, it's easy to believe we are hopelessly lost. I have to remember that the Heart is an insidious thing. I've already witnessed it tricking my mind into believing the corridors hadn't been moving. It could very well be playing the same tricks again. I had trusted Sila when I took her hand in the scriptorium. I had to keep trusting her now.

"You think so loudly, little mouse," Sila teases.

It all looks the same.

"It is," says Sila. "Mostly." I frown at her, holding my lantern aloft to see if she's still teasing me. Her face is as deathly serious as I have ever seen it.

What is it we are looking for, exactly?

"There will be a door," she says. "And that will be the next test, because the labyrinth would dearly love to keep you."

Keep me? You said it liked me.

"It does. We *are* rather alike, the Heart and I. Ah, here it is." For the first time, the darkness shifts and a wall appears out of the gloom with a tall door shut fast. It doesn't budge when Sila tries to pull it open. She glances at the dark above her. "Oh come now, don't you want to let Lorel see what you've prepared for her?"

There is something like an embarrassed silence hanging in the air. Almost bashful. Then, with a soft sigh, the door opens just a touch. Somehow it only serves to settle a scowl on Sila's face.

"So eager to please," she huffs. She turns as I go to follow her, forcing me to stop short and look up sharply at her. "Whatever happens, just keep walking. Do not stop for me. I can take care of myself."

What?

I give her an alarmed look as she grows taller, eyes going dark, blood welling in them and the shadows bleeding out of her. "Just keep walking," she says. It echoes in soft whispers as she turns and wrenches the door fully open. We hardly have to step through it before we're plunged into darkness.

Chapter 20

Lorel

My lantern's dull light tries to hold back the darkness, but it's a thick, light absorbing thing and I am a poor mage. The light in the lantern trembles as I shiver.

"Keep walking, little mouse. I will follow," whispers Sila from somewhere behind me.

Fuck. I take a deep, trembling breath. In the labyrinth, I had Sila to guide me through its twists and turns. I am not as sure of myself here. I put one foot in front of the other and hope the ground intends to hold. That it won't just swallow me down, never to be seen again. Sila would never allow it.

My footsteps echo into the dark, bouncing back to me and away again. Echoes mean there are walls, at least. This darkness isn't endless.

I can hear my heart thumping in my ears, feel the desire for flight as well as any prey animal would. I hope it doesn't give out before this ends.

I've been in the caves of the Glade before, where the silken glow worms live. Little pin pricks of light that wax and wane in the darkness in some kind of arcane rhythm as they dangle and dance on long thin threads. I'm reminded of them now, as a dozen tiny glowing orbs twinkle to life around me. They shift along with me as I walk, like eyes watching me in the dark. A chill runs down my spine and then I feel the brush of shadow and darkness that I know is Sila. There is a snarl. Something damp touches my cheek. Not Sila. I fight down the urge to retch.

My lantern light shivers with me, blurring as my eyes water and a vile feeling crawls over my skin. The air moves again and I flinch, only to brush the back of my hand against something softly scaled and damp in the dark behind me. It's too much. It's too much and I have to keep going. Another snarl cut off with a screech. And another.

"Don't let the light catch you, Lorel. Keep going. I'm here," murmurs Sila in my ear. Another sigh of air ends in a damp scream. I want to call out for her. I want her to take my hand and lead me out of here. I don't want to have to walk into the dark like this. I can't do this.

You could stop.

I stumble, halting to throw the lantern around in an attempt to find the source of the voice that isn't a voice. I remember it, clear as a bell being struck. The thing that had spoken to me in my dream. That had woken me in the infirmary. The Library's Heart.

You needn't go on like this. Give up and I will take care of everything. You need never worry again.

The dark presses in again, the lights drifting closer, the air moving. Screaming. Screeching. Creatures in the dark, I realise. All around me, and Sila striking out at them as they try to ensnare me. I stumble again as I try to walk on.

"Keep going, little mouse."

I'm breathing hard and fast, as if I've run miles. I must keep going. Never mind that I don't want to. That I would rather curl up and die. The lantern light feels as indistinct as I do, being pushed and pulled by the darkness. Those glowing lights are still circling me. Blinking out of existence one moment. Returning the next. There are so many of them. Sila can't possibly hold them all back.

Give up. I will win in the end anyway.

I trip on the edge of a stone tile and my lantern clatters out of my hand as I hit the ground hard. My ears ring and I can hardly see the lantern through the pressing dark. It's that same thick fog of labyrinth darkness that is so unlike Sila's shadows. So much less welcoming. I try to feel my way forward as the darkness crowds in. I must keep moving.

Finally, in the dark, my fingers find the metal of the lantern. I grab it with one hand as my other hand settles on something damp and smooth. Soft and fleshy. I try to scream. Nothing comes out.

I hold the lantern up and the light glances off of thousands of glittering scales. Thin translucent flesh is pulled tight over rows and rows of the creature's thin ribs. Huge cavernous eyes turn on me, completely devoid of light as it opens a gaping wound of a mouth full of needle-sharp teeth. The stench of its breath is overwhelming, threatening my stomach's stability again. From the top of its head dangles a tiny ball of light on fleshy thread. Behind me, Sila lets out a sound of pure fury and outrage.

Give up. Rest.

This thing is going to consume me. Sila is too far away, fighting her way through its children, and I have nothing I can do to protect myself. I don't want to join whatever other unfortunate souls have been consumed by it, nor to leave my flesh to rot with theirs.

Give up. Stay with me.

Time slows as death comes for me. I throw my hand out in front of me and it moves too quickly for how slowly the creature shifts. As if I can do anything to stop the horrific creature from lurching forward and bringing its gaping maw over me. As if something so feeble could prevent the Heart from keeping me.

Give up.

"No," I whisper, closing my eyes. I feel the word pass between my lips and my ears begin to ring, the sound rising into a high-pitched scream. It rises higher, and higher until it is nothing and everything.

Then suddenly, silence.

The darkness falls back with a hiss, and it is no longer that impenetrable black fog. It is just darkness. The creature still looms over me, but it moves as if trying to walk through tar. Air moves past my cheek and my lantern light catches the shadowy edges of Sila as she tears into the beast with talon and teeth and fury. I close my eyes against it all as sound rushes back in, relentless and overwhelming. The air around me sighs, as if disappointed. I feel lightheaded and bloodless, though I have taken no injury. Too warm. There is the sound of my lantern hitting the floor again and rolling away.

"Lorel?" Sila whispers.

Her hands grab my arms as I tip backwards. She holds me up as I blink at her, my vision dark at the edges. She is herself again, blood tracked down her cheeks and caught in her teeth. Her hair a wild tangle bleeding into the shadows. So tall and fierce and strong. She is so lovely, even like this. Maybe, particularly like this. My thoughts are paper thin, crumbling at the edges, and I feel like I am being consumed by fire. Her arms come around me, lifting me with ease.

Sila cradles me against her, and I rest my head on her shoulder. Press my face into her neck where her cool skin soothes the heat in mine. I cling to her with all the strength my weary limbs have left as my thoughts drift away.

The light changes as we exit the ghastly chamber. When I glance around the protection of Sila's hair, we are back in those dimly lit halls and rooms, with the horror fading behind us.

Sila carries me effortlessly onwards. I hold on to her as if my life depends on it. I recall a memory that feels so distant now, of a cool body pressed against mine as fever had burned through it. I had thought it was a dream at the time. When the poison had tried to take me. When Sila had tried to fulfil her orders.

I must doze, because when I blink back to wakefulness, the labyrinth has changed again. There is a dull soft light just barely kissing the interior and it no longer looks like the Library. There are no books anymore, only a long shadowy mural-covered hall. Sila's footsteps click against marble tiles. Indistinct statues stand sentry on raised plinths. My mouth is pressed against Sila's skin, and the scent of it, earthy and sweet, fills my senses. I wonder what it ta—

Dawn King have mercy on me. I find myself suddenly very awake, wrenching my face away from her skin.

"Are you with me again, little mouse?" Sila asks. She sounds her usual teasing self, but there is concern strung tight underneath it. "I'm afraid I lost your lantern."

I wriggle and Sila stops to let me down, gingerly lowering me to the ground. She hovers as I test my legs.

I'm okay. What happened?

I can barely make out her face in the dim light. The shadows it casts are so deep and she is entirely unreadable.

"The Heart prepared a rather nasty trap for us," Sila

says. "And I couldn't keep them all back from you. As for you, I do not know. You told me you are not adept at magic. That was no simple magic, Lorel."

I didn't— I can't— What do you mean?

Sila's voice is steady and patient in the dark. "When you were recovering from the poison, you had a fever. When I found you, crushing yourself into the wall, you had a fever. Right now, you have a fever." She reaches out a cool hand to press the back of it to my cheek. I can feel the way it soothes my skin still. Ice cold as my skin burns. I stare at her. "What magic did you do that night, Lorel?"

She is a ghost in the dark. The curse stirs, sharp as a hissing cat, and I remember. Vividly I remember.

I had tried to soothe it, the curse, to push it down. A memory of pain arcs through my chest, leaving me breathless and I double over, clutching at my sides.

I had gone back to my room. I had been afraid of something. No, not just afraid, terrified. The curse had been a feral thing, trying to scratch and claw its way out of my throat. I had choked on it, not wanting to let it out into the world. My fingers were coated with ash and ice cold. My lips were going numb. I am caught up in the memory now as I try to pull in air like I am drowning. I am back there, in my room as the curse tears and screams. I push it back. Push it down. I feel a rib crack, and then another, and hope that this is only in the memory, even if the pain of it feels real. I push it down again and there is blood on my tongue, running from my nose. I dig my fingers into my sides, nails gouging deep. Another rib. My fingers as I clench them, cracking as I try to hold the curse down.

Then there is darkness, and my ears begin to ring. The sound rises until it crowds all of my senses. And then it cuts out. Silence. My skin burns. My throat burns. I press myself against the cool of the wall. I press as hard as I can, desperate for the feel of it against my skin. It gives way, soft, as arms come tight around me. Fingers threading through my hair, clinging to me.

I open my eyes.

My bones are still intact. The taste of blood on my tongue recedes. The cut on my hand stings from the pressure I had placed upon it. My breath comes in silent gasps and I am pressed against Sila as if I had tried to crush myself against her body in place of the wall from my memory. My skin is still burning. Tears burn at the back of my throat. I sob silently into Sila's chest, no longer caring about if I should. I let her hold me as if she cares. It's painful to try and cry so wholeheartedly without being able to make a sound.

To be unable to put a voice to the miserable realisation that in the end, whatever this cursed silence was, I had done it to myself.

Chapter 21

Lorel

It takes some time for the tears to stop, for the overwhelming pain of it all to recede. Sila just holds me, as patient and still as the statues around us. It doesn't really go away, the dull ache resting alongside the curse. How can it when neither of them have anywhere to go because of me?

Because it is clear as a well-lit light sigil that the reason the curse is still curled up in the cavity of my chest is because I trapped it there. Trapped it along with my voice, my sighs, my whispers. All of it locked away.

I've soaked through Sila's blouse and it clings to my cheek as I sit there, pressed to her chest. How miserable to be so useless that when you finally manage to use magic, you use it to take away your own voice. To be so afraid of something, everything. To make myself as small, and plain, and unremarkable as I have always been. As I have always told myself I wanted to be.

"Lorel?" Sila says. Her voice is wound through with concern and sorrow. That must be nice. To have the ability to say one word, and have it mean so much.

Irritation prickles under my skin and her fingers tense as

I pull back from her, as if she is afraid to let me go. I am not worthy of it, this misplaced affection of hers. Of these feelings that neither of us should be feeling. Feelings that I will crush down with the rest of it.

I sit back on my thighs and wipe my eyes. The labyrinth is silent and still. I take a deep, silent breath. Sila's face is shadowed, tracked with blood. Something has cut through her sleeve, gouging up her arm. I clench my fist, feeling the fresh scar tissue of the bargain on my hand. I had been foolish to bind her to me. I am nothing but misfortune.

Sila reaches out a hand, touching my jaw, and I wrench myself away from her.

I'm fine.

"Lorel—"

Don't. Don't pretend that I am anything other than what I am.

Sila drops her hand back to her lap. "And what is that?" she says, voice flat. Eyes dark and unreadable.

Useless and foolish. I was worth nothing in the Keep. I am worth even less now. Who does this to themselves? To finally do something of worth, and make themselves into nothing.

My hands are all sharp, jerky movements and I know she sees every one of them. I want to shout the words into the dark, and I can't, and I think I might cry from the frustration.

Sila sits silently, a long dark shadow. Then she sighs heavily. "It is a shame I will never get to tear the limbs from those who have made you believe this of yourself," she says, low and regretful. "Come, scribe, we must keep moving."

The way she says *scribe* carves through me and leaves all my buried feelings bleeding out of me. I was the one who had put distance between us first. That Sila should call me that should not hit me so hard. It's what I had wanted, after all. For her to treat me as a Librarian should treat a scribe. It should not hurt so keenly.

I let her walk on, wondering if the Heart will take me here. Turn me to stone so that I don't have to feel anything anymore. But the heaviness in my limbs does not come. And I do not wish to be left alone here, after all. I do not want to lose her to the darkness.

I stand, and with each step that I take, something settles in me. I want to blame it on the curse, with its cold, dreadful weight, but worse than that dread is the regret. It tangles and snarls on itself. Sinks a sickly feeling into my stomach. Something is horribly wrong.

Light catches the edges of Sila's figure up ahead, her image reflected in the massive ornamental mirrors that line the corridor. A thousand Silas in a hundred mirrors.

The labyrinth has arranged itself in a perfect replica of the Court's long mirrored hall of reflection, right down to the wallpaper and the scuffs in the tiles. The painted ceiling rising high overhead appears accurate until I look too long and catch the subtle changes that turn it from the tale of the Dawn King's Ascension to something much darker. Something that might be called treason.

It shows the Dawn King standing between two women. Then, one woman is in chains, and the second is crowned with starlight. Later, the crowned one lies dead over the altar, blood as black as ink staining the rest of the painting as the corridor continues.

"Scribe, you are falling behind," Sila says, her voice drifting back to me down the long hall. I tear my eyes from the ceiling and back to her. She's still walking on, as if she knows exactly where she is headed. And she must, because she has walked it centuries ago. The hall of reflection has only one destination— the chapel. The altar.

The click of her boots is fading, and I am seized by a desperate fear not to lose her. To not let her go on alone. Certain that if I do, I will not see her again. Not alive. I feel sick with the knowledge and I am moving, running as quickly as my tired legs can carry me.

My own boots beat out a harsh rhythm against the tiles as I race to catch her up. I cannot lose her. I *cannot*. Dawn King strike me! Why am I so afraid of everything?

The darkness presses in, crowding me as I strain my ears for a sign of her presence. A strip of bright light up ahead is the only thing that illuminates the darkness. It casts her in golden light, and my breath catches, silent as every other breath tearing through my lungs, to think that she might go through without me.

Chapter 22

Sila

My heart feels as if it is being crushed, only it is too fragile for it and it is shattering. Turning into tiny shards of white hot fury. I don't know what to do with heartache, but I know what to do with anger. The all-consuming feeling of rage that there are people up there in the Citadel who will continue to live and breathe. People— *vermin*— that had held power over Lorel and used it to turn her into a creature of such self-loathing. She hides it so well, but the labyrinth is bringing all of her emotions to the surface. Peeling back the layers of skin and muscle to get to the heart of her.

I'm done with the Heart's games. It can play with me, as it has always done, but I will not allow Lorel to suffer it any further. She had looked so wretched. So small and fractured, and I had held her as if she was mine.

She had clung to me as if I was hers. I fling a shadow from my hand, striking at a mirror and shattering it.

The Heart is playing with me, because the hall of reflection is not this long. My memories of my life before my death are threadbare. That life had been little more than a fleeting moment compared to the age that I have lived since. Just a whisper through the world, rustling the pages, shifting the dust. The end of it, though, I remember that. A jagged wound cut across the end of one life and the beginning of another.

My shadows hit another mirror, and it is a reflection of myself, all the pieces I am breaking into. Enough is enough.

Speak to me, you wretch, I call out in my mind. Feel the way the shadow and space shifts as the labyrinth's ancient sentient being turns its attention towards me. I can feel its presence in every stone and paint stroke and piece of shattering glass.

Hello, my dearest Librarian.

I feel a tug on the tether where it catches under my heart. That faint, tenuous line that is keeping me anchored here, preventing me from fading away. The Heart, reminding me that I have already broken one lifeline, and I cannot break another. Lorel's footsteps echo in the dark behind me, her little boots clipping along the stone.

So, you will do the same as he, in the end, I tell the Heart. I feel its indifference in the shifting shadows.

Only one of you walks out of here, whispers the Heart. *It is your choice.*

Is that a promise? I ask.

Yes.

Then I have made my choice.

You will die again.

So be it.

It is silent for a long moment as I walk on. The door to the chapel finally gets closer, golden light spilling from within. Exactly the same as that day, back when the sun had still shone. Back when fae blood gave him his power to keep the dark at bay. Now the blood of the fae has faded through the generations and his power is waning. I doubt Lorel has ever seen the sun or felt the warmth of its light. And the light that spills out is *warm*. I hold my hand out to feel it against my skin, and the warmth of it is overwhelming and soothing all at once.

I have no wish to leave Lorel now. I would have made her mine, with time. I think of her face pressed against my skin as I carried her, and the way her fingers dug into my arms as she cried those deep, heart-wrenching sobs. She does not deserve the fate that lies at the centre of the labyrinth, and I will give my own blood to the Heart before I give it hers.

If it is between me or her, it will always be her.

She is just a scribe, Librarian. Nothing worthy of you, the Heart murmurs. Its ink dark presence lurks at the back of my mind.

Then why do you want her? If she is nothing?

I always want, Librarian.

No, there is *something special about her,* I reply. I believe it, too. More than just my own feelings and desire for her. Lorel had silenced something in herself so brutally, something that should have swallowed her whole. Whatever magic she possesses has the ability to stop the will of the Library's Heart. I have lost many scribes or researchers to the Library. It is a known hazard of the labyrinth, and something all Librarians grow accustomed to.

Those times had been nothing like this. The Heart had called to her, permitted her entry on her own merit. It had tested her emotions to find the ones that it could best manipulate. Lorel comes to a stop beside me, and a cold wave of dread neutralises any warmth from the sunlight.

Her chest is heaving, her eyes panicked as she gasps down air. As silent as any corpse at rest. I must make it to the altar before her. The chapel door beckons, as if in welcome. I turn to step through and small, soft fingers clamp around my wrist, holding firm. I look down at her hand, white-knuckled, and make a soothing noise as I gently pry her fingers away.

"Stay here," I tell her. "Whatever you do, little mouse, do not follow me." My heart, slow and heavy, thumps in my chest. It will not do so for much longer, but hers will keep going. I cannot look at her face, with her salt-marked glasses, and her puffy red eyes.

"I will return shortly," I promise, because unlike the Heart, I am not bound by my promises. I push through the chapel door and step into the blinding sunlight.

Chapter 23

Lorel

THE METALLIC SCENT OF BLOOD WASHES OVER ME along with the warmth, the sunlight blinding in its sudden intensity as Sila steps through. If she thinks I will let her go through there alone, then she has underestimated me. I step up and push through the gap in the chapel doors, and it is as if I am trying to move through honey. I push through until it gives, stumbling into the chapel.

I hold my arm up against the light as my eyes adjust. The chapel itself is exactly as it ever is. Exactly as it ever has been. White marble colonnades rise up high overhead, the domed ceiling rendered with a mural of the first sacrifice, entirely allegorical in nature. Gilt details catch the light that filters in through the tall glass windows that line the chapel. The light is brighter than I have ever known it. True warming sunlight, constructed by the labyrinth. It is not the only thing wrong with the picture.

Bodies lie strewn across the floor. The channels that run through the stone down from the altar are flowing with blood, warm and pooling over. Encroaching upon the toes of my boots. Accounting for the metallic taste that rests heavy on my tongue.

They are each dressed in sacrificial robes of white. All of them stained red. All of them staring, lifeless and discarded.

Sila is already halfway to the altar, where one of the dead stands, ceremonial knife in hand. I don't like this. Everything about this feels wrong. The curse stirs in my chest, restless. The Heart's strange presence brushes against my consciousness.

Are you going to let her do this again?

I feel the way my lips try to form her name. To call out to her. Entirely futile— she is going to do it again. The Heart has set out this horrific tableau for her because it is only intending to let one of us leave, and Sila has decided that it should be me. That I should stay outside this room while she enacts her first sacrifice, again. That in spite of everything, she is still trying to protect me. That she is pushing down her feelings with as much success as I am. I do not deserve her. I do not deserve this devotion.

I am fever-hot as I surge forward. I slip on the slick stone, falling hard on my knee, and blood soaks into the fabric of my skirt and leggings. I push back up, fingers grasping for purchase, the blood making it impossible to hold onto. Even if I had the energy left to do so, I cannot silence Sila or still the room in the way I had before. I can only try to reach her before they cut her throat again.

I push myself up, and the bodies near me start to shift.

To move.

To rise.

To reach.

Fear pushes me onward as they drag themselves towards me. The fingers of the closest grasping for my skirt, my legs— anything that it can grasp to hold me. The Heart is a *prick.*

I stomp down hard on the hand of one— bone and flesh crunching together. I stumble around the reaching arms of another. The bodies furthest away are rising now too, heads twisting strangely on their necks. The flesh of their throats cut open in wide, gaping wounds. I am not athletic by nature. I'm not sure I can outrun them.

I try to dodge one, and another grabs me from behind. Sila is getting further away from me, walking as if in a trance. The dead drag me to the ground, grabbing at my clothes and limbs. I use whatever I have to kick and hit. To tear at their flesh. To claw my way out of their grasping hands. I'll use my teeth if I have to.

There is another crunch of bone and flesh, the ripping sound of a limb tearing from one of my assailants' bodies. I can feel the Heart watching, amused. I can't scream with my voice, but if it can speak into my mind, maybe it will hear me scream back.

Is this all just a joke to you? Why don't you do something useful and maybe you'll get what you want.

There is a thoughtful shift in the Heart's strange presence. Sila is nearing the altar and fear is all I know. I thought I knew what it was to be scared. I was wrong. Nothing will ever be like the fear of losing her.

I'm barely halfway across the room, trying to crawl my way across it as blood soaks into my dress, dragging me down with the weight of it. The dead try to pull me back under them. My silent screams of exertion are all I have. My bloodied fingers and broken nails.

I'm only making sure you truly want it.
Oh fuck you.

I kick back at the bodies, twisting to make sure it lands. I bring my foot down on another, and another. The fabric of my dress gives way under the hands of yet another, and I stumble back. My hand braces against the floor and I push off, free of them. I trip up the slippery set of stairs up to the raised platform.

I throw myself between Sila and the altar. The Dawn King only knows what I must look like. She blinks at me, unseeing, and then her eyes clear. Panic fills them. Fear twisting at her features.

"Lorel, no—" She grabs for me, but the hands of the altar maiden reach me first.

Blood splatters across Sila's face. There is a hot line across the skin of my throat. My blood.

Sila's eyes turn pitch black. She screams, and everything goes dark.

Chapter 24

Lorel

THE AIR IS COLD. OR I AM BURNING UP. IT'S HARD TO tell, anymore. When I open my eyes, I am lying in a box. Shadow presses in and writhes against it. There's a low light from underneath me that reflects off the glass walls of the box. No, not a box. A coffin. The kind they use to hold your body before they inter it in the catacombs.

Am I dead, then? I relinquish the book I am holding and reach up. I expect a wound or a gash, but there is nothing. Just the smooth fall of my throat. Dried blood flakes away against my fingers, but it isn't wet. It isn't bleeding. There is nothing else to suggest the blade had ever bitten into my skin at all. It's even difficult to tell if the blood drying into the fabric of my dress is my own, or soaked up from the chapel floor.

I rest my hand back on my stomach and find soft, time-worn leather there instead. The book. There's enough room to bring it up to my face. Red leather, no title, dry and as brittle as the last time I saw it. Leather and paper flaking like the blood from my skin. It is the book from my memories. The thing we had come here to find. I grow uneasy looking at it. I have turned it over and over so many times in my mind that I had stopped believing it to truly be real.

I had picked up this book, and then I had run terrified to my room. I had silenced myself brutally and kept the curse it had given me inside me. Crushed myself in the process. For the first time, the curse sits quietly in my chest, not even stirring as my thoughts brush against it.

Perhaps that meant I had done it, then. The Heart had taken me instead of Sila. She is free of me now. My heart aches with the thought of it and so I turn my attention to the Heart of the Library.

Is this where you're going to keep me?

The Heart's attention shifts, brushing up against my consciousness.

Perhaps. You'll be safe here, little vessel. Even Sila knows that, much as she fights it.

Sila. *Has she not gone?*

Can't you hear her?

The sound is muffled by the glass, and then it clears, as if the Heart has let it in. Sila's voice, furious and defiant. "You will give her back, or I will tear you down myself."

The Heart sounds amused as its attention turns back to Sila.

Is that so? Even your own bargain is telling you that's a bad idea. You know I can keep her safe here.

Sila lets out a sound of pure frustration.

Do you really think you can keep her safe?

The silence is as thick as the swirling shadow, trying to find purchase on the glass. Sila's shadows, trying to find a way through.

I reach my thoughts out to the Heart, turning its attention back to me.

Why do you want me?

Because I have given you a gift, and it was a gift not easily earned. I need you to speak it and mark the traitors' downfall.

But I can't speak.

There is a feeling of the air sucking in and rushing out. The Heart sighing.

No, you cannot. It will take time to break the silencing, but I will do it and I will hold you until it is done. None will touch you here.

"Please," Sila says. "Let me take her place as I had intended. Let her go." She cannot hear what the Heart speaks to me. She is pure, abject sorrow. As if she has become a melancholy wraith from an old faetale, wandering dark halls searching for a lost love. The Heart turns away from me again.

Without you, she is unprotected. Unsafe. They have come for her blood already. Who will protect her when they come again?

Long dark fingers press through the shadow against the glass. They scrape along it, a wretched sound. Sila.

"I will," she whispers. Blood drips onto the coffin. Thick dark red, almost black spots settling against the glass. I press my fingers to where hers had been a moment before. I scratch my broken nails against the glass, seeking purchase. I need to be with her.

I remember Sila's quiet fury at the curse mark on my skin. At the claim that someone or something had made upon me. That someone might have dared to claim what was hers.

I remember her gentle touch when she had found me in the scriptorium and the Lightkeepers lay dead around us. How ruthlessly she had taken their lives, and how soft those same hands had been combing through my hair.

I remember her journal and the way I had been a mark and become Lorel. Her obsessive notes and far-reaching research as she tried to save me. As she tried to keep me.

I remember her voice as she told me that finally, in her long life, there was someone that she did not wish to see dead.

All of them are impossible things. Things that should never happen.

Librarians did not fall in love with scribes. Scribes did not imagine themselves in love with their tormentors and guardians.

Ancient fae creatures like Sila should have no interest in simple fleeting creatures like me. It should be of no conse-quence if I am dead or alive.

Instead, it is *everything*. I had pushed her away, and she had walked to her death to try and save me from the Heart.

I had not wanted to see Sila go to her death again. I had not wanted to lose her in the labyrinth. Because I do not want to just be a scribe to her. I want to let her obsession devour me. I want to let her have me, however she wishes to have me. I want to be hers.

We have come so far and I will not lose her now.

Heart, I call out and the Heart's attention again turns to me. I can't feel any strong emotion from it now, just indiffer-ence. As if Sila is little more than an unruly child.

Is there another way to break the silencing?

If an existential being could look side long at something, the Heart would be doing so.

Yes.

And if I agree to break it, and speak what you wish me to speak, will you let me go?

There is a drawn-out contemplative silence from the

Heart, as if it has all the time in the world. It probably does. The Heart's attention shifts back to Sila.

Librarian.

The shadows stir and shift furiously.

"If you want to keep her, then I will stay with her," says Sila. "I will stay until you see fit to release her back to me."

You cannot stay here. You would lose yourself.

"I do not care," Sila says, raising her voice. "Is throwing myself on your altar not proof enough that I would give up my life for hers?"

In my glass coffin, I choke back the sound of grief that tries to escape me. I don't know what I have done to deserve Sila. I had never wanted attention. I had never wanted this. Yet Sila has seen me, anyway. Seen me and decided there is something worth seeing. There is no way I am going to give her up.

The Heart sits silently.

You would do that for her?

"Without hesitation. As surely as I have devoted myself to you and to my queen," Sila says.

Would you put her above all others? Even your queen?

"I already have, have I not? Can you not feel that you are my only tether now? What more do I have to do to prove myself?" Sila's hand comes down on the glass, leaving a dark smudge. The shadows flicker like flame.

I hold my breath, waiting for the Heart's verdict.

Be still. I must consider.

I feel the Heart's presence turn back to me.

Little vessel. You will read the book again and remember it. And when the time comes, you will speak it. You may be afraid of it. I do not care. That is my demand. Will you submit to it?

I do not have to think on it. Whatever I was afraid of before, I have a new fear now that far outweighs it.

Yes.

The word sits burning and binding in my thoughts.

There is a wry feeling from the Heart. *I should have thought to put such a command on the book in the first place.* It turns its grumbling back to Sila. *You will protect her, the vessel. I take your bargain, and bind you to it. You will break her silence and until the words are spoken by the vessel, you will protect it.*

"I do not need a bargain or an oath to bind me to do so. I would do it willingly," Sila says.

I would still have your oath.

"You have it, as you always have."

Then it is done.

Without thinking, I hold the book up in front of me. My limbs do not feel like they are my own as I take a steadying breath. My fingers crack the cover, and the glass coffin shatters around me.

Chapter 25

Lorel

SHARDS OF GLASS CATCH AGAINST MY EXPOSED SKIN, opening a hundred tiny cuts, each bright red against the chapel's gloom. I have barely a moment to fear before shadows swirl around me, catching the glass and scattering it to the far corners of the nave. As the shadows fall back, Sila coalesces at their centre, a wretched figure standing among heaped bodies and rivulets of pooling blood. There is nothing but the sound of her ragged breathing and the clink of glass as it clatters across the marble floor. I can barely focus on any of it with how the words of the book run through my mind. They dance across my tongue as if in waiting.

A curse— of a kind. A prophecy that will become true once spoken.

I now know why I had been so afraid that night. The Heart is tired of bowing to the Dawn King. It had chosen me as the vessel to bear its message out into the world, only it had chosen poorly. It had not known what I was capable of doing to myself out of fear. Even I hadn't known. The words of the prophecy fade, settling into my chest. Pooling back into that ever-present creature that has lived there since I first opened the book.

The glass cuts are tiny things that sting and dry quickly. I stare at them as I sit up, weary down to the bone, and as I flip my hand, I see that the scar from Sila's bargain is gone. Only the still-healing wound of my foolish slip with the knife remains.

Sila shifts in a flicker of shadow, comes to stand in front of me, tall and impassive. I don't hesitate to collapse against her. Rest my ear against the soft swell of her breasts. There is the quietest, slowest sound of a gentle heart beat. This must be how it sounds when it races, for surely it is lucky to beat even once a year. No wonder her blood runs so slow, her temperature so cold.

Sila tips my head back and I do not begrudge her for checking that my throat is still intact. I do not think I would have handled watching such a thing happen to her quite so well. Her fingers brush gently from my jaw to my collar, and she makes a small, mournful sound. It is something ancient and sorrowful, a keening note of grief that rings out through the dim chamber.

"When— *fuck*—" Sila says, voice raw and catching in her throat. She brings her hand around to cup my cheek. "I thought I had lost you."

I reach out and wind my fingers in the soft silk of her blouse, craving that point of connection. She's so very close like this. I search her face. Those dark eyes, half lidded as she looks down at me. The soft contours of her cheekbones splattered with my dried blood, and her dark tears. How could I have ever thought her terrifying? Her eyes flick to my mouth as I swallow, my silent breath parting my lips as it rattles through me. A slumbering warmth in my body that has nothing to do with the curse that slumbers within me, and has everything to do with how she's looking at me. Sila's fingers move to cradle the back of my neck as she leans down—

The Heart's presence surges back to life within the imitation of the chapel. A wave of fear and panic and righteous anger washes over us. Sila's face turns into a lovely picture of alarm and frustration at her patron's sudden reappearance.

You must go. You must go now!

A gilded door appears at the back of the sanctuary, as if it has always been there. The Heart's warning clamours around us, urging us to move, to go, to leave.

Sila gives me a look that I can barely begin to understand. It is the heartache of a missed chance, and a fear that chance might never come again, both wrapped up in the Heart's urgency. I promise myself there will be another chance. I cannot think it will be otherwise.

Sila loops an arm about my waist, lifting me easily from the altar and setting me on my feet. This close, her sweet flower scent mixes with the copper scent of blood, and I grip her blouse tighter.

"Are you able to walk?" she asks, her arm still firm around me. I test my legs and nod. I don't know how much further my legs will carry me. I don't know how much further Sila's legs can carry me if mine fail. I hope this door is a shortcut, given the urgency and the rude interruption.

The door leads to a stairwell that looks similar to the one leading from the entrance. Sila takes my hand, her grip vice tight, and leads me up into the dark. It's a toothless kind of dark now, and no longer clouds our minds. Sila's pace is almost as quick as it had been when we walked through the Greater Library and none dared stand in her way.

The Heart's fear makes my heart race and drives me on after Sila. We exit far more quickly, and the disorientation as I leave hits me as badly as it did when I entered. Only this time, it feels like I am being reassembled. Like the labyrinth has pulled me apart and made me into something new. Maybe it has. Maybe it already did.

I don't even have the chance to take a breath of air before Sila's shadows wrap around me and pull my body sharply up against the wall. They pin my arms and legs in place with a grip as implacable as she is. I struggle weakly as my sight adjusts to the light, showing me what exactly had caused Sila to hide me in her shadows.

Mercias stands almost where we had left him— but he is not alone. Three Lightkeepers stand before him. Another lies lifeless on the floor, and near the feet of one Lightkeeper, lies the unmistakable form of a Librarian, deathly still, her dark blonde hair spilling across the floor. My heart feels like it stops. *Not another one.* I struggle against my bindings, but they only hold me tighter.

Mercias blows out a breath of air. "There you are," he says, before he drops to his knees and activates the sigil to close the Heart of the Library.

"Here I am," Sila says, taking up her position beside him.

Mercias glances at her as he stands again. "Fuck, you look awful."

"Charming," she says, turning her attention to the Lightkeepers. "To what do we owe the displeasure?"

Their leader smiles lopsidedly at them both. I recognise his face. Once it belonged to a boy that had grown up alongside my sister. Now it belongs to a man leading an incursion into the Library. Jaime. His hair is shaved close to the scalp, his features sharp and his brown eyes are calculating.

"As we informed the Librarian here, we are following the trail of the scribe known as Lorel," he says. His hand rests on the pommel of his blade. There's no leather binding on it. I remember that too. There wouldn't be— it wouldn't last because he's a fire mage. I have a distinct memory of him threatening to set my hair on fire when I was younger.

He'd been whipped for it. Back then they'd still thought the hair on my head was worth more than his flesh. I suppose he was relishing the opportunity to track me down and drag me back to the Keep as prey.

"Following a trail," says Sila thoughtfully. She's shifted to face them fully and I can no longer see her face, only the way she holds her body tense, as if ready to pounce. "Ah, of course. Blood magic. I suppose her sister is cooperating? How upsetting. Fortunately, you will not find that same cooperation here." Shadow snakes around her fingertips. Mercias shifts his stance, mirroring Sila's. I search the faces of the other two Lightkeepers. One of them, light-haired and green-eyed, smirks, his eyes bloodshot. A blood mage. I can't imagine my sister cooperating with these people, but she *is* one of the King's inner circle. Deception and contrivance are a matter of life and death. If my death ensured her own life? Well...loyalty is rare to come by in the pit of snakes that is the Keep.

"We only intend to take the scribe into custody. Ask her a few questions," Jaime says, trying to sound amiable. Trying to sound like he's being reasonable after he's clearly used the dead Librarian as a cover to sneak into places he has no right to be.

"On what grounds?" growls Mercias.

"That's privileged information, I'm afraid," Jaime replies.

"Hardly a convincing line," Sila says darkly.

"Look, if you insist on resisting—"

"What I insist on is you leaving," snaps Sila. My little scribe heart quails. I even catch Mercias flinching. "You have no authority here—"

"I have the authority invested in the Lightkeepers by the Dawn King himself," Jaime cuts in.

The blood mage shoots him an alarmed look. *Interesting.*

"No, you don't. Because if you did, we wouldn't be having this conversation over the dead bodies of our peers," Sila says.

Jaime rolls his eyes, turning away from Sila to the blood mage. "Is she still here?" he demands.

"Yes," the blood mage whispers. "So close I can practically taste her."

"Your own blood will coat your tongue before I allow you near her," Sila snarls.

"Librarian tricks." Jaime spits on the ground.

I stare at him, aghast. Even Orielle hasn't done something that disrespectful before. The absolute nerve of him. "There's only one way to deal with this. Bar the door, get rid of them."

No. Fear scratches at my heart, a fluttering bat trying to get free. The third Lightkeeper moves to close the door, her hands already forming the sigil to lock it fast.

The door closes itself before she can finish, and the Lightkeeper barely has a chance to look around before a dagger is burying itself in her throat. She falls to the floor, blood bubbling from the wound as the blade dissolves into shadow.

Chapter 26

Lorel

As the dying Lightkeeper hits the floor, chaos erupts. Jaime and the blood mage move swiftly. A wave of heat washes over me as fire bursts from Jaime's hands. He doesn't need the simple sigils of everyday magic, not when he has command of the potential burning energy in the air. Sila counters it with her own darkness, smothering it. I can feel the way the shadows around me pull, as if it's costing her to keep me hidden. I grit my teeth and tug, but the shadows don't give. Perhaps it's for the best. I could hardly be useful even if I were free.

Jaime's sword lights up with flame as he arcs it through the air to slash at Sila. Mercias moves to meet him, and the blade glances off a shield of darkness. Mercias pushes the Lightkeeper back and Sila follows, catching Jaime's arm with her blade, the two of them moving in a well-practised rhythm of strikes and parries. Mercias' form flickers, never in one place for too long as Sila's shadow self surges around him. Jaime keeps himself between the blood mage and his opponents.

My heart hammers in my chest. Mercias catches the

Lightkeeper's arm as Sila tries to snare it with shadow. The rot sets into Jaime's skin where Mercias' hand touches. Jaime's sword clatters to the ground and I think for a moment that perhaps things won't go so badly after all. The moment is broken as Jaime draws a knife from his hip and slashes it across Mercias' chest.

"*Fuck*," Mercias hisses, letting go. It's a shallow wound, barely anything to remark upon, and then Jaime lifts the knife dripping in Mercias' blood and throws it to the floor by the blood mage.

Sila surges forward, a roiling wave of dark shadow and sharp blades, and Jaime grabs his fallen sword and throws himself at her. There's a cry from Sila, a dark splash of her thick, black-red blood against the floor and then Mercias is there throwing his shield into Jaime and trying to find purchase on his skin. Sila snarls, throws away her blades and becomes a nightmare incarnate, all long talons and razor sharp bloody teeth wrapped in swirling shadow.

"Grab it!" Jaime shouts, shoving back against Mercias and lunging at Sila. Mercias' form flickers out of sight and back again as Sila clashes with Jaime. She is entirely reckless, and I flinch with each cut, each hit, her body takes.

Mercias flickers and throws himself across the room. The blood mage grins as he slides to a stop by the knife and grabs it. Still grinning at Mercias, he raises the knife to his mouth and licks it. Mercias' blood coats his tongue and he speaks a word, a command. Mercias chokes, stills, and drops to the floor like the dead. I cry out without thinking, but my own enchantment continues to keep me silent. Keeps me hidden. All I can do is watch Mercias' skin turn grey. Everything is happening too fast.

Sila lets out one of her fae screeches, and kicks Jaime hard, sending him face first into the stone floor. She turns on the blood mage like a vengeful ghost. He keeps grinning as he reaches down to run his fingers through Sila's blood, splashed across the chamber floor.

No. He can't. I scream and not a sound comes out. The shadows do not give way. I feel them dig into my flesh as I try to pull myself free. He licks Sila's blood from his fingers and he speaks the same horrific word that had sent Mercias crumbling.

And nothing happens.

It takes a moment for the blood mage to register it. His face turns to shock as Sila bears down on him, and her long talons sink into the flesh of his chest. Blood gushes down her arm. The look on his face is almost amusing. There's a pause as Jaime groans, lifting himself from the floor. Then there's a sickening crack as Sila tears the blood mage open. I cannot look away.

Mercias' body heaves as his blood moves through him again. He gasps for air and groans as he pushes himself up. Sila stands between Jaime and the locked door, and he must know the odds are no longer in his favour.

And I know there's no way he's going down without a fight.

Sila tosses the blood mage's remains carelessly aside. I can't see Jaime's face, but I can see Sila's. Her features are warped and monstrous. Her eyes dart to Mercias and then she moves, swift as candle light.

Jaime reignites his sword. He brings it down over Mercias, who throws up a shield between them. The sword glances off it, and Jaime brings it around again for another strike. There is fear in Jaime's eyes as he turns, desperate to take at least one of them with him. Mercias grits his teeth, his face grim. I don't know how long his shield can keep up. It flickers as Jaime brings his sword around.

And then Sila is there between them, catching the sword with her body, the blade sinking deep into her side. My throat is raw as I scream. It's a futile, silent thing. I hope this is some cruel nightmare made up by the Library, because it surely can't be real. We've only just escaped one horrific fate. This cannot be where it ends.

Sila grins, one of her horrific nightmare smiles that slices across her face. Her long taloned fingers sink into Jaime's skin and her shadows finally find purchase, gripping him tight.

"You won't even have the chance to regret this," she whispers as her shadows wrap around his neck. He struggles, trying to pull himself away from her. Shadow creeps over his skin and pushes into his mouth and nose. He tries to scream as it smothers him. Sila holds him viciously as his body convulses and then she lets him go. His sword goes with him, clattering to the ground. The shadows holding me weaken.

Sila blinks slowly, stumbling back and Mercias, half-raised on one knee, catches her as she drops. Her form fades back to normal as she does. Her head falls back over Mercias' shoulder, lifeless. I wrench myself free of the last of her shadows and throw myself across the room to her.

Chapter 27

Lorel

Mercias lowers Sila gently to the ground, and I crumble to the floor beside her. There is blood, her blood, everywhere, and it's pooling alarmingly underneath her. I look up at Mercias, who gives me a wry, tired grimace.

"So you're still alive," he says. He almost sounds relieved. "Elris will be pleased."

She's bleeding so much.

Sila blinks up at me as the door unlatches, swinging open. I push her shadowy hair back from her face. A face that is still a little too sharp, her eyes still entirely black. She blinks, unseeing.

You need to go and get help. You'll be faster.

Mercias' fingers tighten where he holds Sila. "She'll bleed out."

Not if you move your arse now. I'll get her to her room.

"That's impossible," he says, staring at me.

You just saw her. I'm sure you've seen her before, even. You know it's not. I'll get her there, just go.

"*Fuck*, alright," he says.

I pull Sila into my lap, taking her weight from Mercias

and letting her fall against me. She almost topples me. Mercias gives me one last curious glance before turning, his form flickering like lantern light as he disappears from the room. No wonder Librarians could always sneak up on you with talents like that.

"Lorel," Sila says, gently calling me back to her. Her eyes focus on my face, her smile soft and heart-rending.

There has to be a way to stop the bleeding. She's fae. The wound is deep where the sword had bitten into her flesh, but surely she can survive this. She can't just go and die. I hadn't even thought for a moment that she could die, again, but here she is looking even more ghastly than usual and *fuck*. Tears burn my throat and eyes, but I had long since run out of them in the labyrinth. I cling to her. I need to get her out of here.

Sila moves, resting her fingers against my arm. Her long, talon-like claws are gone, but her hands are covered in blood. Hers, theirs. Between the chapel and this, now we're both covered in it. The air is tinged with the scent of it. I'm running out of time.

"Go back to the Library, little mouse," Sila whispers. "It can protect you far better than I can."

I stare at her. Such a beautiful, delirious creature. I did not bargain with the Library for our freedom for it to end like this. Not so soon. I will not go back to the Library.

"Lorel?" It's barely a whisper now.

I don't have time to sign her an essay. I take her face in my hands and lean in to press my lips to hers, quick and firm. Her lips are as cold as the rest of her, but soft. So much softer than I expected. If this turns out to be the only time I get to kiss them, I'll drag the whole Court down into the Heart of the Library myself and set it all on fire. When I pull away, there is a metallic tang on my tongue. I give her my best withering look to tell her what I think of any further protestations, and tear at the edge of my bloodied dress. I'm sure that if I can just keep her with me, we can get back to her rooms. Back to safety. I shift her, trying to wrap the makeshift bandage around her. It is a useless effort. There are tears of frustration stinging at the corners of my eyes, burning at the back of my throat. I will myself not to panic, to get my bottom lip back under control. I can't lose her like this.

Sila reaches for me, and her fingers caress my jaw. She leans back, tipping her head back against my shoulder.

I'm not going anywhere.

It's a struggle to sign it. I don't even know if she can see it, with how soft and unfocused her eyes are. Or even read the signs from this angle. Please let her understand.

Take us to your rooms, Sila. Please.

She stares at me, as if the sky has opened up and the sun has shone through the clouds as it hasn't done in millennia.

"Alright," she says, with a breathy laugh that feels a world away. She hisses as she lifts herself and wraps an arm around my waist. She pulls me tight against her and rests her head on top of mine. Shadows come up around us and I grip her tight, squeezing my eyes shut and taking a deep breath. I don't know who to pray to anymore, so I cling to her and hope that my faith in her will be enough to get us through.

Chapter 28

Lorel

IT IS DARK IN SILA'S ROOMS WITH NO LANTERNS LIT and the sigil hearth is quiet. The shadows relinquish us upon the rug and I gasp silently, desperate for the stale air of the room. We must have been in the Library's Heart for at least a week with how the air tastes against my tongue. Sila leans like a dead weight against me, almost crushing me. She is so cursedly tall. I need all that muscle to come back to me so that it can move itself. I push her up, cradling her head carefully as I lower her to the ground.

I have no idea how long Mercias will take to find help, and I have no real natural ability for healing. She's still bleeding, and all I have going for me is that I've had to copy many medical tomes. There is a cushion on the nearby armchair and I grab it. I have to shift her again to stuff it underneath her. I try not to worry that she isn't breathing. Try to remind myself that she doesn't need to. I ball up my skirts against the wound and lean my body weight against it, willing the bleeding to stop. If I can just get it to stop, everything will be alright. Mercias will bring help, and Sila will heal, and she'll kiss me properly this time. Dawn King have mercy on me, I want it so badly.

I can hear my heart thumping in my ears. I lose count of them as time slides by, the time spent in the labyrinth catching up with me. My eyes are growing heavy. Where is Mercias? I need to keep my eyes open, keep the pressure on her, keep—

The door rattles open, and so do my eyelids. Shit, how long had I been asleep?

"Sila! Fuck, this is a mess—" Mercias says as light blooms. His companion is holding a lantern aloft. Lune.

"Lorel!" Lune pushes the door shut and abandons Mercias, leaving him to find his way through stacks of books and debris to light the sigil in the hearth. He should be able to move easily through the dark, but even then I'm not sure what kind of value that has in Sila's warren. Lune drops her case to the floor and sets her lantern down near Sila's face. I look away. She looks on the edge of death and if I have lost her, I don't want to know it yet. I don't want to see her face stilled. I grip the fabric of Sila's shirt tight.

"Come Lorel, let me have a look," Lune says.

She's gentle as she tries to shift me. I move reluctantly. Mercias grumbles his way through Sila's stacks, lighting every lantern he finds. I sit back and I feel as bad as I had that first time I woke in the infirmary weeks ago. My muscles cramping and my bones aching, and everything creaking like the scriptorium doors on a bad day. Only this is so much worse.

I watch Lune's hands as she gingerly pulls back the cloth of my skirts with a grimace. They were already soaked in blood, now they are heavy and dripping with it.

"It's clean, and the bleeding has stopped," says Lune. She hisses as she lightly presses her fingers to the skin around the wound. Lune's eyes go faint and distant as she checks Sila's state with her magic, then they widen. "Her pulse—" She frowns as she and her magic try to make sense of Sila. "It's so slow."

"As would yours be if you were as old as she is," says Mercias from across the room. "As long as it still beats, she'll recover."

"A Librarian thing then, is it?" Lune says, giving Mercias a sceptical look. "Very well. We need to get this cleaned up, then I'll deal with the wound as best I can. I don't think there's much I can do for her other than that."

I clench my fists in my skirt, staring at Sila's hand lying limp against the rug. I wish she was awake. I want her to tell us what we need to know and what we can do to help her. Though mostly, I don't want to need her to do any of that at all.

"Lorel?" Lune asks, carefully easing my hands out of their fists. "Can you fetch hot water? Mercias can help me move her to the bed."

I finally glance at Sila's deathly pale face. The dark shadows under her eyes are darker than usual. There's blood everywhere. I stare at her profile, the gentle light catching the soft edges of her face, her lovely full mouth. Mercias thinks she will live. Her heart still beats.

I nod and push myself stiffly up from the rug. Lune is watching me, sharp eyes missing nothing, clever mouth holding her questions because of Mercias' presence.

In the washroom, I activate the sigil for the hot water and wash my hands in a daze. It takes some time for the water to run even close to clear. With all the excitement gone, I'm more tired than I've ever been, but I refuse to sleep until Sila is tended to. I find clean cloth and a shallow wash basin under a pile of old clothes. I top the basin up with hot water and carry it through.

In the bedroom, they've made Sila comfortable, and Lune is fussing through her case. Mercias is sprawled in an armchair, looking exhausted, head resting in his hand.

"Thank you," Lune says, taking the basin from me. She's pushed Sila's things aside on the bedside table to make room for it. I hang back awkwardly, unsure what to do with myself. I watch as Lune carefully tends to the wound and then have to look away when she stitches it up. It had been bad enough to have her stitch up my own flesh. Mercias appears at my shoulder, an alarming shadow. He's watching Lune, his eyes startlingly clear when I look up at him.

"Sit, scribe, and get some rest," he says, keeping his voice low. "Sila will need you well rested." He puts his hands on my shoulders and squeezes them, raising his voice for Lune's ears this time. "Cupbearer, do you have everything you need? I should inform the Head Librarian of the breach."

Lune is silent for a moment as she finishes what she's doing. "I'm as well equipped as I can be. Go, I can take care of them." She sets herself back to her task.

"Very well," Mercias says. "I'll take my leave." His fingers tap nervously on my shoulders, and then he is gone in the blink of an eye, the door closing behind him in the other room.

Lune breathes a deep sigh. "I don't know what's going on here, but I know it'll be better if you wash and get out of that dress."

She looks tired. She must have been near the end of her shift when Mercias fetched her. I let out a bone deep rush of air, with not a sound to accompany it. It doesn't startle me so much anymore. I nod at Lune, who seems satisfied enough to continue tending to Sila's wounds.

I hope that what Mercias had said is right. That as long as her heart still beats, she'll recover. My fingers ache as I stand watching the bath fill with water. I wash my face and hair in the washroom basin because I know once I enter the water, it'll turn to muck from the bloody filth that covers me. I scrub myself pink and my nails raw, trying to get it all off.

I need Sila alive. Without her, I wouldn't survive. Without her, I think my heart would die first anyway, mourning every lost chance and missed opportunity. Because it had hurt enough to think the Library would keep her from me. It hurt more to think that a reckless strike of a sword might do it instead.

"What in the name of the King is going on here?" Lune says, trying to keep her voice down.

I am wearing one of Sila's ridiculous blouses and nothing else because there was little else to fit me. Its large sleeves are awkward as I try to write a reply to Lune. She has done what she can for Sila, and removed us from the bedroom to the living area. I can see the silent shape of Sila in the bed, through the open door from where I sit. I don't want her out of my sight if I can help it.

Lune is giving me an assessing look, and I try not to fidget under it. She's used her magic to check me over, and though I am covered in bruises and tiny cuts, there is nothing immediately threatening my well being. It makes a pleasant change.

"I thought she was returning you to your rooms," Lune follows up. "Not her own rooms."

She did. Only—

"You're here willingly, aren't you? If you're not, I can get you out. We can leave," she says, eyes darting in the direction of the bedroom. I fumble my borrowed pen in alarm.

I won't leave her.

Lune stares at the words I've written, and my heart thumps in my chest.

"What's happening here, Lorel? I don't like this Librarian's interest in you. No good ever comes of that. I see the scribes and the researchers when they visit the infirmary." Lune's face is set in a dark scowl. I knew that, as well as any other scribe, as surely as I knew Sila would not harm me. Could not harm me.

I returned to my own room. I thought—

I'd thought that I needed to go to the scriptorium, that I'd needed to try and find out why someone had tried to poison me.

It doesn't matter. I've been trying to find the cursed book. Sila has been helping me. We found it in the Heart of the Library.

Lune stares at me, her mouth hanging open. "And I suppose the Heart of the Library decided to run her through then?"

My eyes dart to the doorway, making sure Sila is still there.

No. When we left, there were Lightkeepers. They'd killed a Librarian.

Now Lune is deathly still. "What were— How were they—?" she stutters. "Why?"

They were looking for me.

"You? So they have determined to return you to them? Or they have decided you are a risk," Lune says.

I hiss silently through my teeth, gesturing at her to keep her outraged voice down.

Surely that's not why.

"Why else though?" she insists. I pause. It's been ten years since I left the Keep. Left the place that had been my home, to join the Library. I had thought they might have forgotten me, like a piece of unremarkable paper. Other scribes have easily been forgotten by the Keep. I knew that of Sybri's sisters, only Anora visited her— never Lenore. Not since Lenore had joined the Keep and the Lightkeepers. But Orielle has always visited me, even when she shouldn't. The image of her sitting on my desk gnaws at the back of my mind. As does the blood mage, as his body is torn asunder, who could only have tracked me with my sister's blood.

Chapter 29

Lorel

LUNE LEAVES ME PROMISING TO RETURN TO CHECK UP on me tomorrow. I deflate against the closed door, my eyes going immediately to the dark shape that is Sila, resting. Lune doesn't trust her, and I know she has good reasons not to. They were not so different from the reasons I had told myself, when Sila's arm had first come around my shoulders. It was different now. The Heart of the Library had bound us to each other and I would not be parted from her.

I cross the room quietly, my legs still aching, and stop at the end of the bed. She's still a mess. Lune had sewn and cleaned what was urgent, but she hadn't seemed as hopeful as Mercias. I grip the footboard and my fingers protest. She's so peaceful beneath the blood and dirt. Is this how they laid out her first body in the catacombs? Would I lay out her second the same?

I will the tremors trying to shake through my body to stop and fetch the basin and cloth from the bedside table. I return with more hot water, and a clean towel, and take up the space Lune had occupied earlier. I wring out the cloth and the water trickles over my hands and back into the basin with a gentle sound. My hands are steadier now as I press the cloth gently to her face, unearthing her from the week's trials. Tracing her cheekbones with the cloth and carefully lifting the blood from her lips. Lips that I had kissed in a moment of panic. That I wanted to kiss again. That I wanted to hear my name from again. The curse stirs, as if it is trying to be a comforting weight. I rub the healing salve Lune had left me for my scrapes and bruises into the worst of the cuts and scrapes across her face.

That done, I turn my attention to her hands, and feel the way my mouth tries to smile, strained and painful. She has certainly not kept them to herself in the time that I've known her. Possessive since the very beginning. Even as weary as I am, I treat each finger, each nail with care. Cleaning each little cut or scrape on one hand, and massaging Lune's healing salve into her skin, before moving around the bed to reach for her other hand to repeat the process. It's not a wide bed, but there's space for me there if I want it when I'm done.

And I do want it.

When her hands and face are clean, I set the basin aside and crawl onto the bed beside her. Underneath the harsh aroma of the salve and the tang of copper, there is still the scent of her— steady and earthy in spite of it all. I curl into her side and let my head rest on her shoulder.

"Little mouse?" Sila murmurs, her voice thick with sleep. Her fingers flex and I tangle mine with hers. She grips them back, implacable even at the edge of death. Sleep is trying to claim me already, but I manage to tip my head back and press my lips to her neck. An attempt to reassure her. She shifts, her lips pressing against my hair as she breathes in deeply. She makes a pleased sort of hum before her body relaxes again into sleep. It relaxes every muscle in my body to hear her speak, feel her move again. Sleep overcomes me, and at least this night, my dreams are quiet things.

I have never felt so keenly how many places a person can ache as I do when I wake. I must have slept deeply, because I've barely moved from where I fell asleep. My head is still resting on Sila's shoulder, her fingers still tangled with mine. I groan silently as I shift, wincing as I stretch out my legs.

"That's a lovely sight," says Sila, her lips near my ear. I twist around quickly, pushing myself up so that I can see her better. She is awake, just. Exhaustion is clear in her face, even if there is a teasing light in her eyes. There is a tightness in her face, and her colour is all wrong still. I pull my hand free of her grip.

The Dawn King have mercy, you're awake.

Sila's mouth twists in a grimace. "Don't thank the Dawn King. Thank the Library and my fae blood."

If that's who I need to give thanks to, to have you back, then so be it.

Sila opens her mouth to reply and stops, her gaze flicking over me. "Are you wearing my blouse?"

I needed something to wear... but I can find something else today.

"No," Sila says, reaching out to tangle her hand in the blouse's fabric. "I like you in my things. Marking you exactly as you ought to be."

My heart thumps in my chest. *Marking me?*

"As mine," she says, pulling me to her. Her lips meet mine, and I gasp silently against her mouth, opening it to her. Her fingers tangle in my hair and it turns from a simple press of lips, like my chaste offering had been, to something that steals in as if it can take more than just my breath away. To something that quickens my blood and sets my skin alight. If this is how a fae steals a soul, then Sila can have mine. As long as she never stops kissing me like this.

She has to, after a long indulgent moment, to let me gasp silently for air. She nips softly at my lower lip, her eyes dark, her mouth kiss damp and she's so very beautiful like this. I try not to let my thoughts wander to how lovely she could be. She rests her forehead against mine, her fingers still locked in my borrowed blouse. She sighs wistfully.

"You do not know how much I long to hear you gasp. Hear you whimper for me," Sila murmurs. "Hear you say my name."

I can barely summon a thought because Sila has kissed me and all I can do is think of her lips over mine as my mind tries to catch up. She smiles softly at me and kisses my nose before letting go of my blouse and falling back against the pillows. She looks weary again. Tired right through.

How long?

She smiles softly and closes her eyes. "Truly? Since I first saw you. After the Ascension, I was tasked with watching the scriptorium to watch for you— for the target," she says. "I fancied for a moment what it would mean if it were you, if I were to press my blade to your throat. Would you whimper? Would you beg?"

I stare at her, because the Ascension, the celebration of the Dawn King's coronation, was months ago. She opens her eyes again and they're clear as they look at me. I had not seen her before the day I returned to the scriptorium— but she had seen me. Watched me from her shadows. She had known when I had read the book, and she had known when I was in strife afterwards. When she had found me in my room.

"I never thought for a moment it would be you, but it did not stop me thinking of you," Sila says. "It did not stop you from consuming my thoughts. And I have so very much time for thinking."

I feel unmoored. Adrift. Not because Sila had been observing me and obsessing over me for months now. Once the thought might have sent me running, now it only makes me hungrier for her. I want her to devour me as wholly and completely as her kiss had promised.

No. I am unmoored because in the end my body, my blood, is still a gateway to the Dawn King. No matter what they had said when they allowed me to join the Library all those years ago. Only now, the Library had a claim on me too. I had become a bridge between the two. A bridge that the Library had exploited. A bridge perhaps that the Light-keepers could exploit too.

It could only have been me.

Sila's brow twitches in a frown. "What do you mean?"

When they found I had no magical gift, they called me a foundling. The Lightkeepers. The courtiers. The Dawn King. My parents had long been dead from the night cough, or I have no doubt they would have executed my mother for trying to pass me off as my father's child if they could have. Except that they were wrong. He was my father.

Sila sits up, her frown only deepening as she makes sense of each hand sign. It isn't done to speak of it outside the Keep. Even if the other factions suspect, they do not know. People rarely ever leave the Keep. I was still not entirely sure how I had been allowed. I often suspected that for all her protestations otherwise, Orielle had been involved.

My father is descended from the Dawn King. I am

descended from the Dawn King. Who else would the Library choose in a room full of scribes? Of course it was me.

I stare miserably at my hands. Even now, even after so long, I can't escape it. I try to steady the tremble starting in my hands and bite down on my quivering lip. I feel sick to think of it. Sila's hand finds mine and her fingers run over my palm and grip my wrist. She runs her thumb over the veins, stark against my skin.

"We never found your book," she says softly. I slip my hand from her grip with great reluctance.

I did. In the coffin. I read it and I have promised to speak it.

Sila is staring off through the doorway when I look up at her. She is a world away, her eyes focused on something that doesn't exist.

"That's why the Library tasked me with breaking your silence," she says. "It wants you to speak it."

I can see the way her mind is turning over, her thoughts flicking through every note she had ever made on curses and magical afflictions. Her expression fractures as she comes to the inevitable conclusion. She looks at me, stricken.

"Words once spoken, made true. A prophecy?" she asks. I nod. "Then—" She reaches out to tug down the collar of the blouse. The curse mark is as present as ever. It's darkened at the centre, and it radiates heat. Like an ember dropped on my skin and pressing through it, burning through me.

"It's eating you up," Sila says. Her eyes go distant again. "Like your fevers." She drops back against the pillows again, her arms going limp. She is wearing through what little energy she has recovered, her body still trying to pull itself back together again.

Does it usually take so long for you to heal? I watched

the way you fought. You take hits like they're nothing more than an inconvenient paper cut.

Sila gives me a sidelong look, and I think half of it is made up of the way sleep and recovery are trying to take her. "That cursed Lightkeeper and their sword. I should have known it was sanctified, since they'd sent a blood mage." She hisses as she shifts.

I knew a little of sanctified weapons. Blessed by the Dawn King, to ward off evil, wielded only by a select few of his Lightkeepers. Of course, it would be like poison to Sila.

You need to rest.

"Only if you promise me you'll eat," she murmurs. I let myself smile, then.

I'll eat. I promise.

She nods, satisfied, and allows sleep to take her.

Chapter 30

Lorel

I RUMMAGE THROUGH THE KITCHENETTE AND FIND some pickles, stale bread and some of the salty powder that makes a clear soup that makes the bread edible. It's a world away from that first meal from the Librarian's mess hall, but since the last thing I ate was that awful bread in the Library, it tastes almost the same.

It's quiet with Sila resting. Sila isn't usually loud by any means, but when I've curled up to sleep in her bed, it's usually to the scratch of her pen, or the dull soft sound of the blotter. The quiet rustle of turning pages. The smell of old paper and damp earth. The scent of blood still clings in the air, still marks the rug by the hearth. There's no sound from the bedroom. Everything is still, and it makes me anxious. The curse stirs, restless.

I stand to go and check on Sila, when there is a gentle knock at the door. I still, my heartbeat kicking up.

"Lorel? May I come in?" Lune calls softly through the door.

Relieved, I open my mouth to call back a reply, close it with a grimace, and then turn myself reluctantly away from the bedroom door. Lune's face is a picture of anxiety that eases only slightly when she looks at me. Sila's mirror earlier had shown the way dark shadows are pooling under my eyes. How I am starting to look a little worn and thin around the edges. The curse eating away at me to sustain itself, just as Sila had said. I step back to give Lune room to enter.

Lune lets out a relieved sigh as I close the door behind her. "I hate the Librarian's quarters. I always feel like I shouldn't be here, despite my special dispensation." She drops her case to the floor and pushes a bundle of clothes into my hands, before she grabs my face with both hands, the tingle of her magic tickling my skin. Her frown deepens. "I can see something is wrong," she says, clearly frustrated. "But it won't show me anything."

She lets me pull away to find something to write with in reply. I set the clothes aside, grateful for them, and also not. I'd liked what Sila had said before she'd kissed me, but I also can't very well wander around in only a shirt and nothing else.

I'm fine.

Lune looks to the ceiling as if asking for patience. "You're not, but if you're not going to tell me, then I can only hope you know what you're doing," she says. Her eyes flick to the bedroom door. "And that it isn't her doing."

"I can hear you, you know." Sila's voice is weak, but clear as she calls out. I follow Lune into the bedroom, where Sila is propped against the pillows, almost exactly as I had left her. She looks worn still, but improving.

"Librarian Sila, you're awake," Lune says. It is as cold as I have ever heard her, any pretence at bedside manner entirely gone.

Sila smiles, and it's one of her sharp toothed ones.

"Cupbearer," Sila says, greeting Lune with her title with equal ice. The use of Lune's title is a clear warning.

Once there would have been a Cupbearer to tip the poison into Sila's willing mouth before she stepped towards the altar. In all the years since its inception, the ritual of the sacrifice has remained the same. Now, Lune was the Cupbearer to others like Sila. To each sacrifice that had walked to the altar in the past decade.

Lune's jaw stiffens. "I'll need to check your wounds," she says, as if she'd rather crawl through the corpse of a cave mole.

"I know your tone is only because of your care for Lorel, and so I will let it pass," Sila says. "You may inspect your handiwork."

Neither of them thaw much. Lune's jaw is set in a stubborn line and Sila observes her as she might watch the scriptorium on a dull morning. I perch on the end of the bed and watch on anxiously.

"You're healing remarkably well," Lune mutters, already able to pull out the thread she'd used to stitch Sila's skin back together.

"The Library takes care of its own," says Sila blandly. Lune has her roll onto her side so that she can inspect the whole of the wound. Lune's frown persists.

"Does it now?" Lune says sharply. A chill prickles over my skin and I go very still.

"You are lucky to even be in this room, Cupbearer," Sila says. The tone of her voice makes me want to hide in a closet until she's gone.

Lune straightens, relinquishing Sila so that she can settle back against the pillows. Lune's eyes pass over the room, littered with the debris of Sila's long life. "You're lucky I haven't reported you for holding a scribe," Lune snaps back. Sila narrows her eyes.

"How about we call a truce," Sila says, watching Lune intently. "For Lorel's sake."

Lune sets her jaw. "Fine."

"Besides, I have other concerns." Sila's eyes turn to me. "Like why the Lightkeepers are pursuing a scribe that happens to be a Dawnchild."

Lune looks at me as well. "So you have told her," she says. She looks conflicted. I wish she'd trust me in this.

Yes. I thought it had become relevant.

Sila reads my hand signs aloud for Lune's benefit. Lune sighs deeply, rubbing her face with her hands.

"I know we don't talk about this, but you know my thoughts on this. And with this last incident? You're not safe here," Lune says.

I catch the very slight upward tip of Sila's eyebrows. "And what are your thoughts on this matter?" Sila asks.

I grit my teeth.

"That Lorel should leave," Lune says. She's set her jaw again, like she's ready to settle in for a fight.

Sila narrows her eyes at Lune. "Leave the Library?"

"Leave the Citadel," Lune says. "A scion of the Dawn King with no magic? These actions prove that he clearly had no intention of letting you go—"

"Lorel isn't without magic," Sila says.

Lune looks quickly between the two of us. "*What?*"

But they don't know that.

"No," says Sila. "Which only adds more weight to the Cupbearer's theory. To the Dawn King, you are a weakness."

I stare at them both and think of what the Heart had said. That the words I would speak would mark the traitor's downfall. There was only one being of equal standing to the Heart. Only the Dawn King. He is the traitor.

"No, what do you mean Lorel isn't without magic?" Lune demands.

This is a mess.

"Have you never wondered at Lorel's fevers?" Sila asks her.

Lune purses her lips. "I have, of course I have. I can feel the magic in them, but I've never been able to figure out how they happen. You're saying her magic does it?"

"I believe so. We are still trying to understand it, because I have never seen its like before, either," Sila says. "And for what it is worth, I agree. Lorel needs to leave the Citadel. Magic or not, the Lightkeepers are going to great lengths to take you back, or kill you." I look at Sila, alarm chasing my blood through my veins. "And I will not let them do either."

I'm not going anywhere without you.

"I did not say you would," Sila replies, holding my gaze. It burns through me.

I heard you tell the Heart it was your only tether. That means you'll die without it, doesn't it?

"What's Lorel saying?" Lune asks, wary.

"Lovely things," Sila says softly. I purse my lips.

There is a flutter of a laugh from Lune. "I'm sure," she says, coming to stand by me. "I can arrange it."

"Such interesting connections you have, Cupbearer."

Lune is silent for a long moment, her dislike of Sila warring with her honest heart.

"I see the effects of the night cough. I send people to their death in the hopes it will end it. These plagues and problems have a root, but I don't believe in the dark anymore," says Lune. She has a faraway look. I reach for her hand, gripping it tightly. She looks down at me. "I won't send you to your death, Lorel. I can't let that happen again."

It works exactly as she had intended, even if it doesn't make her hurt any less real. And it doesn't change that I would be risking Sila's life, to take her from the very thing I was sure was keeping her alive. I couldn't take Sila from this place with me.

But outside the Citadel? I hardly knew how I would survive on my own. Magic or not, the outside world was a dark and cruel place, bereft of sunlight and ruled by blood and violence. It was no place for a scribe, and as my eyes meet Sila's, I know without a doubt that now she has me she will never let me go again. That she will doom herself all over again to keep me, and that I can never let that happen.

Chapter 31

Lorel

In the end, Lune and Sila had agreed that I should go. I had said nothing. I could not forget Sila had called the Library her only tether left. She would go with me in a heartbeat, I knew that, but if it meant removing her from the very thing that kept her tethered in this world? I couldn't do it. I couldn't bear the thought of a world that didn't have Sila in it.

And really, in the end I am just a speck of a moment in her long existence. Something to be barely remembered, and found tucked in a box at the back of a drawer one day. Sila will be alright without me.

My hands are shaking so badly I fumble the spoon of dried herbs as I try to place them into the teapot. I can't be certain that *I* will be alright, though. When Sila had kissed me, it was in the same way she looked at me. Devouring and all-consuming, and the memory of it sets my blood alight and my body aching. It makes me think of tangled limbs, and skin against skin, and I have never wanted something so badly. Never been so desperate for someone as I am for her. And if I let her have me, I don't think I will ever be able to let her go again.

And that would be the end of her. I cannot condemn her like that.

I dust the herbs from the counter with a deep, silent breath and promptly drop it all across the floor as I hear a gentle thump from the bedroom. Sila.

I rush through the living space, catching my knee on one of Sila's book stacks and sending it tumbling. I wince and grip the door frame tight, staring at the empty bed in front of me. The sheets crumpled and creased around where she had been. It's then I catch the salt and earth scent of hot water drifting from the washroom, the door left ajar. I make to call out to her, to make sure she hasn't slipped, and stop as the air passes my lips without a sound. I cross the bedroom in a few quick strides and knock.

I barely get a third knock in before the door is pulled open, and Sila, steam-damp and wearing only one of her long blouses, stands before me. She smiles.

"Hello, little mouse. Are you here to join me?" All the weariness of the past days has bled away from her. There isn't a single blemish or mark left. I keep my eyes on her face, determined not to let them stray to her long legs and the hint of thighs that could easily crush me.

I heard a noise. I thought— well— You look better. Well. You look well.

Dawn King flay me. I am stuttering with my hands.

Sila's smile widens as she leans in the door frame, her tall figure looming over me.

"Just the taps, protesting as they do," she says, tipping her head. She reaches out, tugging at my collar. "I still prefer you in my blouses."

I can't very well walk around in just a blouse.

"Why ever not?" she asks. I try to swat her hand away and she catches it, a frown scratching itself across her features. "Lorel. Your hands. Why didn't you use the salve?"

I tug my hands back, still scratched and bruised, some nails torn down to the quick. I hadn't because it hadn't occurred to me to do so. Sila had needed it.

I'm fine.

"My Dark Lady save us if we ever learn what you think it looks like when you are not fine," says Sila. She rests her hand on my neck, sliding back my collar where bruises line my skin. Magic or no, there isn't enough fae blood in me to hasten my recovery. The fingerprints of the Heart's phantoms still linger, purple and angry. Her eyes are as dark and fathomless as always. Her face is as still and furious as the time she had found the curse mark. Her fingers run over my skin so gently, and I am reminded of the labyrinth. How easy it would be to lose one's mind.

"I'd like these better," Sila murmurs, lowering her mouth to my skin. "If I had put them there myself." She presses her lips to the marks and they are cool against the flush of my skin. And mercy, what would it be like to give in? To go and bathe with her, the steam billowing and inviting, the sound of the water promising. Sila's eyes dark, just a breath away, and wanting nothing more than to possess all of me. What would it be like to be *hers?*

Tearing myself away makes me want to weep, to scream, to cry out— but I must. I cannot be hers. I will lose myself. I will lose Sila. I will damn us both. And of all the things Librarians can do with scribes, this thing I want with her is not one of them.

"Lorel?" Sila frowns at me. Confused, I think, more than anything else.

Enjoy your bath.

I can't look her in the eye as I sign it, and then, just like a mouse, I turn and scurry from the room.

The washroom door clicks shut not too long after. I hear it from where I am curled in one armchair, my arms wrapped tightly around my knees. My glasses press into the bridge of my nose, threatening to give under the pressure. I was lucky, really, that I still had them with me.

I groan silently. Sila is going to want to talk about it. There is no getting around that. Maybe I should leave now. Find Lune and just go. Run.

I take a deep breath, and the silence around me holds. The overwhelming truth of it all is that I don't want to run. I don't want to leave without her. But I am afraid. Terrified that I might cause her death. Terrified that I might never see her again. Terrified that she might never touch me. Terrified that she might, and that I wouldn't know what to do in return to please her.

It doesn't matter how far I have come, I am still as full of fear as I had been the night I had locked up my voice and thrown away the key.

A sudden sharp knock at the door crashes into my thoughts, and I have only a moment to wipe my eyes on my sleeve before Mercias strides through the door without any further invitation. He clicks the door shut behind him.

"Scribe Lorel," he says, turning. There is the tiniest hint of a frown touching his features and a sharp look of alarm in his eyes. "Are you well?"

I think I have misunderstood him.

Sila is recovering. Recovered, even.

The frown deepens. "Has this caused you some distress? I asked if you are well, scribe."

Oh, I hadn't misunderstood at all.

No. I'm glad of it.

"You look it," he says, dry. "Where is Librarian Sila?"

In the bath. I can take a message for you.

Mercias snorts and it's such an undignified sound I can barely reconcile it with the man. I can barely reconcile his sudden kindness with his usual preference for being an arrogant prick. The silence stretches out.

"Perhaps Sila has tea, somewhere under all this mess?" he suggests.

I stare at him. He stares back.

"Right, well. I'll see if I can find it myself." He disappears into the little kitchenette, and after a moment I follow him like a curious ghost. He's giving the teapot a quizzical look, one eyebrow arched at its state of disarray. "Interrupted, were you?"

Sila—

"Mm, Librarian Sila indeed," he says, throwing extra herbs carelessly into the pot. He fills it with water, scenting the room with a bright, grassy scent.

"I'd ask why you haven't returned to the scriptorium," Mercias says, staring at the wall. "But I rather wonder that the healer didn't drag you back to the infirmary." I tug at my collar nervously and he looks at me with narrowed eyes. "Still not speaking then? Curious."

I can't even say it's the working hours, because I have no idea what the hour is.

I can't go back yet.

"No? I suppose this has to do with the Lightkeepers?" He tips his head as if coming to a decision. "And I suppose there really is no safer place. Librarian Sila, it appears, would defend you with her life."

She did the same for you.

His mouth twists in a wry grimace. "Yes, she did." Mercias pours the tea into two cups and every little nerve I have is on edge, wondering why he needs two cups, and then he holds one out to me. "Librarian Sila and I have known each other for decades. I can only hope I would do the same for her."

Is this for me?

"Sila doesn't drink now, does she?" he says. "Take it before I drop it, I'm not a fire mage."

I rescue the cup from its potential fate, holding it carefully between my palms. There's something soothing about it. Comforting. Who the hell is this man and what has he done with Mercias?

"There must be a table somewhere?" he drawls.

I back out into the living area where the little table sits, the threat of it disappearing again ever present. Mercias settles into a chair and I hover.

"Scribe Lorel, sit down." His tone is such that I sit without even thinking about it. That particular Librarian intonation requires immediate compliance.

I fuss with my cup and take small careful sips as Mercias surveys me, taking in each little scrape and bruise just as Sila had. Only the look in his eyes is rather different from hers. He sighs, pinching his nose between his fingers as if it pains him to even be here.

"Elris is rather disgruntled that you haven't returned to work, you know. He's already lost one scribe, so naturally he's rather distressed at the idea of losing another."

I stare at Mercias. I hadn't considered that I might be missed. Or even that anyone would care that I was gone.

But, I reason, Elris has always been kind to me. Sybri too. Still, how does Mercias know?

Are you familiar with Illuminator Elris?

Mercias smirks. "You could say that. You know, I could have you returned to the scriptorium if you wanted."

I—

"I won't," he says, with a huff of a laugh. "She seems attached to you and I wouldn't dare Librarian Sila's wrath. So I'll have to put up with Elris' displeasure instead. Fortunately, he's easy enough to deal with."

I stare at him. He surely can't mean what I think he means.

Are you saying—

"Yes," he says.

But that's forbi—

"Yes."

My hands hang in the air. Mercias is bedding Elris. He has as good as admitted it.

Does the Head Librarian know?

"Naturally," Mercias says, inclining his head. "And naturally, I take the punishment for it. Not that it changes anything."

I stare at him again. Elris' warning makes so much more sense now, for all the good it did.

"Of course, if you tell Elris I said that, I'll deny it," he says mildly, sipping his tea.

I take a sip of my own to stop myself from staring.

I'm sure I won't get the chance.

Mercias hums thoughtfully. "Yes. The Lightkeepers. I have informed the Head Librarian of the incident. Librarian Idemay will be interred in the catacombs in due course. The bodies of the Lightkeepers have been returned to the Keep. What's left of them, anyway." His face is impassive but a cold fury burns in his eyes. His jaw clenches. "The Head Librarian knows why they came here and has increased surveillance. If they are willing to send a blood mage after you, then they must want you rather badly."

I don't know why.

It's so much easier to lie with my hands than my tongue. Not that I think he believes me for a second. He watches me for another long moment.

"Very well. That's all I came to say. Please pass it along to Librarian Sila." He sets his cup down.

I'm sorry.

Mercias narrows his eyes at me. "About Elris?"

I nod.

"Don't be," he says. "I'll take care to distract him well enough."

And with that, he takes his leave. I stare into the depths of my cup, turning Mercias' words over in my head. I'd been so focused on Sila's mention of her tether, been so concerned with her brush with death, that I'd forgotten her other declarations. Her demand to take my place, her insistence that she had already put me above all others, her oath to protect me, and I know, with bone-aching certainty that there is no world in which Sila allows me to go without her. Just as Mercias takes his punishments for loving Elris, Sila would bear even death for me. She wouldn't have it any other way.

Tentative fingers thread through my hair, as soft and gentle as ever. I tip my head back to look at her, freshly bathed. Fully dressed again. Her smile is soft and a little regretful.

"I think it is time that you and I had a talk, don't you?"

Chapter 32

Lorel

Sila's fingers let my hair fall away, and she
moves around the table to take up Mercias' vacated seat.
She gives his cup a look and pushes it aside.

"What news did Mercias bring?" she asks. She's
circling. Trying to find steady ground again after I had
upset her neat footwork with my panic.

*He has informed the Head Librarian of the altercation,
and the bodies have been removed. The Lightkeepers have
been returned to the Keep.*

Sila hisses. "Far better than they deserve. I should have
liked to have them nailed to the front door."

They would take that poorly.

It's an understatement of the worst kind. They would
seek blood for blood, and blame the Library for starting a
faction war. It would not end well.

"They should consider themselves lucky that we have
not taken their assault so," Sila says, dark eyes blazing. She
tears her eyes away from me, her shoulders shuddering as
she masters her anger. The shadows curl at the edges of my

vision. Sila takes a deep breath, turning back to me. "Sorry, little mouse, I'm getting carried away again."

I'm sorry I ran away.

There is the barest twitch of her eyebrows. "You have nothing to apologise for, Lorel. Nothing needs to happen that you do not want to happen."

I stare down at my hands, all I have to try and explain myself.

There is only one thing that I don't want to happen. I never want to see you dying in my arms again. I could not bear it. Never mind the Heart's binding, I know you want me to leave. I know I cannot let you come with me, even though I know I cannot stop you. I don't know what I've done to deserve you, and it is tearing me apart to think I cannot have you. To know that it would tear me apart even more so if I did. Because I should leave you, and you should let me go.

Sila watches my hands, intent, eyes intent on my face when they still. Her expression is soft, and so lovely, and I could cut myself to pieces on it.

"Oh Lorel, how can you not know yet? I would follow you even into death. I already have. When I did not press my blade into your chest and still your heart, I chose. You cannot condemn me. I have already done that myself."

My heart. My breath. My thoughts. The very blood in my veins. All of it stops, for a moment. All of it catches on the thought that Sila wants to keep me, forever. That I am not just a passing thought or amusement to be thrown aside. That long before I had even truly noticed her, she had already given everything up for me.

And I cannot save her. Leaving her will not save her. Denying myself will not save her. I had been entirely foolish to think that I could. There is little that Sila would let stand in her way. And now, there is little left standing in my way.

Sila smiles at me, dark-eyed, from across the table. "Now that's a promising look," she says.

I shouldn't.

Dawn King have mercy on me, I *will*. To hell with the rules.

Will you take me to your bed?

Sila reaches out a hand, plucking my glasses from my face and setting them neatly on the table. "Nothing would please me more," she says. "But you must tell me what you want of me, and you must tell me if you want me to stop."

What I want of you?

"Yes, little mouse."

I do not know. I've never gone to bed with anyone.

I have the pleasure of watching Sila's eyes widen, to see the way the blackness of her irises bleeds out across the whites.

"No one?" she says, intent.

Not a soul.

My heartbeat is racing, prey-quick. Sila looks at me like she intends to consume me where I sit. "I like that, rather more than I ought to," she says. There is heat within me, warm and pooling, and she won't kiss me still. She hasn't even let her fingers make contact.

Let me please you. Let me have you. Let me give you everything I have. It's yours. Let me be yours.

Her dark eyes are bright, ravenous things. And still she holds back. She wets her lips, and I have never been more aware of her tongue, or how much I want it tangled with mine again. I shift at the aching warmth between my thighs, the way every part of me is aware of where she is and where she isn't.

"If you want me to stop," she says, a little breathless. "I want you to tap me with your fingers." Her arm shifts and her fingers tap my shoulder sharply. "Do you understand?" She turns her hand palm up to me, expectant. It takes me a moment to understand what she's asking of me. I tap her palm back just as sharply, and her fingers wrap around mine. I could sigh at the relief of it. I want to demand more of it.

"Nothing that you don't want, Lorel. If you don't like something, if you want to stop, if it's too much, if you decide you want to read a book instead. Anything at all, tell me. Stop me, do you understand?"

I nod, and grip her hand, pulling her over the table, grasping for her blouse as I press my lips to hers and kiss her with all the hunger that's been lying in wait inside me. I'm clumsy at first, and then Sila takes control and I surrender to her clever tongue. She breaks the kiss, allowing me a moment to breathe and I use a simpler single handed gesture.

I understand.

"Good," she murmurs.

Her fingers curl into the fabric of my collar and she drags me back to her. Her mouth is not soft or gentle. It demands mine again and I offer it up to her, everything up to her. Her arms come around me, sliding across my clothes and holding me up against her, my toes inches from the ground. Everything goes dark and airless for a moment, and as my vision clears, the bedroom appears around us.

"I told you I liked you in my clothes," she murmurs, setting me down on my feet. "But I think I'll like you dressed in my shadows just as well."

As the shadows draw away, they take my dress with them, slipping it from my body. They tug at the ties of my shift until it's falling over my shoulders with a whisper. Sila steps from her trousers, and pulls her blouse over her head with a tumble of hair. The shadows unfasten my utilitarian breast band and drop it to the floor. I gasp, quiet as the shadows touch my skin, drawing the last of my clothes away and leaving me bare in front of her.

When I look up again, Sila's eyes are dark from edge to edge. Hungry. It's almost enough to distract from her naked-ness. Her bare full chest, where I have rested my head so often these past weeks. Her strong shoulders that I have clung to— that I imagine myself clinging to in an entirely different way. The smooth curve of her stomach, the points of her hips, and her thighs. The Dawn King have mercy on me, I would happily drown in them. Drown in her.

So why is she just standing there?

Are you just going to look, or are you going to touch me?

Sila's smile widens, smug and satisfied. "If you think I'm going to rush this, little mouse. I'm afraid I'm going to disap-point you."

I make to move closer to her, and her shadows tighten— just a gentle pressure keeping me in place. If I could, I'd plead with her name and taste it on my lips. I know it would bring her to her knees. Bring her closer. As it is, my entire body is awake under the weight of her gaze. She tips her head, gaze raking over me and then finally, she closes the gap between us, leaning down so that her breath is a gentle ghost across my skin. Her hair, soft and gentle where it brushes against me. The scent of the bath and her hair oil clinging. Surrounding me. And still she isn't touching me.

Sila.

She must be able to feel the movement of my frustrated hand signs through her shadows because the soft breath of her laugh flutters over the soft skin beneath my ear. Her lips brush across it and it sets my flesh alight. I whimper and it's silent. Everything is silent, and still, and careful. I don't want her to be careful.

"Tell me what you want, Lorel," she whispers, between the lightest of kisses down my neck. "Whatever you demand of me, it is yours. I am yours." Her hand slides around the back of my neck, tangles in my hair and tugs, baring my throat to her. I gasp silently as she nips at my jaw. Kisses down my throat to my collarbones. "And you are mine."

I ache. It is no longer a simple want to have her skin against mine, to have her fingers against me, to have her mouth back on mine, stealing my breath away. It is vital. Imperative to my continued existence. It scours through me and I push against the barrier that keeps the curse locked away. That keeps my voice locked away. She kisses across my breasts and I tear at the wall I built. It is my bloody nails dragging me across the chapel floor. My desperate plea to the Heart. A hungry search for a locket through scholarly detritus. A desperate need to call to her.

I rip at it, shred it with every part of my being and every piece of me that wants to meet and be matched by her. And as I pull at it, the magic I had woven unravels and her name tumbles freely across my tongue.

"Sila," I gasp.

Sila stills and the curse stirs and I hope that the curse and I have made some kind of peace for now because if it decides now is the time to come forth, then I will set fire to the Heart in retribution. A long heartbeat later, the curse settles, and Sila's shadows loosen. I thread my hands through her hair, bring her mouth to mine, and pull her with me as I fall back against the bed. The sheets are soft against my skin and they smell of her. All damp earth, salt, and decaying wood, laced through with that insidious floral scent that reminds me of funerals and incense. Sila braces herself over me and I kiss her still. She's smiling.

"Lorel," she murmurs.

"What I want," I say, breaking the kiss, blinking as I hear my breath again for the first time in months. I relish the feel of each sound in my mouth. "Is for you to devour me. Consume me. Show me that I am yours. Ruin me for any other, because there never will be. I am yours."

She is still all over, eyes wide, mouth a soft shape of surprise. "Your voice," she says. "It's sweeter than I remember it."

"It will be all the sweeter for calling your name," I insist, tugging her closer. Demanding her skin against mine, her limbs tangled with mine. Because she is mine. "Give me everything."

"Alright," Sila says softly, and she suddenly seems more. Where the shadow begins and she ends, I do not know. Her mouth is on mine and she's kissing me like she did that first time, leaving my mind blank as she ensnares every wisp of thought.

She presses against me, presses her thigh between my legs where I am damp and aching and I moan into her mouth. Her nails drag over my skin, her fingers press into my hips as she holds me there and grinds against me. She licks up the skin between my breasts, over the curse mark.

She kisses it as if she can suck the mark from my skin with her mouth alone. Her mouth on me, her hands firm against my body, her thigh grinding against me. It leaves my thoughts nothing but the faintest wash of watercolour. I can barely breathe, barely think, and then the pressure of her thigh gives.

"Sila," I gasp as the edge of building heat slips away. So very different from anything I've ever done for myself.

"Tell me you are mine," she says, her mouth demanding against my skin. It leaves me gasping and writhing against her.

"I am yours," I say, breathless. "Sila—"

Her name turns into a moan as her fingers slide between us, against me. Press into me. I thought I had known what pleasure was. Satisfactory, but nothing to bother another being with. Something to barely bother myself with. But as I gasp Sila's name, as she gives me everything I want, everything I have asked for, I know there is nothing, and there never will be anything that compares to this. There will never be anything I want more than her.

And if she is condemned, then I will be condemned with her.

Sila sends me tumbling, gasping, crying out into release and I am everything, and nothing, all at once.

I gasp beneath her as I come back to myself and she bundles me against her as she rolls onto her side. My limbs are as loose as warm honey and I drift a little on the soft and hazy bliss of it, enjoying the press of her body against mine, the tangle of our legs, and her fingers, gentle and soft as they comb through my hair. Fingers that can tear through flesh just as easily as they can bring it pleasure. I press my face into her neck and feel the slow, determined beat of her heart through her skin. I feel her laughter through her chest.

"You are exactly as lovely as I thought you would be," she whispers. I smile against her and bite at her jaw. Lick at her skin. She tastes of salt and earth under my tongue.

"You taste of the grave," I tell her as her breath catches. "I like it."

Sila's fingers curl into my hair again, pulling me away so that she can look at me.

"Little mouse," she says, wicked and dark eyed.

"I want to touch you," I tell her. I don't know if I'm still allowed to make demands.

"You may touch me however you wish, if it will please you," Sila says.

"I want to please *you*," I say. "But I don't know how, exactly." I had thought I knew some of it, but I had not realised the depths of my inexperience.

Sila kisses me and it's soft and sweet, and cold as mountain water. Then her arms come around me as she rolls onto her back, pulling me astride her. She smiles up at me from under long dark eyelashes. "I can assure you that at this moment there is little you could do that would not please me. So why don't you start with what you would like to try most?"

It shocks me, that little revelation. That this lovely creature of darkness is just as wanting, just as aching for me, as I am for her. She takes my hands and kisses my injured fingers.

"Be careful with these. You might have to be creative," she says, pleased.

I lean down to kiss her, because it's the first thing that comes to mind as I stare at her mouth. Sila lets me. She doesn't push back or try to take control. She permits me to make my demands.

Chapter 33

Sila

LOREL RUNS HER HANDS DOWN MY BODY, HER TOUCH feather light— tentative. It is as sweet as she is. As she had been gasping beneath me.

A little frown creases her brow as she makes a study of me. Traces the shape of my body with her fingers and her mouth like a feverish dream. I grip the sheets tightly, gasping at her gentle worship. Her short dark hair curls are damp, sticking to her cheeks as she looks up at me, dark eyed. Ravenous. Tentative, but not nervous. Not afraid. She really is a magnificent creature.

"Sila?"

"Yes, little mouse?"

"How long has it been since you were with someone? Like this?"

"Some time," I tell her.

She softly caresses my breasts, making it difficult to concentrate. It has been an awfully long time since I had given myself up to someone else like this. Ever since the queen had raised me again anew, I had been loyal to the purpose she had given me. And I had abandoned it all for Lorel. She alone has brought me back to myself. I had been a shade for so many years until she brought back emotions I had not felt in so long. True fury. Despair. Fear. Desire. Wanting and a fierce need to possess. To protect and hold and have.

And now she is *mine*. It takes all my restraint not to roll her under me again.

Lorel presses her fingers into my breasts and I gasp.

"They're so soft," she says.

I realise I have invited torture. Beautiful, delightful torture.

"Your mind was wandering." There's a soft smile at the corner of her mouth.

"Very rich of you to say, She-who-thinks-too-much," I say, resting my hands on her hips, fingers against the soft crease of her thigh. She laughs, and it takes my breath away. Hearing her voice, my name on her lips, was one thing. Hearing her laugh, light and careless? I hadn't even considered what that might be like. It tears through to the heart of me, and nestles against my soul.

"You're staring," she says, still smiling. Still lovely, with her eyes half-lidded.

"I have never heard you laugh," I say. I am sure I had not even heard her laugh in all the months I had watched her, before the book and the curse.

"And now you've heard me make many sounds," Lorel says, dipping her head to my chest. Sucking at the skin, teasing with her tongue. The weight of her pressing against my hips, the soft flesh of her breast brushing against my stomach, her fingers digging into my sides, all of it together drags a sound from deep within me. I had not been flippant. I am touch starved and desperate and Lorel, with her paper and ink scent and honey and salt taste, sets my skin alight. Makes me ache in a way I thought was lost to me.

"Each of them a delight," I say, strained. My fingers flex, digging into the soft skin of her backside. To think she knew nothing of her own power. Over me, over herself. Even with her voice recovered, Lorel was holding the curse back. My sweet little mouse, so small and fragile, is such a fierce thing. It is maddening, the way she drives all sensible thought from me.

"Sila," Lorel murmurs against my skin. She licks a hot line of aching need up to my collarbones. "I really do like the way you taste."

"Fuck." Heat surges through me as I think of all the ways she could use her tongue. I tangle my fingers in her hair, pulling her up so that I can kiss her hard. "You are a mouthy thing," I tell her. I kiss her again, pushing my tongue into her mouth, hoping it will somehow quell the desire I have to push her down between my thighs. She smiles, and it is as sweet as I have ever seen it.

"I've never been very good at holding my tongue," Lorel says. "Or my hands." Her hand slides over my hip and she digs her fingers into the soft flesh of my thighs. "So soft," she groans. Surely Lorel had been made to drive me out of my mind.

"Lorel—"

She cuts me off with a kiss as she presses her thigh against me. I moan into her mouth and I can feel her smile. Feel the way it pleases her from where she is pressed, hot and damp, against my thigh. I want to hold back, want to let her have this first time in bed with another. I am trying so very hard not to overwhelm her, because even if it had been centuries upon centuries, this is still something we are not equal in.

Lorel watches me intently, and I can see her tucking away each gasp and moan. Noting the effect of each touch. My fingers flex in her hair and her smile is a wonderful, maddening thing.

"Sila," she says. My body responds to that, too. "I asked for everything, didn't I?" Her fingers still, her thigh rests against me.

"Yes," I say. It comes out more ragged than I would like. My fingers tense in her hair again. "Tell me what you want."

"I want you to use me, the way you so obviously want to," she says.

"Lorel—"

"I can feel you trying to hold yourself back, trying not to overwhelm me. Don't. I want you to overwhelm me."

I search her determined little face for any sign, any indication at all that she might have misspoken. I cannot find it. May the Dark Lady have mercy on me.

"You know what to do if you want to stop?" I ask her. Lorel removes her hand from where it had been resting and taps my thigh. Three quick, hard taps. I pull her in to kiss her again, hard and demanding and desperate.

"Such a lovely creature," I say, tightening my fingers in her hair. Her eyes flutter closed and I tug lightly. She gasps, her mouth falling open.

"Sila, let me have all of you," she whispers. "I want all of you."

"You have me." I loosen my fingers and Lorel wriggles down my body, wetting her lips as she looks up at me. She is so beautiful. So eager. I comb my fingers through her hair again as she breathes in.

"I love the scent of you. Like damp earth and funeral flowers," she sighs, leaning into my hand. Searing heat tears through me again and I need her. My scribe. My little mouse. *My Lorel.*

I grip her hair and push her down. Her face, her mouth, is hot against my ice cold skin and she makes a desperate, wanting noise that I feel all the way through me. I feel the needy way she kisses me, open-mouthed and hungry and *fuck*. This will not take long at all. I grind back against her, keep my fingers wound in her hair, as my breathing comes faster. Becomes more desperate. Every part of my body is alive from the sound and feel of her.

Because I had never thought of myself as dead, but I am coming to realise that I hadn't been living, either. Even with my tethers at their strongest, I had been little more than a ghost of myself until Lorel had caught my eye. Had awoken me from the long, deep slumber that was my existence. And here? With her mouth on me, and my hips pressed against her, and her fingers digging into my thighs? I am alive again. Alive and hot and wanting. Unravelling and made anew, again, as pleasure claims me and tears through my body, dragging a desperate noise from within as I come entirely undone.

My breathing is rough as I release her and drag her back to me. Kiss her damp mouth, and taste what she tastes. Hold her sweet face with her slightly unfocused eyes and her small pants as she looks at me. I smile, a slow thing that creeps across my face, and push my thigh between hers. Lorel gasps and bites her lip as she presses herself against me.

"Do you want more, little mouse?" It is not as sultry as I would have liked, but it hardly seems to matter.

"Yes," Lorel says, desperate. "I want more, I want you, I want—"

I grasp her hips and press them down against my thigh as I grind it against her. She moans beautifully.

"Everything, I know, little mouse. I am yours, Lorel, and whatever you want from me, it is yours. Always."

I kiss the next sound from her lips, because it is mine.

And I am hers.

Chapter 34

Lorel

Sometime during the night there is a knock at the door, and the shift of the bed as the cold press of Sila's body leaves me. From the other room, I hear the murmur of voices, and when Sila returns it's not to bed, but to her closet.

"Sila?" I mumble. She stills.

"Hearing you speak is going to take some getting used to, little mouse," she says. There is a soft smile in her voice, and a thread of iron, too. At odds with each other. Fingers appear from the dark, pushing their way through my hair. A brush of lips against mine.

"Are you going somewhere?"

"There has been an incident in the scriptorium. I won't be long, I promise," Sila says. She kisses away any further protestations.

"Alright." It's made up of more syllables than it requires as sleep closes over me again. She has rather exhausted me and I have not a single concern in my entirely content state.

The door closes with a click and as I drift off again, the curse stirs, and shifts, and starts to wake.

. . .

Something feels off when I wake. My chest feels tight, and there is a painful, burning ache in my throat. The room seems airless. Suddenly too small, too close. I might be choking on something. There is something on my tongue. Words.

I drag my consciousness to the surface, clawing my way through the darkness. The sheets fall away as I sit up and try to calm my racing heart and get control of my breathing.

Words burning on my tongue. The prophecy. A curse for the Dawn King.

Sila had upheld her part of the Heart's bargain, now it is time to uphold mine. I open my mouth to speak, and there is the loud, telltale sound of an axe meeting wood. The dry, ancient wood of the door splinters under the blow, and I know that someone has broken down Sila's door. If they are in the living area, it won't be long before they find me here.

The curse shrinks back, like an uncertain cat. The words slip away from my thoughts, away from my tongue. I don't have time to move before the axe strikes the wood again and the bedchamber door gives way to a pair of Light-keepers, lanterns held high. There must be even more in the hallway behind them, the telltale flicker of battle magic flashing in a chaotic back light.

I am alone. Sila is gone. I have a vague recollection of her lips and her fingers. A promise.

A trap.

I try to kick back the sheets, and they tangle around my legs. Sila might be in danger. I need to get to her—

"There!" shouts one of the Lightkeepers.

My blood turns cold, as if someone has walked over my grave. Sila is not the one in danger tonight. I am.

They charge through the space, Sila's journals tumbling to the floor. I free my legs before the first of them reaches me. He grabs for me, seizing my bruised arm. I cry out as he twists it, dragging me closer to him. I kick out, and I scream, and I refuse to go quietly.

"Help me grab her," the first assailant calls to the other. "Hold her— *Fuck!*"

My heel connects with his face in a crunch of bone. He holds on in spite of it and the second Lightkeeper joins him. He tries to grab me, which is awkward for him because I am entirely naked, exactly as Sila had left me. I scratch at him with my free hand, rough-edged nails digging into the flesh of his arm. I try to twist away to the other side of the bed and the second Lightkeeper grabs my flailing legs. I catch him under the chin for his troubles. He holds me down as I thrash, unwilling to give me up. I'm dragged back and the first Lightkeeper with the broken nose grabs for my arms. I catch his cheek with my nails, a hair's breadth away from his eyes. He cries out, but it doesn't take him long to try again, and my limbs are already weary. I do not have Sila's ability to recover so well.

His hands close around my arms and twist them behind my back painfully.

"Fuck," he says, breathless, as he presses his knee into my back.

"Be easier if we could just kill her," says the one holding my legs. He says it like I have been the one to ruin *his* evening.

"We could call it an accident," the other replies, leaning in.

"Fuck you," I spit back.

He sneers at me.

"Where the fuck is Beryl?" hisses the other.

"Here," comes a woman's voice, short of breath. Lantern light blooms across the room. I recognise her face. Mousy brown hair and pale grey eyes set in a hard, mean face. A water mage, and another of my sister's peers.

"You'll need to pacify her," says the first one, the one with a broken nose. He sounds a bit nasal. Good.

"I can see that," she says, dry. "Get out of the way."

Broken Nose lets my arms free and I twist, snarling and reaching for whoever is closest. Beryl moves swiftly and within seconds my limbs turn as light as air. All the fight goes out of my body. My mind struggles as sedation magic coats my thoughts, leaving them soft and syrupy.

"Lively, isn't she?" Beryl says.

I push through the sedation. "Fuck. You." It's a little slurred, my tongue growing heavy. My body goes entirely limp, my thoughts drifting like an angry, futile storm over an indifferent mountain. I catch Beryl's expression, an unsubtle sneer as she looks me over. Casts her eyes over the bed and discarded clothes. I manage nothing more than a small growl. Entirely ineffective.

"Wrap her up so she's decent and let's get her out of here. I've had enough of Librarians for one day."

The two Lightkeepers jump to her command, pinning my arms to my sides and wrapping me in Sila's silken bedsheets. They still smell of her, of us. I am tossed over a shoulder like nothing more than a sack of grain.

The hallway is littered with the injured and dead as we pass. There is the occasional muffled noise or abrupt movement. I try to keep my eyes open. I feel the curse shift, and my thoughts clear somewhat. My eyelids don't feel quite so heavy. Even the curse is sedated by the mage, a pale image of itself.

My thoughts are still slow, drifting, but one burns through, bright as a flame. I need to stay alive long enough for Sila to find me.

Because I have no doubt that when Sila returns to find her bed empty and bloody, she will come for me.

Chapter 35

Sila

THE SCRIPTORIUM IS IN A STATE OF DISARRAY. I thought I had left it in a mess when I rescued Lorel, but I had nothing on the current chaos. The shelves and desks are pushed out into the corridors, books and supplies scattered everywhere. The Cupbearer is negotiating with a young woman. She sits at the centre of it all, clutching the body of another. Around her are the bodies of two other scribes, long dead before they were brought to the scriptorium, and three Lightkeepers, recently departed.

"Is that—?"

"Yes," sighs Mercias. "Noela."

Mercias' trainee Librarian. She'd only recently pledged herself to the Library's Heart. It seems the Heart is being generous with her, if the black marks across the scriptorium courtyard are anything to go by.

"Is she clutching a scribe?"

"Yes."

"Dawn King have mercy. Have we all taken leave of our senses?" I rub my temples. Think of *my* scribe tucked up safely in bed. So much for the rules, for us or the wretched Lightkeepers.

I follow Mercias into the central courtyard. The Head Librarian had summoned us, since we are currently in charge of the scriptorium, and it is not the first time Lightkeepers had been found here. Mercias crouches down next to Noela. Something tugs at my consciousness, and I frown down at them.

"Noela," he says with a gentle growl. "Let the healer see to her while she's still breathing."

I make a huff of noise. So *gentle*. I turn away to confirm my suspicions— the dead scribes have been long dead. They have been placed here, but for what purpose? And how did Mercias' trainee end up in the middle of them?

Mercias eventually comes to stand beside me as the Cupbearer is finally allowed to see the injured scribe in Noela's arms.

"These are the other missing scribes," he says.

"Other? You did not say." Though it explains why they all look a week dead or more.

"Hmm, did I not? Possibly because the last time I saw you, you were taking one of the missing scribes into the Library's Heart," he hisses, low. There's a sharp, painful tug at my heart.

"That was unrelated," I tell him, scowling.

"And then you almost died on the way out," he continues.

"That is possibly related," I say, frowning down at the corpses. At least there will be more hands available to clear this mess up.

"I figured," he says. "*Fuck*, this is brazen. Even for them."

"Court-sanctioned, perhaps?" I turn my attention to the

Lightkeepers. What is left of them, in any case. There is necrotic tissue damage still eating at their skin. "Impressive." I nudge one with my toe, glancing back at the trainee. "The Heart must have liked her."

"Perhaps the Heart knows something we don't," suggests Mercias.

I suppose the Heart knows I intend to leave. It will need to do better than a trainee if it hopes to replace me.

"Yes," I say softly. "It probably does."

"I don't understand though," Mercias continues. "Every time there have been Lightkeepers so far, your scribe has been at the centre of them."

Something like ice drops through my stomach. I look at him in alarm. Because he's right. She has. There is a tugging sensation again, sharp and painful. *Dark Lady have mercy on me.*

"I've left her alone," I say, my skin prickling. For the first time in a long time I feel nauseous. Properly vile. There should be nowhere safer than my rooms. They should not even know she is in them. The Heart's bargain strains again, a sharp pain shooting through my chest.

But these were people who had delved into the Library, only stopping short of stepping into the Heart itself.

"Sila—" Mercias reaches out to me and I grab his arm, my long nails digging into his skin.

"I need to return to my rooms, *now*."

Mercias makes a very pretty picture in his alarm. A bell begins to ring through the Library's halls.

"*No*," he says, surely thinking of his own lover.

I turn and I run and as soon as I am able to reasonably do so, I shift into the shadows. I slide through all the dark spaces back to my room, hoping I have not made a terrible mistake.

Chapter 36

Lorel

I hadn't ever thought I would see the inside of the Keep again. It is another world, with its austere walls carved into regimented blocks, its plain wood doors, and the tall imposing ceilings. All the ornamentation is saved for the Dawn King's palace that sits above, bloated with all the gold and beauty it denies everything below.

I don't catch any of the words that pass between my captors, but I can tell that we are ascending. That worries me. To be in the Keep is bad enough— to end up in the palace would be a nightmare.

My captors turn off to take me into a plain, unmarked room, and relief sweeps through me. I do not wish to come to anyone's attention here, least of all the Dawn King's.

I'm dumped unceremoniously on the floor, and I hit it hard, still tangled in the sheet. With the sedation still in effect, all I can do is lie there and stare at the sigil hearth. No dull, insipid lights here. Only the best and brightest will do.

The Dawn King only knows why they've dragged me back here.

There are footsteps across the stones, the sound of the door reopening and then closing again.

A chair is dragged over with a screech, and someone drags me up and sets me in it, draping the bed sheet over me. Beryl appears in my line of sight. I get a good look at the markings on her coat, and I realise she is not just a Light-keeper, but part of the Dawn King's inner circle. One of his dreaded Lightwardens. They had protected me once— until they hadn't. I don't expect any mercy from this one.

Beryl's mouth makes the shape of a smile. It does nothing to soften her face and does everything to make her resemble the creature from the dark room in the labyrinth. She kneels in front of the chair and takes my hand, looking at it with mock regret.

"Now," she says. "I'm going to give you back control of your limbs, and you're going to wash and dress. The Dawn King wishes to see you, and I'll not allow you to go dressed in little more than a bedsheet."

I take a moment to get enough control of my tongue to reply. "I'd rather go naked," I say. It comes out a little mumbled.

Beryl grimaces. "You seem to be under the impression that I was asking for your preference. I was not, so let me make myself clear," she says. "You were a scribe, were you not?"

I don't much like her use of past tense. I am still a scribe. I belong to the Library. Not to these dusty archaic halls.

"I imagine your hands are rather important to you, then."

Fear grips my chest. *No.* Beryl takes my little finger with one hand. I have no control over my body and no means to resist what is about to happen, but I still try to pull my hand away.

Perhaps it is a blessing that the sedation remains in effect, because it means it doesn't hurt quite so much when she snaps my little finger up and back. I let out a strangled cry, my eyes watering. Beryl smiles up at me, still holding my hand. This time the smile is sincere, and it is clear there is nothing she would like better than to break every one of my fingers. I tremble, the pain and shock of it sinking through me.

"Do I make myself clear?" Beryl asks.

The thought of not being able to paint, or write, or sink my fingers into Sila's thighs is enough to convince me that this is not a fight worth fighting.

"Yes," I manage. It's barely more than a whisper.

"Good," says Beryl as she rises. "Jareth, set the finger, but don't heal it. I expect our visitor could use the reminder of what she has to lose if she decides to misbehave again." She leans in over the chair and lowers her voice. "Your sister may have the Dawn King's protection for now, but how long will that last, I wonder? Be a good girl now, hm?" Beryl pats my cheek sharply, and the weightless feeling in my limbs bleeds away.

My slow, foggy thoughts clear, and then the man, Jareth, is grabbing my broken finger, and I can hardly think at all.

I'm left alone after that, with nothing but the throbbing pain in my finger and my bed sheet for comfort. At least it still carries Sila's perfume. I bury my head in it and breathe it in. Sila will come for me, only now I hope she won't. I'm not sure she can stand against the Dawn King, but for me, I know she will try.

The curse stirs in my chest. It feels feeble, and a little

dazed, like it's in sympathy with everything that has happened since the Lightkeepers broke into Sila's rooms. Under everything, the dark coal-black mark on my chest is burning. Time is running out for both of us.

There is a knock at the door, which seems absurd, and then the door opens and the quiet of the chamber is being turned upside down. It's as if I had never left the Keep, the chaos that floods in exactly as I remember it. A woman marches in, followed by two men carrying a bath. Another woman carries a fashionable dress, two more carry cases of accessories and shoes, and another man has a case that suggests he's going to try and do something to my hair and face. Overseeing them all is Inetta. My sister's handmaiden, and a force of nature who does not ever back down from a challenge.

She takes one look at me and proclaims, "No, this won't do at all." She claps her palms together. "Stand."

I do, the sheet huddled around my shoulders. I remember this part of life here— this ritual of dressing. An army of people, all existing only to dress courtiers up like dolls for their roles in the Dawn King's circus of a court. Orielle had always thrived in this place. I had withered.

"No, don't hang onto the sheet like that." Inetta swats at my hands, and I wince, dropping the sheet to the ground. She grabs my hand roughly, but not unkindly. "Beryl," she hisses. "The nerve of her to think she can lay a hand on a Dawnchild."

I shrink back from the title and the way it settles sickly in my stomach. It has been a decade or more since anyone has called me such a thing. Since I had thought of myself as such. I'd been naïve to think I could be free of it.

Inetta holds my hand gently between hers, and the pain eases. "There now. Let's see to all these other scrapes of yours." She does not heal the broken finger completely. It still aches, but perhaps the damage won't be so lasting now. I do not begrudge her the caution in the slightest. Inetta is a clever woman, and she hasn't survived with my sister all these years in the Court without knowing how to play its games.

Inetta heals as many of the cuts and bruises as she can— and there are more than I thought— and while she works, the rest of the envoy prepare the next stage of torment. A water mage fills the bath, a fire mage heats it. The hairdresser sets himself up at an empty table, and the remaining attendants lay out some of the finest clothing I have ever seen. It's all colourful silks and florals, ribbons and pearls, and they are lovely beautiful things, but I prefer my sturdy woollens and my dependable leather boots. As I stare at the beautiful costume laid out for me, I wish I was stronger, that I didn't have to go along with this. Not again.

"Right," says Inetta. "Into the bath."

I allow myself to be ushered across the room and submerged under the water. Inetta and another woman take no time in starting to scrub me.

"Really, I'm sure I can—"

"Nonsense, Lola, you are in the Suntide Court now. You do as you are bid," says Inetta, rubbing soap into my hair.

I grit my teeth. Of all the indignities I have suffered today, this is the worst. Being called by my childhood nickname somehow digs in like a thorn. As if it wasn't enough to be dragged from my lover's bed, have my finger broken, and be called a Dawnchild by the same people who had happily called me a foundling and my mother a whore. Now I must also sit and be called Lola, and do as I am told, like a dutiful child.

Because on top of everything else, these are not the people who truly mean me harm. Inetta is as close to an ally as I will ever get in this place. I should just be grateful that, for now, I'm still alive.

Once they have scrubbed me to within an inch of my life, I am pulled from the bath and dried off. I endure the whispers and looks the two women give each other. Inetta has already cleared away Sila's kiss marks, and I'm sure they'll speculate later for their own enjoyment. Fury seethes through me. If I am to die, I would have preferred to be left as I was.

The splint is redone on my finger, which is looking less swollen, though still aching. That ordeal over, they start on the next one. I set my jaw and grind my teeth as they begin to dress me. First a clean shift, then stockings, garters, stays laced comfortably, petticoats, hip padding, all the pieces of the gown pinned into place, jewellery, my short hair puffed up and set, cosmetics applied to my skin so that I look less like a rogue prophecy is draining my life force. And silk slippers to finish it all off. I'm so tired and I haven't even left the room yet.

If the Dawn King had any mercy, he would have skipped the torture before he killed me.

"There, that wasn't so hard now, was it Lola dear?" Inetta places a slim gold band upon my head. "Perfect."

"How do they do this every day?" I ask. I can barely recognise my own face in the mirror.

"How does anyone do anything?" Inetta replies. "Do scribes not sit and copy letters for hours?"

It's not entirely what a scribe does, or at least it isn't all that a scribe does, but I suppose, to another person, it might be tedious. I touch my face lightly as I lean towards the mirror, peering at this strange version of myself. I turn to

Inetta before it overwhelms me. "Take me back to the Library," I say.

Inetta gives me a pitying look. "Lola, darling, they should have never let you go there. You are a Dawnchild, one of the King's own blood. If this is where he wants you, this is where you will stay." She pulls me to her side and lowers her voice and speaks quickly. "Lady Orielle does not know you are here, and if you run, Beryl has been given permission to do what she thinks is necessary to subdue you. I do not know why you have been brought here, but do not think that all of this is for your benefit. If you bring harm to my lady, I will hand you to Beryl myself. Do you understand?"

My blood turns to ice, and I hide my trembling hands in my skirts.

"Yes," I say.

Inetta's voice returns to its usual cheerful tone. "You have always been such a sweet girl, Lola. I am sure the Dawn King will find no fault in you."

Chapter 37

Lorel

IN THE HALLWAY, LIGHTWARDEN BERYL STANDS WITH three other Lightkeepers, waiting to escort me to the King. Inetta takes her leave without so much as a backwards glance. If this is to go poorly, Inetta can't be seen to be friendly with me. Far easier to make amends later, if required, than to pick the wrong side.

How dare she warn me of bringing harm to Orielle of all people. Orielle has far more to answer for than I do. I would have been content to be forgotten by this place, but she held on to me. She had been there when the poisoning had occurred, she had given them her blood to find me, and now here I am being pulled back into the Keep and the Court's games.

Beryl grabs my arm, dragging me along with her, and my entourage follows. We go up again, and the plain stone walls and dull tapestries give way to marble and gold and painted murals. Here, the King's palace pierces through the mountainside, emerging out into the open air. It is the only part of the Citadel to do so. Where the rest of us exist in darkness, his palace is filled with the filtered light of the outside world. Stepping into the palace has always felt like stepping out onto the open mountainside— dangerous and highly inadvisable.

I am pulled along hallway after hallway, and above, the ceilings are painted with swirling clouds. We pass the closed doorway to the hall of mirrors, and my eyes catch on it for a moment before I am pulled onward. I had walked these hallways so often as a child, in the wake of Orielle's skirts. Even then, the hallways were cold, dead, echoing things and there had been no welcome in them. It is no wonder terror has always come easily to me. I was raised on it.

Finally, Beryl pulls us up short in front of a door with two Lightkeepers posted either side. A gentle chatter comes from inside, and both guards tap their foreheads in a salute. One turns to knock on the door, sharp and loud in the empty hall. The chatter on the other side ceases immediately.

There is a pause, and I can imagine the performance going on inside. It is always the same. The guards will look to the Dawn King, who will give them leave to open the door— or not. It is too much to hope that he might change his mind this time.

The doors open with a whisper and Beryl pushes me into the room. Her footsteps follow behind me, loud in the chamber's silence.

The Dawn King accepts audiences three times a day, first in the morning when he wakes and is dressed, second when he takes his morning meal, and third at the midday meal. I have trespassed on the midday meal. The long room has the same extraordinary scale as the rest of the palace and is occupied by a table set out with the finest of foods. At the far end sits the Dawn King, presiding over his chosen few.

He's a tall man, almost as tall as Sila, his hair once black now bleached white by the centuries. His eyes, a pale blue, intent upon his conversation partner. There are twelve of his chosen at the table. I'm surprised to recognise some of them. It is a table of ghosts from my past. Edrian, who had sat beside me in our history lessons as children, and has grown into a dangerous-looking man. Asther, who had once braided ribbons through my hair for a ball, and now sits at the end of the table in a gown that rivals any that we might have daydreamed of together. Cadence, who had excelled at everything she did and was constantly trying to outpace us all, sitting at the Dawn King's right hand.

One by one, they each turn to look at me. Each trying to hide their confusion, muttering and staring, until the last of them at the King's left turns. Orielle cannot hide her shock, or the way the colour drains from her face. The King watches my sister with a faint air of amusement. I cannot help but see there is an empty chair at the closest end of the table.

Orielle's chair scrapes across the floor as she rises. "What is the meaning of this?" she demands. "Lorel, why have you come here?"

"I haven't come here. I was dragged here," I snap back. "Don't pretend ignorance."

"Pretend ignorance? Lorel, this is the last place I would want to see you," says Orielle.

To her credit, her fear seems genuine. Doubt creeps in, the kind of cold trickle that quickly becomes a drowning flood. Inetta had said she didn't know I was here, but that doesn't mean she hadn't been involved. I clench my fists and wince at the pain of my broken finger.

"The blood mage. He used your blood," I say. It has no conviction to it though. No backbone. The assembled courtiers mutter amongst themselves.

"No," says the Dawn King. Silence falls as he turns his gaze on me. "They used mine."

The world stops. The table turns to stare at the Dawn King now. As well they should, since each and every one of them had called me a foundling. Each one of them had turned their back on me when I had been found to have no magic.

I was happier when they thought of me like that. My desire to be in the same room as any of them is non-existent.

"Come, child of my blood. Won't you dine with us?" the Dawn King says, motioning to the empty chair. Beryl behind me makes a bored sound and shoves me forward. I stumble, unwilling to walk into the trap the Dawn King is setting for me. It's hard to breathe and my chest is on fire. As if something is trying to tear its way out.

I stumble into the end of the table, gripping at my chest — my throat— and know this is no usual panic. I know this feeling. Remember it. I grab for the edge of the table to hold myself upright, pulling at the tablecloth. This time, I can barely feel the pain in my hand as I clench the fabric tightly.

The curse is stirring, furious and angry, and my body is no longer my own. Finally, I give it over to the curse. I cannot hold it back. Something else looks through me, looks at the Dawn King, who is suddenly sharp and attentive.

The words fall from my tongue in a strange voice. Each word burns through me as it is spoken. I can no longer see my sister, or the room, just the King's pale blue eyes.

"Shadows cling to gilded lies.

Five stars fall from shadowed grace.
Through death's dark gate, a path unwinds.
To rend the veil of blood and bone.
A crown of dust, an empty throne."

And then I am suddenly and entirely empty. My ears ring, and I feel hollowed out. No one moves as I cling to the table, breathing heavily. I look down and thin, bright red blood drips from my nose, staining the soft blue fabric of the table-cloth. I taste it on my tongue. It's the only warning I get before my body heaves and blood pours from my mouth and nose, bleeding across the end of the table. Asther, the nearest to me, leans away. The weight in my chest is gone. It had once felt like unyielding dread, and then had come to feel like comfort— and now, I was startlingly, terrifyingly, alone.

I wipe my mouth on the back of my hand. It comes away bloody.

The Dawn King stands from his place at the head of the table and the silence of the room is heavy as a shroud. It is broken by the sound of his clapping. Despite his slow, mocking applause, dark anger burns in his eyes. His courtiers are unsettled, shifting in their seats and trying not to look at me or him.

Orielle sits down, hard. She looks as bloodless as I feel. She stares at nothing as if for once in her life, she'd prefer the quiet of the scriptorium.

"Oh, well done," the Dawn King says. "These are the tidings you bring to my court? Then come, my child. Sit at my table." He motions me forward once again.

Beryl comes up behind me and grabs my arm. "You heard the King," she hisses, shoving me down into the chair.

I go without a fight. My throat is dry and raw. I wet my lips and taste blood still.

The King sits, turning his attention back to Cadence and drawing her into conversation, as if nothing had happened. Orielle is staring at me, one ghost to another. The other courtiers begin to laugh and chatter again. It is as if I had merely performed a parlour trick. Something to be remarked upon in the same way as an acrobat or a musician. It doesn't feel quite real, sitting here, but it never has.

My blood seeps down the tablecloth until it drips to the floor. It pools on the plate in front of me, like some kind of macabre garnish. I might as well be dining at the sacrificial altar itself. I clench my hands in my skirts, ignoring the pain in my finger. A spot of blood falls into my lap, slowly followed by another. Perhaps at least my bleeding nose is slowing. I'm light headed, nothing but a phantom sitting at the end of the table. I feel eyes on me and I meet the Dawn King's cold and ruthless gaze. Whatever he has understood from the words I had spoken, he is afraid. He believes them to be true.

I blink and the look is gone, replaced by the same pleasant and unreadable mask that I have always known. He returns to his meal, laughing at something the courtier to his left has said and I don't know what to make of it. This place has always confused me.

I look down at my hands. The shadows that cling to the gathers of my skirt shift and move, and my breath catches. Another drop of blood drips from my chin into my lap. A moment later, the guards in the hallway scream.

And relief and agony sweeps through me all at once, because she has come for me.

Chapter 38

Lorel

I TWIST IN MY CHAIR, TURNING TO SEE. IT ISN'T horror I feel as the shadows stretch, reaching out to wrap around the guards stationed by the door. They don't have a chance to take a step back. Don't have a moment to know that the danger is upon them. Darkness bleeds across the doors like a misplaced ink blot and the guards shout, trying to twist out of the silky shadows that hold them fast. And then they can't scream because the shadow is in their throats, dragging them, shuddering and flailing, into the growing darkness.

For a moment, all is silent. Then next to me, Asther screams. In an instant, the most powerful mages in the Suntide Court are scrambling, making an awful noise as they try to escape through the back of the chamber. A loyal few stay, Cadence and Edrian among them. At the head of the table, Orielle is staring at me. Nothing that has happened yet has helped her to regain the colour in her face.

"Lorel!"

She pushes out of her chair. The Dawn King moves, as

quick as light, to grab her arm, holding her fast. His expression is smug, eager even.

"I will deal with this," he says to her. "Sit, child. And do not move." He rises, releasing Orielle, and stalks towards me. I stumble up from my chair. I need to run. If I can get to Sila, then we can leave— I hit a solid body standing behind me. Beryl.

"Hold her," he calls to the Lightwarden. "You two, stop the wraith." Cadence and another courtier follow the King as Beryl grabs me, dragging me back against her.

"What did I say about being good?" says Beryl, grabbing my hand and putting pressure on my broken finger. She tries to get purchase to break another finger.

The shadows are pooling now, spreading across the wall. Consuming it. A figure forms in the shadows, far taller and more horrific than I have ever seen her. I struggle against the Lightwarden's implacable grip, as she puts pressure on my fingers, pushing them in a direction my fingers should never go. I stamp on her foot, and attempt to kick out at her, but my skirts get in the way.

Cadence and the courtier pass us. They hardly spare me a glance. I'm reminded of Jaime in the Library. At the beginning, when he thought he was going to make it out alive. Arrogant fools, the lot of them.

"Let. Me. Go." I twist in Beryl's grasp, try to find anywhere for my nails to get purchase.

"Fuck, you're like a feral cat," she snarls.

"Good," I hiss, teeth grit against the pain. There's that same numbing sensation as earlier, and then my limbs go limp again and I collapse against her.

"There's a good girl," Beryl says, patting my cheek. I bare my teeth at her as she turns to the Dawn King. He stands between us and darkness, watching two of his favoured mages go to their death.

The shadows reach out and Sila stalks out from the darkness, a beautiful, horrific spectre. She creates a jagged, vaguely human shaped void in the light-filled dining room. This is not Sila the Librarian anymore. This is Sila, the wraith.

Her long, talon-like nails click as she stands before us all. She is a constantly shifting shadow drenched in blood. It drips from her eyes, her mouth, her hands, and coats the floor with each step she takes. Her limbs are stretched out like a shadow before a lantern. Her pale face is a blur of moonlight pierced by black, jewel-bright eyes. The two courtiers hesitate, no longer grinning.

Sila doesn't give them a chance to even consider their options. Her shadows stretch out, ensnaring them. The two cry out, casting formless, frantic spells at her. The shadows drag them to the ground, cutting through them, crushing them. Leaving them gasping as they choke on their own blood. Sila steps over them and it is so much like that first time in the scriptorium that my heart feels like it is screaming within me. To think she had been nearly a stranger then. She stands before the Dawn King, and in this form she towers over him.

"Ah," says the Dawn King, sounding pleased. "One of hers." He throws a look over his shoulder at me, smirking. "You know, I waited so patiently to have you done away with. There's so many ways to die in the Library, and yet you kept evading my attempts. It surprised me that you were so resourceful, but this makes far more sense. You had help. After all, you were never particularly useful on your own, were you, Lorel?"

"You—" says Orielle, coming to a stop beside Beryl.

"Ah Orielle. Still poor at taking directions, I see. No matter."

It is the way he says 'no matter' that has me finally understanding.

There is nothing the Dawn King does without reason. Everything he does is to maintain his control of the Citadel and its people. Right down to allowing them to bathe and dress him each and every morning. He doesn't collect up the most powerful mages to use them, he collects them to keep them docile. Turns them into pampered creatures that depend upon him for their comfort. Keeps them snapping at each other, to prevent them from snapping at him. Keeps them loyal, keeps them expendable. And to the Dawn King, this entire room is expendable. The perfect audience that will never talk of what I have spoken.

"You, hold her," says the Dawn King to Edrian. Edrian grabs Orielle and Orielle doesn't resist. She goes as still and quiet as a cavern lake, the kind that will swallow you whole if you step wrong. The clicking of Sila's talons continues in the background, impatient.

"Enough. I believe you have something of mine, Usurper," Sila says. Her voice hisses, echoing through the room like a chorus of hungry ghosts. "I have come to take her back."

"I'm afraid I do not give audiences to the uninvited," the Dawn King says. He claps his hands once and throws his hand forward, palm out. I barely have a moment to understand what he's doing before Sila is engulfed in white fiery light. My breath catches, and I let out a strangled cry. It is the best I can manage under Beryl's sedation.

I can't do anything to stop this. I think of Jaime's sanctified blade digging into her side. Feel sick to my stomach at the thought of her falling to the ground. How does my lovely creature of darkness survive this kind of onslaught?

The light holds, burning bright enough to force me to tip my head away. The heat of it presses against my cheek, and then, in the corner of my eye, I see a tendril of shadow flick through the wall of light. It pushes through the crack it makes and is followed by another. And then more. A tendril whips out towards the Dawn King and he ducks with a laugh, hunger written all over his face. The shadows smother the light and Sila stands unharmed amongst them and I think perhaps the night can win out against the day. Sila is in her full power. She may not have her queen's blessings, but she has the Library's Heart.

And the Dawn King is waning. That's why there was night cough in the Citadel. He was using it to encourage the Citadel to sacrifice its own people.

The Dawn King laughs. "Oh, you are old, aren't you? Tell me, when did I send you to the queen, wraith? I would dearly love to know," he says. He follows the question with a strike of light, called down upon Sila's figure. She flickers in shadow, evading him easily.

"If you cannot remember my name, then I will not be reminding you," she says. She throws herself forward, shadows surging. The Dawn King calls up a wall of shimmering light and the shadows batter themselves on it and roll back and away. "Give me what is mine." She throws herself against the wall of light again and I can see it flickering under her assault. It will not hold against her.

Beside me, Edrian screams and I glance at Orielle. She holds her hand over his eyes as light radiates from her palm, burning at his skin and adding the smell of burned flesh to the copper-soaked blood scent of the room. Edrian lets her free, and she kicks him viciously in the knee, sending him to the ground. The Dawn King ignores them both, instead looking over his shoulder at me.

"The girl? No, I don't think I will. Though you will be far more useful to me than your predecessor," he says, and this time when he waves a hand, a ring lights up across the floor. Light blue, like the doorway to the Heart of the Library. The light snakes in on itself, and Sila hisses as it ensnares her, the light snaking over her limbs and binding her in place. The trappings try to pull her to the ground and her snarls echo throughout the chamber.

"Lightwarden, secure the wraith," he says.

The Lightwarden strides towards Sila. Sila, who is pushing up against her restraints, snarling and clawing at them where they dig into her flesh.

Despite the sedative effect, my heart is racing. I can't let him take her, but I can't move. I can barely hold myself up. Beryl pushes me towards Orielle, who catches me. She clings to me as the Dawn King turns back to us, ignoring the courtiers cowering under the table behind us. The back doors, it seems, were locked.

"Now, what do I do with two unruly children?" he says mildly. "It really is a pity your personality is so defiant, Orielle, since you show such talent otherwise." He frowns at Edrian lying screaming on the ground. "Oh do shut up." He marks a swift line through the air and a shard of light pierces Edrian's heart. He gasps, his face constricting before it relaxes into death.

Orielle grips my arms, and there is a faint tingle of her magic against my skin. The sedative effect drains away from me, slowly giving me back control of my limbs and tongue.

"Let my sister go back to the Library," says Orielle. "Like you promised. And I'll stay here, like I promised."

"Orielle?" I get my feet under me, and Orielle doesn't

let go. So there *had* been more to my freedom than a simple rumour about my parentage. I had thought so, but I also hadn't ever considered that Orielle might have had the ability, or the courage, to bargain with the Dawn King.

"I could, I suppose, but I rather find I don't feel like it," the Dawn King says with a pleasant smile. "And why would I?"

He thinks he has won. I flex my fingers as feeling returns to them. I don't know if it will work— the Dawn King is ancient, and his magic equally so. But so was the Heart's, and I had stopped that before. And the Dawn King was not at his full power.

I don't even quite know how to do it, I just know that at both times I had wanted something badly enough to make it happen.

All I can do is try.

I take a deep breath, trying to remember that feeling in the dark chamber when faced with the Heart's horrific beast. I look the Dawn King in the eye and take another deep breath before I spread my fingers wide and push my mind against the current of time in the room. It comes easier than it ever has, flowing out from me, and I am powerless to stop it. Control of it slips through my fingers. There is the faintest, swiftest moment of alarm in his face, and then everything begins to slow and the Dawn King is caught. I hang on to the thought that I cannot let him win. Cling to thoughts of Sila. Promise that I will leave here with her. I leave no room for doubt. If there is one person in this world I do not doubt, it is my terrifying and lovely nightmare of a Librarian.

All the sounds in the room, the screams, and the crying, the hum of the Dawn King's magic, and Beryl's footsteps as she crosses the marble floor, come together as one high pitched ringing. It rises higher until everything stills. Even Orielle behind me, caught in the moment.

The blue light of the snare holding Sila flickers.

Once.

Twice.

And then out.

Everything is plunged into darkness.

The Lightwarden screams.

Chapter 39

Lorel

I LET GO OF THE SILENCE AND THE DARK SMOTHERS ME. I reach for Orielle in the dark, for where she had been behind me and fear grips my chest. I do not know if my lover will make much distinction between friend and foe. The screams start behind me, a horrific choir, each voice choked off one by one. Gasping and flailing. There is the sound of things— bodies— hitting the table, pushing chairs as they fall. Cutlery clattering to the floor.

"Orielle—" I stumble in the dark, reaching.

"Lorel—" Orielle's hand finds mine, and then it's slipping away.

I trip on something soft and warm. Edrian. I push myself away from him.

The shadows shift and they are solid, physical things as they come around me. They pull me back further, sliding across the floor. They shift and shape themselves like a creature hunched over its prize. There are the sounds of a scuffle. Whatever Sila is doing, she cannot make purchase on the Dawn King. Perhaps if I had held the silencing longer— but no, I can already feel the rising fever under my skin. There is a very real risk I might lose consciousness.

"Enough," says the Dawn King, sharp.

Orielle cries out as a sudden light flares. It sears at my eyes and forces me to turn my head away or risk being blinded. The light glances off Sila's horrific visage, the shape of her where she crouches over me. It reflects off the blood and her long sharp teeth, illuminates her strange pale face, and glittering dark eyes. Reveals the remains of the body of Beryl, strewn across the floor where Sila had left her.

She shifts, her long talons clicking against the marble. Everything is still in the room. The King's courtiers lie in various states over the table, blood soaking into the linen, dyeing it red. The Dawn King's light shines in their dull, dead stares. There is only me, and Sila, Orielle, and the Dawn King.

As the intensity of the light fades, the King stands there, glowing faintly. Orielle is hiding her face in her free arm, grimacing against the light. Orielle's wrist is caught in his hand, and twisted cruelly. She is powerless— the Dawn King is the one person Orielle's own light and magic cannot work against.

I cry out to her, and Sila shifts, putting herself— or part of herself— between us. The Dawn King looks at Sila and for a long, quiet moment, nothing happens.

"Prisilla," says the Dawn King. There is something ancient in his voice. A knowing that is older than I can fathom. "That's it, isn't it? You were as eager to die then as you are now." He tips his chin up, looking between us. "Though it seems you have something to live for now. How interesting."

"Spare me your thoughts, Usurper. I do not care," hisses Sila. "I'll be taking what is mine now."

"Orielle—" I start, trying to push myself up. That familiar burning feeling is settling in now, like my body has become a flame. I can feel it darkening the edges of my consciousness. Weighing down my limbs and making it hard to move. I taste blood, fresh on my tongue, still dripping from my nose.

"This Dawnchild stays with me," the Dawn King says. "As she promised."

No. I can't leave her here. Not now. I rage against my body as it tries to drag me under. Urges me to rest. To quiet. I feel as if I am drowning.

"Go," Orielle says, pleading. She isn't looking at me when she speaks. Her eyes are locked instead on Sila's face somewhere above me. "Take her and get her out of here. Please."

"Yes," the Dawn King says. "Go now, fallen one. Let us see what havoc you wreak."

Sila snarls. She doesn't wait to be told again.

"No, Orielle—" I think I try to reach for her, I don't know anymore. I can't feel my fingers.

"I love you. Always," Orielle calls as Sila's shadows come around me.

Her arms are firm and solid and real as they hold me. I jam my eyes and mouth shut as Sila drags me into the shadows and away from the Dawn King's marble palace.

Chapter 40

Lorel

THE DARKNESS RECEDES, AND I GASP FOR AIR. I AM kneeling on the floor. Sila— or some semblance of her— holds me close. My lungs are burning, my skin is burning. It feels like my head is on fire.

"Sila—" my voice scratches over my scoured throat.

"Lorel, I am so sorry," Sila says. She's pulled me against her body, as cold and soothing as it ever is, as she's returned to a more familiar shape. She's covered in blood and the Dawn King only knows what else, but I press my face into her shoulder anyway. Cling to her, because everything is all too much and now there are tears burning at the back of my throat and trying to spill from my eyes. We have left Orielle behind.

Sila's arms feel the right size again, as they hold me. Her hands are soothing as she strokes my hair. Everything hurts. Aches. My sister had not betrayed me at all. She hadn't even known. And I had left her with the fae king who had tried to kill me. It hurts. Everything hurts, but never Sila. Never her.

I dig my fingers into her bloody blouse. "I knew you would come," I whisper.

Sila lowers her face to my ear, pressing her cheek to my temple. "I will always come. Never doubt that, little mouse," she says. "Even if it is only to go into death with you."

I bury my face in her, try to dig my fingers into her flesh. I want to crawl under her skin and curl up around her heart. Without her, I would be dead, just another body lying across the Dawn King's marble floor. Without her, I would still be nothing more than a ghost trying to convince myself that I was content. Trying to convince myself that it was enough.

I don't know where we go from here, but I know we do it together. And if she starts to fade, or the Library's tether fails, then I will find a way to keep her, even if I have to bind her to my own self.

Sila rubs her fingers soothingly along my jaw. She tips my head back to look at me.

"You are bleeding," she says, touching my lips softly with her fingertips. Outside the safety of her darkness, the world tips a little.

"Oh," I say. "I'd forgotten."

I look down at my chest with its ribbons and silk and try to tear at it, but my arms are weak and I cannot make any headway. My broken finger throbs.

"It's gone," I mumble. "The prophecy. I spoke it."

I want to check my skin, but no matter how much I tug, the pins that hold my gown in place resist me. Sila lays her hands on mine, stilling them. I look up then and realise we are in the infirmary, in one of the private rooms. The door is open and light spills in. There is the gentle sound of coughing and shifting bodies. Sila turns my hand over, her fingers gentle over my bandaged little finger. Sila's eyes are very dark. Dangerous.

"Who dared touch you?" she says, battling to keep her tone even.

"It doesn't matter," I sigh.

"Of course it matters," she says, and there is that echo in her voice again.

"They're already dead. What more can you do to them?"

"Make sure no one ever finds their body," she replies.

I reach up to cup her cheek. "I don't think there is any chance of that," I reply. "There wasn't much left of her." I stretch to press a kiss to her bloody mouth.

"Good," Sila says against my lips.

"I think I'm going to pass out," I murmur. The room spins and darkens.

"Lorel—"

She catches me as I tip backwards and my body jerks to a stop before it can hit the ground. The flow of light from the open door behind us is blocked.

"Librarian Sila?" Lune says with alarm. "Oh thank the King, you have her."

Everything seems a little fuzzy, a little faint. I'm glad Lune is here. I can't remember why, though.

"Cupbearer, her nose is bleeding," Sila says quickly. "And she has a fever."

There are footsteps and then there is the faint, familiar tingle of Lune's magic at my temples. I try to blink the dark spots from my eyes, to tell them I'm fine. It's enough to make one laugh because Dawn King strike me, I am not fine at all.

"Cupbearer," Sila growls.

"Hold her still, please," snaps Lune. "Ah, there it— *fuck*

—" Lune cuts off with a range of colourful expletives. "Why couldn't I see this before?"

"She was cursed," Sila says. "It was not visible."

"But you saw it, didn't you?"

"Of course, but I am a curse too, am I not?" Sila replies.

"Sure as hell seems like it," mutters Lune. "For what it's worth, I blame you."

Sila sighs in response.

"And the curse is broken?" Lune asks through clenched teeth.

"Yes, and she can speak again."

"Good, maybe she can explain herself, then," says Lune.

I don't quite know what Lune is doing, or what she is seeing, but I suppose if there has been something feeding off me— off any residue of magic or life— that it might cause some damage. Somewhere. I can hardly bring myself to care. All I want to do is sleep.

"Not yet, little mouse," Sila says. "We are not safe yet."

I can feel Lune's magic inside my chest, and the chilled way it settles into my skull, under the skin. It feels as if parts of me are being pulled back together and patched up.

I groan. All my limbs are so heavy. It hurts. Everything hurts.

"Don't fight me, Lorel, please," Lune says through gritted teeth.

My breath comes quickly through my nose as my body's instincts to push her out kick in. Pain sears up from my chest through to my nose. I gasp. I hold my breath, trying with everything I have not to fight her. A cry bursts from my lips and Sila's fingers dig into the soft skin of my arms.

There is a tickle in the back of my nose. Lune breaks her connection to me with a shout and I sneeze without warning. Sila holds me up while I cough up a thick, dark liquid.

"There," Lune says, triumphant. Her hand rubs my back. "I think I've got it. Whatever it was. I can't do much about the fever, though. I've tried to ease it."

Sila's fingers comb through my hair, firm and grounding. "Thank you, Cupbearer," she says.

"Of course. She's my friend, too," says Lune. "I'm hardly going to let her die on me if I can help it. What happened?"

"The Dawn King," says Sila darkly. "He let us go, but I do not know how long his mercy will hold."

"Fuck," Lune says. There is a hand combing through my hair. Lune's, soft. "We need to get her out of here."

"Sila." My voice is hoarse as I try to lift my head. It's clearing. It doesn't feel quite so heavy. Sila pulls me to her and I melt against her. Perhaps I can just stay here forever.

"Have you had word from your contact?" Sila asks Lune.

"Yes," comes another voice and I think I must be going mad. "He'll be ready and waiting for you at the fourth hour."

Mercias is in the doorway, watching us carefully.

Lune moves away. "Thank you, Mercias," she says.

My eyes are clearing and I shift my head so that I can see them both properly, my cheek pressed to Sila's chest.

Lune is giving me a perplexed look. "That's not much time. We need to find you something sensible to wear," Lune says.

"Can I not get something from my room?" I mumble.

"I do not think you are in any condition for me to shadow walk you, little mouse, and I will not leave you alone again. Not for a minute," says Sila.

"I'll find something," Lune says, slipping from the room.

That's good, I like that. It means I don't have to go anywhere. The longer I can stay pressed to Sila, and not have to stand, the better.

Mercias steps inside once she's gone. "What happened in the Keep?" he says, keeping his voice low.

"The Dawn King had her," Sila says. "Because she is a Dawnchild."

"Fuck," Mercias says. "Will the Library have any cause for concern then?"

Sila shifts as she shakes her head. "I do not think so. I acted alone, and I think he will be keen to tidy things up now. He knows we will not stay."

Mercias breathes a sigh that is equal parts relief and anxiety. "I've never known the Library without you," he says. "In some respects, I think you are the Library. You are *the* Librarian."

"Do not go getting soft on me now Mercias," Sila says in her haughtiest Librarian voice. She's pleased with his sentiment, though. I can hear it.

Mercias must too, because he huffs a short laugh. "I'll go help the healer," he says. "And you can get that ridiculous thing off the scribe." He looks at me, then. "Good luck to you both." That is all he says before he turns lazily on his heel and leaves.

I tip my head to look at the gown. "Is it so ridiculous?" I ask, tugging again at a ribbon.

Sila gets her arms under me and lifts me as she stands. I cling to her shoulders, her face mere inches from mine.

"It is a lovely glimpse of another Lorel, who deserved so much better," Sila says. "But it is not the Lorel that belongs to me, and that is the one I like best."

She sets me on my feet carefully. I brace myself on her

arms and my legs hold— for now. When she is happy that I won't topple over on her, Sila starts on the pins, collecting them as she peels away the layers of the gown.

"The Lorel that tastes of paper and ink and honey," she says, untying the first layers of petticoats. "The Lorel that gives under my hands, and my thighs, and my tongue."

"Sila—"

She turns me away from her and I expect her to untie the stays next. Instead, I feel her finger slip between my shift and the cord as she runs a sharp talon through it, cutting the stays away from my body.

"The Lorel that fights with her nails, that can bargain with the Heart, that can quell even the Dawn King's magic." Sila presses her lips to my shoulder, bared as she pushes aside the shift. "My Lorel," she sighs.

I twist, reaching for her. Drag her face down to me so that I can kiss her. It leaves me dizzy, but I need to. I have to. "Yours. Always yours," I whisper.

She tastes of blood, and earth, and salt when I kiss her, her cool mouth pressed to mine. Over mine. It is a claiming kind of kiss and I cling to her.

She's so blissfully cool against me. My skin is still feverish, and I have been standing too long. Sila grips me tightly about my waist. I rest my forehead against hers, my fingers wound into the cloth of her blouse.

"I'm afraid of leaving," I whisper, like it's some kind of secret. "Orielle—"

"Made her own choice, little mouse. As I have made mine," Sila says.

"Why are you all so willing to throw yourselves away for me?" There is the barest hint of hysteria in it, as my grip tightens painfully. I can't hold it for long with the way exhaustion is trying to take over me. Exhaustion, frustration, fear— all of it is too much for me to bear at this moment.

"You know why," Sila says, gently taking my hands. "Because you are loved, Lorel, and I hope one day you will understand that you are worthy of it."

I open my mouth to protest, though I've no idea what words I intended. They flee my mind entirely as Sila presses a finger to my lips. Her hand drops to pull down my shift, her fingers skating over my skin. It is, I remember, what I had been trying to check in my earlier delirium. I look down where her fingers rest, the soot black mark of the curse is gone but where the dark ember-like centre had been there is a twisted circle of scar tissue marking my flesh. Sila hisses as her fingers pass over it, and then, quite unexpectedly, she laughs. The chamber is suddenly full of the strange, bright sound.

"You still bear the Heart's mark," Sila says. "A memory of it."

I look up at her. "What does that mean?"

"That I will never leave you, Lorel, and that I will always, always come for you," she says. "Remember that."

Chapter 41

Lorel

LUNE RETURNS IN SHORT ORDER WITH AN ASSORTMENT of clothes and a pair of boots to replace my flimsy silk slippers. Most blessedly of all, she has my glasses.

"Sila had them," Lune says. I am redressed in short order, and swaying on my feet by the end of it. It's only thanks to Lune's earlier intervention that I haven't already passed out. Though it's a near thing.

At the last, Lune settles her cloak around my shoulders. I know it's hers because it smells like her— an earthy, herbaceous scent with the underlying hint of alcohol used for distilling.

"Lune, you can't—" I say, looking at her.

"So your tongue does work, then. And don't tell me what to do, Lorel. I can give my friend my cloak," she says, fastening it with a determined set to her face. "I can hope it will keep her safe when she goes beyond where I can see her."

I blink at her slowly. I had thought myself alone in the Library. I had sought to keep myself apart and be as unremarkable as I could be after leaving the Keep. I had certainly not set out to make friends. I had had none in the Keep. I did not think I had any right to expect to make any here. Each time Lune had patched me up, or cared for me, or had come by with tea to check up on me, I had figured she was only doing what was expected of her. I hadn't thought she might actually care for me.

Elris might miss me because it was hard to lose half your team of scribes, and Sybri might miss the extra pair of hands that helped to lighten her workload, but Lune would miss me and my sad attempts at conversation and inability to be compliant.

"I'll miss you too," I mumble, embarrassed and feeling the tips of my ears warm further. I would miss her with her no-nonsense fussing and persistent optimism. I am wrapped suddenly in a tight, alarming hug, Lune's cheek resting against mine.

"I still don't know how I feel about your Librarian, but I'm glad you're not going alone. It'll be dangerous, but at least you'll be beyond his reach," Lune says quietly. Fiercely. "Now, let's get you out of here."

It's late in the infirmary, the light is kept low. The sound of the night cough's victims echo as Lune leads us out. I pause at the entrance to the infirmary, looking back at the bodies lying in their beds.

"Sila," I whisper. She's at my back, close and hovering because neither of us are sure I won't pass out at some point.

"What is it?" she asks.

"How can he do that to his own people?" I ask. A note of pain that cracks through it. My blood pounds in my ears, the echoes of those coughs both real and memory. My parents, ailing. My father, one of the Dawn King's own blood. Dead so that the Dawn King could have his willing human sacrifice.

"Power," Sila says. "All the Dawn King cares about is power."

I look down at my hands, feel the aches and the fever, and wonder what sort of person might ever be able to stop him. I think of my sister, her golden light so like his, still at his side. A treacherous cavern lake, waiting for a misstep. I have left Orielle behind, but perhaps she is exactly where she means to be.

"Will Orielle be alright?" I ask.

Lune finds me in the darkness, squeezing my hand gently. "She has allies here, she's not alone," Lune says. "Come."

"Alright," I say. I slip my hand from hers and turn away, stumbling as I go. It's not as graceful as I had hoped. Sila catches me, because she always catches me.

"Careful," she says. Some part of me knows I'm not making this journey out on my own two feet.

"On the fifth floor, near the fissure. That's where he'll be waiting for you," Lune whispers. "Go with haste and be careful."

We turn away from the passage that would lead us back to the Library and Scriptorium, and my heart aches as we walk the other way.

Lune watches us from the infirmary archway, a benevolent ghost in the dark. The ache in my chest doesn't let up for a moment.

Sila wreaths us in her shadows and it muffles the sound of our boots on the stone. I'm slow, and I'm flagging, sorrow weighing heavy on my heart, fever burning bright, light spots appearing in my vision. I stumble and Sila catches me, again. I think I must have fallen as the world tumbles over itself and I find myself thrown over her shoulder.

"Sila," I hiss.

She keeps walking, picking up that brisk Librarian pace of hers.

"Hush now and indulge me. You will not make it on your own, and I wish to keep you close," she says, keeping her voice low.

When she puts it like that, it's hard to deny her anything. I flop against her, and she pats my thigh. It's entirely the wrong time to think about what else I'd like her to do with my thighs, but I'm exhausted and I don't know when I'll next get the chance to sleep, let alone be able to go to bed with her again. With all my defenses down, I am consumed by heartache. This time it's threaded through with frustration and anguish and I don't have the space for all these emotions. I want to be back in Sila's room, in Sila's bed, not here mourning the loss of it.

"Little mouse?" Sila says, still quiet. We've made our way down several floors, deeper and lower than I have ever had any reason to be before.

"Are we going to the catacombs?" I ask, matching her volume.

"Yes, and through the caves below them, if I am assuming correctly," she replies. There's silence for another floor. Then, "Will you tell me what the prophecy says?"

I right myself, elbows braced on her back, and tell her. Even as an echo, the words feel heavy and metallic on my tongue. The silence returns and I imagine I can hear the sounds of Sila thinking.

"Do you know," Sila says. "That the Gloaming Queen's Court is called the Evenfall."

"The inverse of the dawn," I mumble.

"Yes. In your oldest myth, the people of her court are called stars," says Sila. "Now they are called wraiths, which is the more accurate term."

Now it is the sound of my thoughts ticking over. My breath catches in my throat. "The Dawn King called you 'fallen one'."

"Yes. I suppose he has made that connection," Sila says. "Though he let us go, which concerns me. He was weakened, dangerous, but if I had been less concerned with you. Well."

We fall into thoughtful silence again, something nagging at the edge of my thoughts. Why had the queen wanted me dead, too? It clicks into place.

"I thought it was the Dawn King," I say. "But the Heart said it was for the 'traitor'."

"It could be both, or either. That would explain the queen's interest. And one star has already fallen," Sila whispers.

She stops suddenly and I notice the sound of heavy boots on stone, the soft clink of metal on metal. I twist to look and Sila lets me go so that I can slide to the ground. She pushes me behind her, placing herself between the dark figure in the corridor, pacing menacingly towards us. Sila steps free of the shadows. They'll be of little use here, I think, as the figure steps into the low light of the nearest sigil lanterns and tips their chin up.

"Vika," Sila says.

"Sila, Sila, Sila. What have you been up to?" says Vika, smiling.

Chapter 42

Lorel

Vika is exactly as terrifying to meet in a dark hallway as I expected. Though the corridor is wide and well lit, she makes it seem small and impenetrable.

"It no longer concerns you, Vika," Sila says. "Now step aside."

Vika heaves a theatrical sigh and gives Sila an unapologetic smile. "I'm afraid I can't. I warned you that there would be consequences. And to find you with the very scribe you were tasked to kill? That's treason, and my hands are tied when it comes to traitors."

"They don't look tied," I say, eyeing her warily as I sway on my feet.

"Lorel," hisses Sila in warning.

Vika's eyes flick to me. "Oh, it talks," she says. "Don't worry, I can succeed where you have failed—"

"If you so much as touch a hair on her head, Vika, you will wish you never knew what it was like to breathe when I'm done with you," says Sila, voice low and dangerous. "Now stand down." Sila has grown taller and darker. Less distinct around the edges.

"You no longer have the queen's blessing, Sila. You can't hope to walk away from this," Vika says, rolling her shoulders.

"I do not need it," hisses Sila. It echoes around us, and even Vika pauses. Then she smirks.

"I do like it when I bring out the worst in you," Vika says, stepping forward. Tiny shards of darkness swarm around her, pieces of black broken glass that catch the lantern light and clink against each other. Her eyes go pitch black like Sila's, from edge to edge, and that same thick, dark blood bleeds from her eyes. All the sharp, handsome planes of her face become lethal enough that if you hit her with your bare hand, you'd lose fingers and be grateful that it wasn't worse. She curls her fingers into a fist and the dark shards embed themselves in her knuckles and shoulders, cutting through the metal and leather of her gauntlets. Pierce through her armour down her spine. She grins.

Sila's shadows come around me, pulling me out of the way of the fight and anchoring me in place as Vika rushes in. Sila moves like smoke, dancing around Vika as Vika strikes out at her. Each time Vika makes a move towards me, Sila surrounds her, or takes the force of Vika's strike with her body, as reckless as the last time I'd seen her fight. Only this time she is alone, and the Lightkeeper had nothing on the vicious, determined mass of muscle that is Vika. Vika grins manically with each dodge and hit as if she has been longing for this fight for a long time.

Sila's long talons strike and glance off Vika's mirror-like shadows, and Vika's fists fail to make purchase as the two move in some grotesque imitation of a court dance. I sag against the wall and Sila's shadows. I cannot do anything here, not in this condition. Just like the last time, all I can do is watch, fever-riddled and barely on the edge of consciousness. Somewhere in the swirl of shadow and darkness, Vika laughs and Sila snarls as Vika is hurled backwards down the hallway.

Sila's monstrous figure stands alert between Vika and I. Vika sits up, wiping blood from her face and smiling widely.

"Finally," Vika says. "A proper fight."

"You are wasting my time," Sila snarls. Vika hauls herself up from the ground.

"Orders are orders," Vika says.

"Fuck your orders," Sila replies.

"No, I think you already did that," Vika says with a laugh. She throws herself forward again.

Sila rises to meet her and Vika dodges, surges, and dodges again. Her sharp eyes are locked on me as she throws herself at Sila, and Sila takes the full force of the blow to her shoulder with a crunch of metal and bone. She grinds her fist in cruelly as she stares at me and Sila pushes back against her. If Vika hit anyone else like that, they wouldn't exist anymore.

Vika grins and pulls her fist back, and this time she sends a shard of shadowy glass at me. I shriek in my panic. Sila's shadows pull me aside as the shard embeds itself in the stone where my head had been.

As if struck, Sila and Vika flinch away from each other in eerie unison. Sila's talons retract as she grasps at her temples. Her shadows flicker and thrash as if in agony.

Vika winces, falling back and making a wretched attempt to shake off an unseen foe. As if the shard had lodged in *her* head — sharp and high-pitched.

"Sila," I gasp. I can feel something weighing on me. Draining me. There is a darkness at the edge of my vision that has nothing to do with Sila's shadows.

"Little mouse," Sila grinds out. "Whatever it is you're doing, *ah*—"

She flinches again and Vika falls to one knee, gripping her head, teeth gnashing, choking back a noise wrenched from deep within her.

"No—" My voice is brittle and sharp. "I'm not—" Surely this isn't my doing. I can't sto—

Chapter 43

Sila

LOREL'S SMALL FORM CRUMPLES AS SHE LOSES consciousness, drained from the magic she has cast. My shadows catch and hold her and the sharp, mind-searing pain that had been lancing through my skull ceases. Vika gasps as it releases her, too. She doesn't stand yet, her breathing coming rough and harsh as she pants. The glittering shards of her shadows move like embers, dark sparks bleeding away from her form and fading in a constant rhythm.

"What the fuck was that, Sila?" she snarls.

I grin at her, wide and sharp-toothed. "Struggling to handle a little pain, Vika?" I need her to stop thinking about my scribe. "Get up, or get out of the way."

"You're not leaving here, not with her alive," Vika says. She spits to the side. Blood coats her teeth as she snarls at me and surges up from the ground. She throws her fist at me again, trying to force me to step around and away from Lorel. I block her and the sharp shadow shards sink into my skin.

"How sweet that you would let me live when I have

betrayed our queen," I hiss. Blood splatters her face and it hardly makes a difference.

"She's not your queen any longer, Sila," Vika says, twisting her knuckles cruelly.

I laugh without mirth. "No, I suppose not." My shadows lash out, grappling Vika, and she twists and slips from them, ducking back before she comes at me— at Lorel — again. "Always so persistent, but you never learn, do you?" Vika breathes heavily, rolling her shoulders. Her shards cut away at my shadows, where they try to push her back.

"You know," she says, spitting blood from her mouth again. "I never expected to see you fade."

"You won't," I tell her.

"No?"

"No."

Vika stares at me, the sound of our uneven breathing bouncing off the walls, my half-hearted attempts to annoy Vika with my shadows constantly cut off by glittering shards. I wait, standing firmly between her and Lorel's prone form. If there is one thing that is always true, it is that Vika's patience is shorter than a breath.

"You're always so fucking sanctimonious," she snaps, darting forwards. She dodges my talons easily, shreds my shadows as I push her back again.

"Always so brash." Vika tries to sweep at my legs, and my shadows react in kind. She tries to grab me around the waist to unbalance me, and I slip from her grasp. She lets out a frustrated growl and returns to her favourite technique — trying to beat me into submission.

I take each hit as she intends, and hold my ground, striking back whenever the opportunity presents itself.

"Losing your temper, Vika?"

"Just give her up. How can she possibly be worth giving up your queen and betraying us all?"

"There it is," I say, kicking her in the stomach. She falls back again for a moment of respite. Her shoulders heave with her frustration and anger. Her hurt. "I haven't betrayed you, Vika."

"You have! You—"

"I do not wish to kill you, Vika. Were we not friends?" I ask, soft in the face of Vika's rage.

Her eyes flicker, looking behind me to Lorel. Her face is cold with fury.

"You would invoke that word, now, would you? To save your skin."

"If I wanted you dead, you would be."

"You're full of shit, Sila," Vika snarls.

She moves again, darting across the space at me. And fine, I am tired of holding back. Shadows surge and curl around her. Vika shifts and dodges. She cuts at me with her shards and I lunge, withdrawing my talons as I grab her by the throat, digging my nails into the skin. This time, *I* snarl.

"Let us go, or I will put my talons through your throat and tear out your heart."

"Are you sure you're willing to risk that?" Vika says, grinning. Battle rage colours her features manic. The soft, gentle sound of metal shards echoes behind me. It would almost be a pretty sound, only it fills me with dread. I glance over my shoulder, to where Lorel is kept up by my shadows. All I can do is grip her tighter to prevent her from slumping into the choker of razor-sharp shards threatening her life.

"I could have them cut her thr—"

I tighten my grip on her throat, drawing blood. Fear, sharp and cold, grips my insides. "I do not want to kill you, Vika, but if you harm her, you will not survive what I will do to you. And trust me, my dearest, oldest friend, when I tell you that there is no one who knows your fears as well as I do. No one else who can make sure each and every one comes true," I whisper, leaning in closer. "We were friends once, and mutual destruction is not what I want for you."

Vika's grin fades. "She's just a scribe. She's *nothing*, Sila."

"She is mine," I hiss, feeling it in my bones and the shadows that envelop us. Vika flinches. "Now call them off. I do not wish to kill you."

"You have more to lose than I do," Vika snarls. We stay locked together, Vika breathing heavily, my nails sinking in a little more each time her body shifts.

"I do," I say, trying to keep as still as possible. I know her shards can react as quickly as my talons. I have faced down a King today for Lorel, kept her alive through multiple attempts to kill her. I can only hope now that whatever camaraderie Vika and I shared, it will be enough to let us all walk away from here.

Vika's face twitches as if whatever she's thinking is causing her pain.

"Fine," she hisses.

All her shadows melt away from her, and another quick look behind me shows they're gone from Lorel's throat. I let her go and she stumbles back, straightening sharply. The whites of her eyes are no longer black, though that same dark thick blood we share drips languidly from her fists. Her's or mine, I could not say.

"We were friends, once. So go, and know that if we meet again, there's no walking away."

"Thank you." I let my own shadows fall away, until I am little more than a weary woman. My shadows lower Lorel to the floor gently.

Vika watches her still, eyes sharp. Closed off. "Go," she says, setting her jaw. "Before I change my mind."

I collect Lorel from where she lies, her face soft in repose with dark shadows under her eyes. A phantom memory of that sharp, mind-rending pain slices through my thoughts. Her magic carries a heavy cost. I can already feel the heat of her fever rising under her skin as I hold her close.

This magic is going to tear her apart if we do not get it under control.

Vika hasn't moved yet. She stands as still as a sentinel, jaw clenched and staring down the hall. I cradle Lorel close and grimace as my blood stains her clean clothing.

"Goodbye, Vika," I say softly.

For a long while after I pass her, it is only my footsteps that echo down the hall.

I breathe a sigh of relief because Vika will not see me fade, and for that I am grateful.

Chapter 44

Lorel

I wake with my head resting against Sila's shoulder. Whatever happened back there has drained me further again. I do not think there is much left to lose. My limbs are shaking and in all the places where I am pressed against Sila, her skin is as cold as the marble of the Dawn King's halls in winter. Vika and the bloody hallway are long gone. There are cuts raked down Sila's face, slowly closing even as I watch.

"Sila?" I ask, shifting.

"Not much further, little mouse," Sila says.

"What happened?" I ask.

"You did," she replies.

"I—"

"Hush. All is well," Sila murmurs.

"You're bleeding."

Sila shrugs. "I have left conversations with Vika in a worse state. I will be fine. You, on the other hand, keep terrifying me."

"I don't mean to."

"I know. We can discuss it when we are free of this place," Sila says.

I fall into silence and bury my face in her hair. She still smells of blood and sweat, but under it all there is the scent of her, as sure and inevitable as the grave.

Sila takes a set of stairs, and the smell of damp earth and decay rises from the stone in the hallway. Here the walls drip, running with water from the natural cave system. Moss clings to the untamed stone, and I know we are at the edge of the catacombs.

There is a main entrance to the catacombs, of course. All wrought in stonework by masters of their craft millennia ago and protected from moisture and plant life by their magic even all these years later. That is not where we are going.

Here, where the crypts meet the Citadel, everything is laid out in long, dark passages. This area belongs to the Barracks and their foragers and metalworkers, but most will not dare to delve so close to the catacombs for fear of disturbing the dead interred there.

Sila pauses, her eyes catching in the darkness, seeing what mine can't. And then, as we move closer, I can.

A deep crack breaks through the wall and floor ahead. It must continue down for many levels, forgotten or ignored as unfixable. It has pulled the floor of the hallway apart, and a gentle mist drifts from within it, damp and earth-warm.

"Here?" I whisper.

"If we are not too late," Sila says, setting me down carefully.

I peel Lune's cloak away from where it has stuck to her bloodied shoulder. The wounds are already closing and her blouse is blood-soaked and torn. I reach out, resting my fingers there. It makes me uneasy, even if it doesn't seem to phase her.

"They will heal," Sila says softly. "This isn't like last time." She threads her fingers through my hair to cradle the back of my neck and leans down to press a kiss to my forehead.

A thump echoes out from the fissure and I flinch, heart hammering in my throat, sure that the floor is about to open and swallow me whole. A lantern light appears, floating above the fissure and a figure soon follows it. A set of footsteps echoes across a plank thrown down over the crack.

"You the Librarian?" asks a rough voice. He appears from the gently curling mist, walking over the makeshift bridge. He's an older man, with rounded human ears and sandy blond hair. His figure is sturdy, the kind of person you'd ask for help hauling books back and forth, and right now his unruly eyebrows are pulled together in a deep-set frown that might be permanent.

"Yes," Sila says. "We are friends of the moon in the glade."

"Right," he says. "I'll take you where the moonlight hides."

"Thank you—?" I ask.

"Corus, but let's not get comfortable here. I don't like standing still for too long if I can help it. Come on." Corus walks back across the plank, and I look at the swollen, damp wood with a deep well of uncertainty.

"I think I best carry you across, little mouse," Sila says.

I don't want to admit she's right, but my legs are already shaking and the fissure runs deep. I let her scoop me up again and I can barely hold on, my arms are so weak. Once we're across, Corus peers at me before he pulls up the plank behind us, stashing it back against the wall.

"You sure she's up for this?"

"We have no choice," Sila replies. "If I have to carry her out of here, I will, but it must be now."

Corus frowns, looking troubled. I watch his eyes flick from blood-stained garments to our faces.

"Right," he says. "If it's as you say. Can she walk?"

"She can talk," I grumble.

"When necessary, and after some rest," says Sila, squeezing me gently.

Corus nods and turns, walking on down the hallway. Sila follows his bobbing lantern light.

It's dark, and I am warm, leaching cold from where I'm pressed against Sila. I press my face against the cool skin of her neck for just a moment.

When I wake again, we are in one of the burial chambers of the catacombs, the room lined with carved out hollows for the dead. It might be slightly warm if everything didn't feel so cold against my skin. The scent of decay lingers, and those who had been interred here so long ago are little more than dust waiting to be swept away and replaced.

Death is simple in the Citadel. A body laid out with no jewellery or adornment, and wrapped in fine linen or silk, embroidered or painted to tell the dead one's story. Lovingly, sometimes, ordinary others. Then the keepers of the catacombs find you a place to rest.

Somewhere down here my parents' bodies rest wrapped in cloth painted by their children. I had been six, and mine had been a clumsy attempt, finessed by Orielle, who had been twice my age then.

"Go to your rest," I murmur, having no desire to wake the dead by thinking of them. Corus and Sila echo it, though Sila says it in a tongue I have not heard before. Likely as archaic as her handwriting.

Corus leads us through the chamber into another, and from there they blur together. Many of the corpses are recent and there are no empty alcoves here. We move from hallway to chamber with no discernible pattern, with only Corus' sure footsteps to guide us. He takes us down further again, deeper into the catacombs. The earth groans and creaks and there is the ever present sound of trickling water. The scent of death and crushed moss fades after a while, from familiarity more than anything else.

Corus doesn't speak as we go, and we follow his lead. It does not do well to speak here.

I lay my head against Sila's shoulder, tucking my face under the curtain of her hair and breathing in deeply. There is the metallic tang of blood that is becoming too familiar, earth and salt, star flower and ash. She is cold and bloodied, but her body is still strong and her stride doesn't falter. I feel safe, shrouded by her hair and held so tightly and so I drift off again, unable to keep my eyes open against the fever any longer.

Chapter 45

Sila

It has been a long, long time since I have feared death. I had gone to my own willingly. My lover had been dead. My friends and family were dying. It had been a simple choice. I had been entirely helpless against the onslaught of fever and cough. I was not a healer, and they would not allow me near my loved ones. My magic had always been that of decay and rot, and there was enough of that without me adding to it.

I had not feared dying. If anything, it had been a relief.

I had knelt, and the Cupbearer had poured her poison into my open mouth. After that, it was like a dream. Golden sunlight in the chapel. Someone screaming. The Dawn King's hand in my hair as he tipped my head back. Then darkness.

They had brought the body here, to the catacombs. I do not remember where, anymore, though I visited once, when I was newly returned. I had wept to see the decoration on the shroud, because it meant that someone who loved me had survived. It had not been in vain. Regardless of what my queen had told me.

The sound of our footsteps echoes off the catacombs' walls and Lorel is burning up again in my arms. And I fear death. I fear it deep in the marrow of my bones. In the depths of my shadows. In the wrenching ache of my heart that constricts my chest. I am only grateful that I have no need to breathe because I think I might be incapable of it.

Something like fear and grief claws at my throat, trying to tear its way free. It is as if I am carrying Lorel, shrouded, to her final rest. I clutch her slight form tightly. She is limp and soft cradled against me. Her heartbeat, like a fluttering batwing compared to mine, is steady and sure in her chest. I grip her and my nails dig in, longer than they should be. I pull them back sharply. There is the whisper of a voice at the edges of my mind. The tether to the Library is pulled taut, stretched to its limit. But that whisper…The Library is saying farewell. Soon, I will be on my own.

Corus leads us down further into the dark until the structure of the catacombs gives way. Water leaches stronger here, seeping through the stone. Stalactites forming on the ceiling, water pooling in shallow basins drip by drip. My vision flares, bright and wider, as it does when my eyes go dark. I blink and it returns to normal. I shake it off. It must just be this place, getting to me. My tether still holds. Faintly, but it holds.

"Here," Corus whispers, before disappearing as he pushes through moss.

He might as well have melted into the stone. I test the moss wall with my shoulder and it gives. I push through. On the other side, a cave opens up, looming overhead. Water runs away from the puddles at our feet and tiny baubles of light glow, creatures or subterranean flowers nestled amongst the crevices and dragging trails of old man's beard moss. The Cupbearer must have cultivated it for it to be so full of life.

"We can speak more freely here," Corus says, voice barely raised above the trickle of the water.

"But not move?" I ask. He has yet to continue walking.

He frowns, the sigil lantern swinging at his side. He's at ease here.

"I don't know what you're running from," he begins. He holds up a hand as I open my mouth to speak. "And I don't want to know. I can see you're both in a state, but you should know that it isn't much better out there. They distrust magical folks, and they'll have never seen the likes of you. I can help you leave the Citadel, but I can't promise you safety."

"I would not expect you to," I say, shifting Lorel's weight. "But there is no safety behind, either."

Corus looks at the bundle of woman in my arms, his face grim.

"Are you sure it's wise to remove her from the Citadel?" he asks, looking back at my face.

"How do you mean?" I keep my tone careful.

Corus keeps quiet for a long moment and then sighs. "It's nothing."

I do not move when he turns to walk on. "Corus. I require an explanation."

"I'm sure I'm wrong," he says.

"Wrong about what, exactly?"

Corus turns back with a noise of exasperation. "She's a Dawnchild, isn't she?"

I find now that I am the one who does not wish to answer.

"I recognise her. I lived in the Suntide Court, once."

"Once?" It comes out as dangerous as I mean it. I shift,

turning my body in case I need to turn back through the catacombs. "I find I require further explanation."

Corus runs his hand down his face. "Don't usually tell people any of this," he mutters. "I did work in the Court — until I had to smuggle my wife and child out."

"Ah."

Silence stretches out between us, the sound of the water filling the space. Corus gives me a hopeless look. "She was fae, and she gave my son strong magic. The Dawn King pays attention to things like that in his court. I suppose he turned his attention to Lady Meline after we left. I knew them. Her parents." He nods at Lorel. "Her mother had strong magic, too."

I stare at him. Dark lady have mercy on me. Lorel had thought her father was the man who raised her, another Dawnchild. But Corus is implying something far worse. I knew little of the Court. Nothing of this borrowing of wives. Apparently, neither did Lorel. I hold her tighter.

"And so you became a smuggler?"

Corus shrugs. "I did what I could, but it's a harsh world out there. I lost my wife to it, eventually. Neither of us would have changed a thing." He pauses, looking surprised. "Don't know why I'm telling you all this."

"Because you were worried that I am stealing one of the Dawn King's children," I say.

"Yes, well—"

"I am. She cannot stay there."

Corus takes us in again, blood-soaked and weary. "You can never let them know what she is," he says.

"Is there any reason anyone should know?"

"Not from my lips," Corus says.

I nod firmly. "Good. Then lead on."

"There's a spot not far along that we can stop and rest

safely," he says, turning and starting on again. This time, I follow. "They'd need a blood tracker to find us there."

I laugh, softly. "I don't think the King will risk that again."

Corus mutters a prayer to the stars. We fall into silence again as the light falls off, the cave's cultivated plant life disappearing. The water trickles on into the darkness and the tether is pulled as tight and delicate as spider silk. It pinches as I walk.

And then it snaps. My steps stutter, but I forge on. I hold Lorel tighter, breathe in her paper and ink scent. Think of her fingers digging into my thighs. Her sweet sighs and her less sweet mouth. I do not know how long it will take, this unraveling of my being, but for now, for her, I will hold myself together.

Chapter 46

Lorel

THERE IS THE FAINT SOUND OF RUSHING WATER WHEN I wake. The gentle sway of Sila's footsteps is gone and I feel her body shift beneath mine as I rub sleep from my eyes.

"Are you awake, little mouse?" Sila asks, gentle hands finding my face. She sits against the wall of a cave. I am settled against her, my face pillowed on her chest. She watches me and her face is soft and fond, and I would dearly love to kiss her.

"Where are we?" I ask, instead. The air is damp with the taste of earth and salt that I would expect from bathwater.

"Corus found us somewhere to stop, so you could rest," Sila says.

Corus crouches beside Sila, holding out a flask. "It's as she says. Here."

I take it and sit myself up with Sila's help.

"I can refill it, so don't hold back," he says.

I stay settled in Sila's lap and look her over. She does not seem weary. Whatever Vika had done to her, it didn't carry the weight of the sanctified sword Jaime had used. The wounds are now nothing more than faint marks across her skin. I brush my fingers over them, just to reassure myself. She must be able to tolerate an incredible amount of pain to fight so. Seeing her fight is equal parts exhilarating and terrifying. She's a magnificent force of shadow and darkness. Entirely reckless. Breathtakingly beautiful. I'm still baffled to have caught her attention at all.

"Lorel?" Sila says.

"Was I out for long?" I ask.

"Not so long, but you were exhausted," Sila says, taking my face in her hands to inspect me further. "Your eyes are clearer already."

I smile at her. "I don't quite feel it yet."

"Because you need to eat," Sila says, entirely sure of it. The rough piece of bread that Lune had shoved at me while I was being dressed seems a world away now.

"That's easy fixed," says Corus, rummaging in his pack before holding out a cloth-wrapped parcel. "You too," he says to Sila.

"I do not need it," she says. "Give it to Lorel, unless you think it is better kept by."

"Suit yourself," he says, swapping the empty flask for the bundle. Two soft buns roll into my lap as I open it. Sila watches me as I eat.

"What is it?" I ask. I take another bite and watch as her eyes track it.

There is amusement playing at the corners of her mouth. "I don't feed you nearly enough," she says.

I make a disbelieving noise. "You're always trying to feed me."

"Because you need it," Sila insists. "And there is something rather sweet about you when you eat."

I stare at her as I shove the last of the bun into my mouth. Sila's eyes flick to my mouth. Corus clears his throat.

"We need to be getting on," he says hesitantly

"Alright," I say, dusting my hands off on my borrowed clothes. I still feel a slight bit too warm. Still feel that ache that will take an age to sleep off. I use Sila's shoulders to pull myself up to standing. My legs protest, but it is only the protest of the unused.

"You sure you'll be right?" Corus asks as Sila unfolds herself to stand up behind me.

I grimace, testing my legs. "I think I'll be okay. Maybe let me know if there is an edge I might fall off? I'd like to avoid that."

Corus stares at me for a moment, until it's Sila clearing her throat.

"Ah, yes," Corus mumbles. "Good idea."

Strange, he looks like he's seen a ghost.

"Come, little mouse, and tell me if you get tired. The caves are dangerous."

"I know," I say, more on instinct than anything else. Because I do know— theoretically.

Corus leads us back out into the caves, and the stale, decaying scent of the catacombs has given way to something earthy and damp. The air is thick with water here too, mixing with a strange murky warmth. The water pools in ever-increasing amounts. First puddles and trickling creeks. It isn't long before they become wide, still lakes and rivers. I had never thought I would traverse the caves that Lune so often frequented, but I had also thought I would spend the rest of my life coming and going from my desk in the scriptorium. I had been so foolish to think the Dawn King would forget me. Even now, the smallest noise makes my heart kick up, worried that we are being followed.

It's easier to bear the loss of it all with Sila at my side. I hadn't thought of my desk much in the days since I last sat at it. It hits me like a blow, now, to realise those ordinary days are gone. The scriptorium, with its dull light and dusty shelves. I won't ever see the faces of my peers again. Not Elris, or Sybri. Not Lune or Orielle. I will never sit down to start the day and check my paints— Dawn King have mercy on me, my *paints*. My brushes. All of that is gone now. I might never paint again. Never hear Elris' gentle praise. Never again hold ancient parchment beneath my fingers.

My eyes blur and I taste salt on my tongue. I brush it away. It's hard enough to see here without being blinded by tears. There will be a time for grief, but it isn't now. I forge onwards.

Our footsteps echo into the darkness, mingling with the steady drip of water, the shifting sound of rock against rock. Creatures slide and skitter in the darkness.

Corus' lantern doesn't give much light, and it gives even less when I have to reignite the sigil when it goes out. I had expected more light in the caverns, more life. In the cultivated caves there are glowing silk worms, the vines that grow my favourite berry, and the small luminous fish that attract the eels.

Here there is nothing but the dark and quiet, the lantern light glancing off the water slick rock, and the occasional wide, still lake.

We squeeze through narrow cracks in the rock, and Corus leads us along the edge of a lake, with the warning that to step wrong is to slip into the dark forever. Sila's eyes, dark and fathomless in the sigil light, tell me that the dark would have to fight her if it wanted to claim me. I shuffle along the edge and see the water break in places, glimpse the wet skin of an eel as it crests the water. I press myself back against the rock, determined not to find out who would win between Sila and a rock eel larger than any I have ever seen in the Library's kitchens.

We make it to the other side without incident, and the path levels. I do not want to think of what else might live within the cold, dark earth. These deep dark lakes. It makes my skin crawl to know that Lune sometimes explores these tunnels on her own. She will soon have to do so again to prepare the poison for the sacrifice, and the thought makes me sick to my stomach. I pull her cloak tighter around me. The herb scent is calming in the dark and oppressive expanse of the caverns.

Corus is taking us further away from everything I have ever known. Taking us through a place both too small, and too big. Too loud, and too quiet. It raises the hair on the back of my neck, and the unsettled feeling doesn't leave me even as the air turns fresh. I catch the barest hint of something woody and resinous. Pine, that reminds me of the guards, when they return from their watchtower postings. The scent does nothing to quell the rising dread and I almost miss the warm, shifting companionship of the curse. How grim.

The cave levels out, widening, and Sila entwines her fingers with mine. Firm. Grounding. It doesn't steady the rapid pace of my heart, or the way my palms sweat, but I'm not alone. I have her. My fierce, dark, lovely shadow.

I don't know how far her tether to the Library can reach. I can only hope it will hold long enough to find some way to stop the unravelling. I have no desire to lose her now that I have her.

She keeps a hold of my hand as I follow Corus through

another narrow channel that goes on for so long, I start to worry that I might be trapped here, even if I were to turn back. Fear grips at my lungs, and then the air stirs and I am tumbling out into the night. Out into the open air for the first time in my life.

It's warmer out here, and it's thick with the scent of pine and woodland decay. I look up at the trees surrounding us and have to look up again. The trees are gigantic, thick around and reaching up high and it is clear that even if the sun shone, it would never kiss the earth here. Fog threads thick as old paint water between them, eddying and pooling between the trunks. It hangs through the treetops and over us like a blanket, ready to smother every living thing. The dark earth is a graveyard of rotting pine needles. They carpet the soil so thickly that the ground seems to collapse in, sinking under the weight of itself.

I shrink back from it all and Sila is at my back, a cool press of the familiar.

"You're alright," she whispers, her breath skating over my cheek.

"It's all so big," I say.

She squeezes my shoulders. Corus is kneeling in the pine needles, understanding something in them that I cannot begin to fathom.

"It's not far to the road," he says, voice quiet. "It's a little way through the fog, but you'll find it hardly matters. Keep your eyes in front of you, alright?" He stands, hefting his pack high on his broad shoulders, and gives Sila a long glance.

Sila looks like she was made for this place, just as surely as she was made to stalk the Library's halls. A horrific apparition waiting in the woods for her next victim. She is surely far more terrifying than anything that can be found in the fog. I take a deep, steadying breath.

"Once we're on the road," says Corus, gesturing for us to follow. "It's a few days to Atratos. My son waits for us there."

The pine needles are soft underfoot, and it's unusual compared to the steady, foot-worn rock that has borne me my entire life. Even the plush rugs of the Court have nothing on it. It makes my skin crawl and my hands itch. I shiver, even in the warm open air.

This is nothing like any illustration I had ever seen. It's difficult to follow Corus' instructions to keep my eyes ahead when everything is so new. So different.

The fog moves as we do, pushed and pulled by the edges of the lantern light so that we are never truly in it. It doesn't flee very far, not with the pitiful light from my sad sigil. I stick close to Sila as we walk. The fog eddies and flows like a living thing. Something darts through the fog nearby, setting my heart fluttering like a bat's wings.

"Just a rabbit," says Corus. "Probably."

"Easy, little mouse," Sila says, squeezing my hand. I take another deep breath. The towering trees are almost comforting, like the granite columns of the Library. I try to convince myself that it's not so different from being underground. Surely the road isn't too far away now.

My foot sinks into the pine needles, slipping in a treacherous hollow, and a light catches the corner of my eye. My ears start to ring. I shake my head to dislodge it. Sila's fingers slip from mine.

"Sila—"

The light flickers and moves and I turn back to look for her.

And find myself entirely alone.

Would you like to know what Sila was thinking when she confronted the Dawn King? Get the bonus chapter here: https://www.elsiehawthorne.com/bonus-content

Something more?

Would you like to know what Sila was thinking when she confronted the Dawn King? Join my mailing list and get the bonus chapter by going to:

www.elsiehawthorne.com/bonus-content

Acknowledgments

To you, dear reader, thank you. I hope you aren't too hurt by the ending and I promise to make it right for you in book two.

To my beloved, thank you for holding my hand through everything, and walking the path before me. I'd love nothing more than to walk it together, always.

To Vivien, for being so encouraging and enthusiastic. I love that you love my girls.

And to Chris, for your patience and encouragement. I hope that you love them.

About the Author

Elsie writes what she loves; sapphic romances set in queernormative dark fantasy worlds. Her writing features possessive nightmare love interests and the intense cursed objects of their affections, always with gothic vibes. She lives with her beloved partner in Tasmania, Australia, and is just as obsessed with her as her characters are with each other.

Join Elsie's mailing list here.

https://www.elsiehawthorne.com/

www.ingramcontent.com/pod-product-compliance
Lightning Source LLC
Chambersburg PA
CBHW030613170726
48283CB00002B/581